# IT LIVES IN THE WOODS

## CREATURE ENCOUNTERS
## BOOK 4

## BORIS BACIC

*Hylophobia is the abnormal fear of forests: it may only apply to deep forests (which is the most common form), or to any wooded area regardless of size. It may be triggered by traumatic childhood experiences, like getting poked by low or fallen branches.*

# PROLOGUE

"Careful where you step!" Jayden called out, a hand instinctively raised.

Isabella was a little ahead of him, peeking somewhere off the trail. She'd been doing that all day long; whenever she saw something interesting, she rushed ahead, disregarding any dangers along the way, despite Jayden's warnings.

He couldn't blame her. This was the third forest they'd hiked in Europe, and each was better than the last.

"Issie!" he called out again, breathless.

The hike had been an exhausting one. Jayden was no stranger to long hikes on inhospitable terrains, but taking on this trail had proven to be quite a challenge. Isabella was tired, too. He could see it in the beads of sweat that coated her forehead, the way her shoulders slouched, and the way her chest heaved up and down.

But excitement fueled her, Jayden knew, and that was probably stopping her from noticing the exhaustion, even though they'd been walking for hours.

"Issie, wait. Slow down," Jayden said with a bouncy voice, even though Isabella had already stopped.

Only when he got closer was he able to see the glow in Isabella's eyes. *Oh no.* He knew that look all too well. It was the look that said there was something marvelous ahead but probably either illegal or dangerous to reach.

Sure enough, when Jayden followed Isabella's gaze, he understood what got her attention so hypnotically. Off the beaten path, the trees descended into a rocky, mossy ravine, at the bottom of which rested something that differed from the green and brown hues that they'd walked past in the last few hours.

"Is that a building?" Jayden cocked an eyebrow.

"Not just one. Look!" Isabella pointed down the slope.

Jayden just then saw it. Not just one house but rows of them, lined up in a makeshift street, obscured by the foliage of the tall trees.

"Wow. What is that?" He looked at Isabella for an answer.

She offered an aloof shrug, his eyes still fixed on this wonder in the forest. "I don't know."

"You said you researched the area extensively online for all the sights, didn't you?"

"Yes, but there was no mention of anything like this."

"Huh." Jayden turned his head to face the village again, his hands on his hips.

His feet were killing him. He was hungry and thirsty, and his shoulders protested over the weight of his backpack, but strangely, a surge of renewed energy swaddled him. He wanted to go down and see the village.

"I'm gonna go check it out. Wanna come with?" Isabella asked.

Of course she was going to check it out. Whenever they went on urban explorations, she rushed to get a closer look at whatever they ran into and only worried about the risks and dangers after.

"Sure," Jayden said.

For the first time since they ran into the abandoned houses, Isabella turned to look at him. Her eyebrows stood high up, her forehead furrowed in surprise. "Wait, really?" She couldn't contain the smile that stretched her lips.

"It's not every day that we run into an abandoned village in the middle of a forest." Jayden shrugged. "But I'm going first so I can test the ground."

"Okay."

Jayden was grateful that he had decided to wear his hiking boots and cargo pants because the wild undergrowth reached all the way up to his waist and poked at him with sharp twigs. The stinging nettles that he plodded across rustled, just waiting for his exposed skin to come in contact with it.

The slope leading down was covered in an abundance of moss, but at least the surface was rocky and made a natural staircase, so Jayden didn't need to worry about sliding uncontrollably to the bottom. At this height, it probably would have been fatal unless one of the trees near the bottom stopped his fall.

Even so, it would still be painful.

Jayden planted his foot on the first step of the ravine, carefully testing how slippery the moss was. The rustling behind told him that Isabella was already slogging toward him.

After the second step down, descending became easier. He had to circumvent the ravine since some of the crags were either too narrow or too low for him to step on them from where he stood. Every couple of steps, he turned around to make sure Isabella was okay. Her gaze was fixated down, intently focused on her footing. She was much shorter than Jayden, so she often had to sit at the edge of the rocky step and drop off to the one below.

They approached the ground much faster than Jayden thought they would. The rocky surface ended, replaced by the soft ground covered by long patches of grass. The houses were just in front of them, merely a few dozen feet away.

The undergrowth and the saplings densely covered the area, which made walking all the more difficult. Jayden's foot sank between the leaves and into the soft ground with each step he took. Twigs snapped occasionally under his or Isabella's boots, echoing prominently in the area.

Something rustled nearby. Jayden knew that it hadn't come from him or Isabella because the sound came from somewhere to the side. Both of them stopped, scanning the nearby area for any activity. After a moment of nothing happening, Jayden resumed trudging forward.

"Uh, what if there are snakes here?" Isabella asked.

"Hey, it was your idea to check it out," Jayden retorted.

"Oh, come on. Not like you wanted to ignore such a sight."

Jayden gave no response to that. He knew that there were no snakes in the area—at least not venomous ones. That was what the local had convinced him of when he'd asked him about it. Isabella was terrified of reptiles, so he had to make sure it was safe for her since he knew she'd completely forget about that detail until it was too late.

Jayden's head instinctively turned in the direction of where the sound earlier had come from, just to make sure nothing was coming at them. A bear mace and a knife rested in his pockets, ready to be used, even though there should be no need for them.

The undergrowth ended when they emerged on a cobblestoned street. "Finally." Jayden breathed a sigh of relief.

***

Isabella spun in a circle. "Wow!"

Her phone was already out of her pocket, her finger tapping on the button to snap photos all around her.

Although most of the houses were made out of concrete, some consisted of wood—and all were destroyed beyond repair. Moss covered whatever was left of the concave rooftops. Vines encroached on the walls and crept into the houses through the empty windows. Weeds and roots poked between the old cobblestones.

"What is this place?" Isabella took a picture of a tall structure with a spire on top of the roof. The top of the spire looked like it had been broken off, and Isabella assumed it used to be a church with a cross dwarfing the rest of the village.

"Beats me," Jayden said. He looked impressed, and Jayden rarely showed how impressed he was. "Must have been a village at some point. This country has a lot of those. Oh, cool, was that a smithy? I'm going to check it out."

Without waiting, he broke into a stride across the street, toward a wooden building with a rusted anvil and some tools sitting in front. Even from here, Isabella could see the wooden beams that stood slanted diagonally across the shop.

"Be careful!" she shouted after him.

"You're one to talk. You always put yourself in all sorts of danger." Jayden spun to face her and backpedaled.

"I know how to take care of myself, Jay."

"And I don't?" He spread his arms.

Just as he said that, his heel loudly caught on a jutting cobblestone, and he stumbled, careening forward with a clumsy half-spin. He just barely managed to stay on his feet. Isabella didn't say anything. She just sucked her lips into her mouth in a "told you so" manner. Jayden frowned and turned away from her.

He walked normally for the rest of the way to the smithy.

Isabella shook her head and continued sucking in the view. Even in its abandonment, the village was beautiful. The destruction from the elements and the moss and the vines only gave it another layer of beauty, like finely aged wine.

Isabella took a few more photos and then recorded a short video of the surroundings. She was about to post it on Instagram, but then she noticed that she had no signal. Posting for her 14,000 followers would have to wait until she was back to civilization (even though the internet wasn't great at the hotel, either).

"Jayden? Anything interesting in there?" she called out as she snapped another picture of the broken spire of the church. She wondered if going inside would be a possibility. Jayden would probably be against it, but there was no way Isabella would find a place like this only to peek from the outside. It would be like going to Starbucks just to smell the coffee.

Isabella lowered her phone and craned her neck toward the house of the blacksmith. "Jayden!" she shouted.

She should have heard something. Either his boots crunching or some shuffling, or in the worst-case scenario, him answering her call. It wasn't like he didn't hear her, especially with the lack of such noise.

Isabella swallowed. For the first time that day, something unpleasant clambered from her gut to her chest. She didn't like it. She shoved the phone into her pocket and walked in the direction of the smithy.

"Jayden!" she yelled once more, this time in an accusatory manner.

She swore she was going to kick his ass as soon as she found him. It was okay if he ignored her in their apartment back home—the place was big, after all, and two thick doors separated their offices, which effectively muffled much of the noise.

But to ignore her here? It made her angry.

"Jayden," she said sternly as she stepped in front of the workshop for a clear view.

But the figure belonging to her boyfriend that she expected to see prowling in the shadows, illuminating stuff here and there with his flashlight, wasn't there. Instead, what greeted her was a small, empty working space. Scattered tools, broken and rotted workbenches, and a forge that could not be reached because of the collapsed roof.

Isabella spun around.

She didn't have enough time to scream when the thing jumped in front of her.

***

"Boo!" Jayden raised his stiff palms in Isabella's face and then broke into a laughing fit.

She didn't scream, but she did become startled. He saw it in the way her eyes and nostrils widened, and the way her face and hands jerked as if electrocuted.

Belatedly, she raised a hand to her chest as if to calm down her beating heart. She looked up at the sky and then shot daggers at Jayden. He stopped laughing, but the smile refused to leave his face.

*Lecture incoming in three, two, one...*

"What the fuck is wrong with you?!" Isabella raised a hand and brought it down on Jayden's shoulder.

He defensively raised his hands against her blows, continuing to laugh at her reaction. Startling her was one of his favorite things to do, whether it was hiding in the closet or sneaking up on her when she was in the kitchen and pinching her ass, or bursting through the door like a cowboy.

He knew she would get pissed at him for doing it in the middle of the woods, but he just couldn't resist it.

"Seriously! What the hell is your problem, man?!" Isabella finally stopped hitting him and slapped her sides.

"I'm sorry! But it was just way too funny."

"No, it wasn't. Seriously, Jayden. Don't ever do that again. Not while we're"—she gestured around her—"here."

The serious expression on her face and the timbre with which she'd conveyed that sentence told Jayden that he'd gone too far. He sighed, his face going slack. "Okay. I'm sorry. All right? I won't do it again. Okay, Issie?"

She paused as if to consider that. Finally, she nodded, much to his relief. Disaster averted.

"Where do you want to go next?" he asked.

"There." She pointed to the church.

*It's going to be old and unstable, and I know you'll want to climb the unsafe structures, and I don't want you doing that,* he wanted to say but chose not to say anything. Instead, he gave her a big nod. That seemed to remove the anger from her face.

They strode down the street, glancing at the surrounding buildings. Jayden expected to see some forms of modern vandalism: graffiti, discarded beer bottles, and other trash littering the floor, but the town seemed untouched, which was amazing.

How did something like this manage to go unseen when it was so conspicuously placed next to the trail? Then again, the trail was deep in the woods, a long way from the closest point of civilization. Whoever decided to trek it probably did so for the same reason Jayden and Isabella did: to enjoy nature, and not go binge drinking all night long.

The church was inaccessible, guarded by the bevy of bushes, trees, and other plant life that clung to it from every direction. A clear stairway led up to it, but mother nature had blocked the path. It wasn't simple vegetation that Jayden and Isabella could jostle through. No, they would need machetes to clear their way through the thick boughs in front of them.

"Aw, too bad," Isabella said, her shoulders drooping in disappointment.

"We'll come more prepared next time, babe." Jayden hung an arm around her shoulder. Secretly, he was glad that access to the church was blocked.

Isabella squinted defiantly at the church, probably trying to think of a way to get through. Jayden got worried that an idea would pop into her head, but then she shrugged and said, "Yeah. You're right."

Jayden flashed her a smile. "Let's see what's over there. I think I saw a path earlier."

They continued until the houses stopped accompanying them and the cobblestoned path merged onto a beaten path.

"I wonder what this place was like back when people still lived in it," Isabella said.

Jayden made a clicking noise with his tongue. "This one street was probably the entire village. That meant everybody knew everybody. And if the neighbors back then in Eastern Europe were the way they are now, then you can bet they knew everything about your private life."

Isabella furrowed her nose at that.

Not long after they started down the new trail, the ground on their left descended to a small valley. Jayden stopped in his tracks.

"What's up?" Isabella asked.

"Look." Jayden pointed down the valley.

Nestled between the tall trees was a clearing and, in the middle of the clearing, a wooden hut.

"What the heck?" Isabella approached to take a closer look. "Look how intact it is. You think someone lives there?"

"I don't know."

"I wanna check it out."

She took a step toward the slope when Jayden grabbed her by the wrist. She whipped around to face him, her hand squeezed into a fist. "No. Too dangerous."

"Come on, it's not so bad. I'll be careful on my way down."

She turned to leave, but Jayden's hand was still clamped around her wrist. Noticing this, she looked at her wrist and then at him, silently demanding that he let go. He did, and then he said, "I'll go first, okay?"

He knew he wouldn't be able to convince her not to go, so he at least wanted to be able to secure the route for her.

"Okay," she said, her hand relaxing.

Noticing that she wouldn't scurry off as soon as her arm was free, Jayden let her go. He cinched the straps of his backpack and approached the start of the slope. Isabella was right. It didn't look too dangerous. The hill was interspersed with trees and vegetation, but nothing like back in the village big enough to swallow an entire adult.

Prudently, Jayden took the first step on the soft, grassy ground, and then another, sidling while keeping his center of balance backward to avoid tumbling. He wouldn't have noticed that the ground had grown steeper had his foot not skidded slightly.

"Shit," he murmured, a hand instinctively grabbing hold of the hill behind him for support.

"Are you okay?" Isabella shouted.

Jayden looked back up. She was thirty feet above him, standing dangerously close to the edge. Climbing back up was going to be a bitch. Damn Issie and her crazy ideas. "Yeah! Hold on a little longer!"

He looked back down. He could see the slope abruptly ending a few dozen feet below him, but the bottom of the valley was still not there. He got on his rear and slid down the wet grass, using the heels of his boots as brakes.

He had good control.

Until he didn't.

He got too cocky with the sliding speed until his heels no longer stopped his descent, instead helplessly sliding across the grass.

*Shit, shit!*

His heel caught on a jutting rock. For a split second, he thought, *Thank God.* Until he realized that his entire balance had been thrown forward and he was leaping across the abrupt ledge and toward the ground twenty feet below.

***

Jayden's scream caused Isabella's breath to hitch in her throat. The loud *thwack* that came right after was sickening. The silence that ensued was unnerving.

"Jay!" she screamed at the top of her lungs, her heart rate going faster than throughout the entire hike today. "Jayden!"

*Oh God. Oh God, oh God, oh God...*

"Jayden, answer me! Are you okay?!"

The silence of the woods was her only answer. And then a groan erupted from somewhere far below. *Jayden!* Isabella sucked in a breath and braced herself to go down the slope.

"Issie!" Jayden's meek voice bounced from the bottom of the ravine.

Isabella stopped. "Jayden! Thank God! Are you okay?! Are you hurt?!"

No response again. Isabella was about to scream, but Jayden's voice interrupted her. "I broke my leg! I can't move!"

*Fuck. Fuck, fuck, fuck, fuckity fuck.*

"Jayden, I'm coming down!" she screamed and took a step forward.

"No!" Jayden's voice pierced the air. "Don't come down! It's too dangerous!"

The words came out with a hiss. It was obvious that he was in a lot of pain.

"I can't just leave you down there!" she shouted.

"You have to! Find help!"

"Are you crazy?! It's *miles* away! I'm not leaving!"

She took a step forward. Her foot was on the slope, but her weight was on the foot higher on the ground. She stopped when Jayden called out again.

"Issie, please! You can't help me down here! Just go!" He murmured something after telling her to go. It took Isabella a moment to decipher the words as, "Fuck, it hurts."

Tears trickled down her face. How the hell was this happening? This was all her fault. Jayden kept warning her that exploring dangerous areas could end with her being hurt, but she didn't listen. And where did that get her?

They were in the middle of a vast forest, far away from any humans, and Jayden's leg was broken. If she could just rewind the time to one minute earlier. Just one goddamn minute so she could stop Jayden's fall. Fuck!

"Hold on, maybe I can call someone!" she shouted in a cracked voice.

The frayed thread of hope that she held onto died when she whipped out her phone and noticed the little crossed circle icon in the corner of her screen. Nevertheless, she went into the call option. It took her a few tries to dial the emergency services with her trembling fingers. The call failed to go through.

"Please, come on!" Isabella cried as she shook the phone in her hands and tried again.

Nothing.

"Jayden! Can you move?!" she called.

She already knew the answer, but she hoped against hope that Jayden would give her a different answer this time. Maybe the pain wasn't so bad. Maybe after the initial shock, he'd be able to skip up the hill on one foot. It wouldn't be impossible, right?

"Jay!" Isabella called again when no response came from her boyfriend.

"I can't!" he shouted.

His voice was weaker. That wasn't good. Isabella knew that by standing in one spot, she was only wasting precious time. She had to find help before Jayden went into shock. "Jayden?! Just wait there! I'm gonna run back for help, okay?! Jayden!"

"Yeah!" he shouted in a clipped tone.

She spun on her heel and bolted down the trail.

***

The pain enveloped Jayden's entire being until it was the only thing that existed. Upon falling, a buzzing filled his ears, along with a throbbing of his torso. That was good because it meant that he was still alive.

But then the pain in his torso receded while the one in the leg remained as a persistent squeeze. One look down there was more than enough for the heat to drain from his face.

The first thing he noticed was the red and white on his cargo pants. Those colors didn't belong there, and Jayden knew right away that seeing that could only be bad. After his brain finally decided to cooperate, the image before him cleared, and he recognized the white as his femur sticking out and the red as his blood.

First came the shock: staring at the mangled mess of his extremity and refusing to believe that it was really there. And then, as if on cue, the sharp pang of pain shot through his leg, and the metallic smell of blood invaded his nostrils.

It was unlike anything he had ever felt in his life. Jayden had broken both his arms on separate occasions, but those weren't open fractures. What he was facing here... the sharp white stick that was supposed to be *inside* him jutting out of the broken skin at an impossible angle, enough even to tear through his cargo pants...

Bile climbed up Jayden's throat. He turned his head to the side and let the vomit shoot out of his mouth. It fell down the side of his face and ear, the smell of copper mixing in with an acidic redolence from his undigested lunch.

The pain was like knives traveling through the inside of his leg. He hissed and groaned, his limb on fire. The urge to grab it, move it—do anything with it—was strong, but he couldn't, and that pained him even more.

But then Isabella's voice came from somewhere far in the distance. He couldn't tell what she was saying at first, but then her voice cleared up somewhat. The pain still clouded Jayden's ability to fully understand Isabella, but she was there, thank God, she was there, and she would help him.

He looked up. Just above him stood a vertical, rocky cliff face. Vegetation guarded the ledge, making it impossible for him to see Isabella from where he was. This was such a big mistake. Even if his leg was okay, there would be no way back, unless they went around to look for a path back up, which might end up with them getting lost.

After a brief exchange, he told Isabella to look for help. Between the pain that dominated his every thought and the need to convince Isabella not to descend the slope, Jayden wanted to scream in frustration. Eventually, she listened to him because she said she would go look for help and that he should wait where he was.

*Not like I planned on running a lap around the woods any time soon,* he wanted to say, but he was too exhausted. His lips were dry, cold sweat washed over him, and a shiver was already setting in.

The patter of receding footsteps somewhere above indicated that Isabella was on her way to get help, which left Jayden in complete and utter silence. He hadn't known he would feel so alone after her departure. A part of him wanted to shout after her to come back, to not leave him down there, but he knew that the only rational solution was for her to come back with someone.

*What a pain in the ass,* he thought as he looked at his leg once more and allowed his head to slump backward on the uncomfortable rock.

This was going to be such a hassle. Isabella would need to look for the authorities, and they would need to put together a rescue team to get him back to town and give him medical treatment. Two things comforted him about the whole thing, though.

The first one was the fact that he knew the authorities would waste no resources saving one of their own citizens. The second one was the fact that he took out medical insurance, which was not at all high in Europe.

That almost made a smile creep up on his face.

Jayden stared at the tall canopies of the trees blocking the sky. It was much darker in this part of the woods. Then it hit him. It wasn't just the woods. Daylight was burning fast. It wouldn't be long until nightfall took over.

Would the rescue services look for him at night, or would it be deemed too dangerous? Would he even survive until morning? What if there were dangerous animals nearby? What if the smell of his blood attracted predators?

Jayden dismissed those thoughts because they made him panic. And because he couldn't think from of the pain.

Fuck, he was so thirsty. His bottle of water was in his backpack, but he was lying on it, and there was no way he'd be able to get up into a sitting position without arousing more pain in his leg. He would ignore the thirst, for now. When it got really bad, he would bite the bullet and fetch food and water from his backpack.

What about taking a leak?

*Well, I hope you brought an extra pair of diapers*, he mocked himself.

Time slipped away. It could have been hours or minutes. It was impossible to say. The only thing that Jayden was sure of was the constant pain. The throbbing and the burning never abated, but extra pangs of pain crashed over his leg in waves, strong enough to force him to clench his jaw and moan.

He wished that he'd brought some painkillers with him. He was prepared for all sorts of situations that he could encounter on a hike, but he hadn't thought about the most basic thing: first aid.

Isabella. This was all her fucking fault. If only she had listened to him for once and agreed not to go exploring a dangerous-looking place, none of this would have happened. Then again, it was inevitable. Isabella was the kind of person who didn't learn until she got burned.

Jayden was glad that it was him who got hurt, and not Isabella, because now he would never let her live it down. He would make sure to remind her of it every time they got into an argument.

*Oh, you're angry because I left the toilet seat up? Well, remember that time we went hiking in the woods and you wanted to go down a hill and I ended up breaking my leg and needing surgery?*

She would learn her lesson after all this was done. After all the panic was over and Jayden woke up with a cast on his leg, he would crack a joke about his broken femur, and they would both laugh in relief, and she would promise never to go exploring abandoned places again.

Shame that it took a broken leg in the middle of the woods for her to see the dangers, but it was what it was.

Something rustled nearby. Not something light that scuttled through the leaves before burrowing into its den. No, something heavy that caused the ground to crunch.

Jayden's head instinctively went up as he scanned the area. Was it Isabella with the rescue team? No, it couldn't be. She'd only left a short while ago. No way would she be able to return so fast. Unless she ran into someone along the way? Maybe a forest ranger or something like that.

"Hello?" Jayden called out with a hoarse voice. Then again, louder, "Hello?!"

More rustling, but no response. If this was a person, surely they would have said something.

A twig snapped somewhere. In the absence of all the other noise, it was too loud. Then it hit Jayden. It was *quiet*.

Deafeningly so. No chirping of the birds or buzzing of the insects. Nothing. That could only mean one thing.

A predator was nearby.

Jayden propped himself up on his elbows. Even just that action sent another twinge through his already painful leg. He reached a hand toward one of the side pockets and unzipped it, giving a silent thanks that the object he was looking for rested against his healthy leg.

He fished out the bear mace and fumbled with it in his hands until it was pointed away from him, his forefinger ready to squeeze the top of the can and spray the substance on the approaching animal. He held out the mace in front of him, his head darting in various directions, trying to pinpoint where the rustling was coming from.

"Hey, whoever you are, stay away!" he shouted, mostly because he knew that shouting was one way to warn the bear that he was not alone in the area and, therefore, stop him from coming closer.

The rustling grew closer. Moreover, it quickened. Mixed in with the sound of foliage breaking under something's weight plodding through it came the unmistakable sound of footsteps.

And they were growing faster.

What started as shy, probing steps turned into full-on dashing through the forest. Jayden's head and hand holding the mace whipped around in a futile attempt to locate whoever was in the area. He realized too late that the footsteps were, in fact, coming from behind him.

Something crashed into his back, sending him toppling onto his stomach, the bear mace knocked out of his hand. His leg exploded with new, unimaginable pain. Jayden barely had time to recover when something sharp stung his neck.

He tried to scream, but he couldn't. Warm liquid trickled down his neck, and he knew that it was blood.

*His* blood.

As if that wasn't enough, something brushed through his hair and grabbed a firm grip on his scalp. It pulled his head back until it was raised enough for him to see the bear mace resting in the grass, mere feet from him.

This time, Jayden screamed. It was interrupted when his head violently snapped to the side with a loud pop that reverberated in his skull. His head slumped uselessly to the ground, his temple hitting the dirt.

Any resistance that Jayden wanted to continue exhibiting was gone because he couldn't move. He couldn't breathe. All he could do was stare at the grass and the trees as shuffling ensued around him.

When the sharpness in his neck burrowed deeper, he prayed for it all to be over fast.

***

Isabella ran until she couldn't run anymore; until her legs and lungs burned and until the tears dried from her eyes. She then resumed walking, until she was able to run again.

She had made it back to the village and then looked left and right, her panicked mind trying to remember which way they'd come from. Everything looked the same over here. She recognized the house that she and Jayden had seen first on their way down, and she knew that the trail would be right up there.

She plodded through the deep grass, stumbling along the way until she reached the elevation. From there, she climbed the hill using all fours, but it was too high for her to reach some of the rocky ledges. She had to go around and find a better foothold, and it only made her hyperventilate more because she was losing precious time.

Jayden was down in the valley, his leg broken, and night would fall soon. In her frenzied mind, Isabella tried to calculate how long it would take her to reach help. They'd left hours ago. *Hours.* It would be hours until she was able to reach the town for help and come back with the rescue.

When Isabella finally climbed the top of the ravine, her head whipped around. There was no trail. Why was there no trail? She was sure that it was supposed to be—

There it was, just thirty feet away from her. She pushed through the undergrowth, ignoring the branches that abraded her exposed arms. Once her feet were on the beaten path, she broke into a steady dash. She wanted to cry some more, but she couldn't let herself do it. Jayden needed her help.

The tinge of orange that poked between the foliage told her that she and Jayden had overstayed in the woods and that daylight was burning way too fast. She didn't let that discourage her. She ran past the familiar curves of the trail, painfully reminded of how far she still had to go.

She ran until she couldn't run anymore, until her legs shook like pudding and her lungs couldn't heave in more than a whiff of air. Until night fell. But she didn't stop. Her torch illuminating the path in front of her, Isabella continued with a steady gait, sobbing during those times, breaking into occasional jogs. Surely she was close now, right?

Something rustled off the trail.

Isabella froze in her tracks and swept the beam of the torch across the trees where the sound had come from. She couldn't see anything.

"Is someone there?" she called out, hopefulness clambering from the deepest recesses again. "Please, we need help! My boyfriend is hurt! Please!"

Her voice cracked when she said that, new tears sliding down her cheeks, shuddering. But then a sound made her go stock-still. A low groan erupted from the trees, deep, guttural, raspy. One that could by no means belong to a human being.

More rustling, approaching Isabella.

She didn't wait to see what it was. She spun on the ball of her shoes and dashed down the trail, her body filled with newfound strength. On cue, the thing in the trees broke out of the undergrowth, its footsteps stampeding after Isabella.

She suppressed the urge to scream as she ran, her mind racing with only one goal: get to safety.

That thought was short-lived when her foot got yanked backward and she fell headlong on the hard ground. Isabella's flashlight dropped out of her hand just as she whacked her face on the dirt, a shockwave sent through her nose, mouth, and gums. She had dislodged and chipped some teeth, that was for sure.

She planted her palms on the ground to push herself up, but before she could do that, she helplessly slid backward, away from the flashlight, deeper into darkness.

Isabella's screams were not heard by anyone that night.

***

Sometime later, the door of the hut opened, and the two hikers were dragged inside.

# CHAPTER 1

Dylan squinted against the afternoon sun. The day had only begun, and he was already irritable again.

Now that the time had come, he wasn't sure why he had agreed to go on this trip. One look at the person sitting on the sidewalk next to him was enough to give him his answer. A cigarette dangled out of Mickey's mouth, a plume of smoke billowing from the tip. He had been awfully quiet, which was so out of his character. It made Dylan realize that he was probably hungover from last night. Dylan liked Mickey more when he was hungover, he figured.

When Lexi first recommended the hike as a farewell activity before Dylan left to go back home, he wasn't too thrilled with the suggestion. Not only did he hate hiking, but he also didn't want to make his departure so official because it meant having to say goodbye to all of Lexi's friends and family, which meant a lot of hugging, kissing, and drinking.

He had politely declined her offer, but then she brought it up again last night at the house party. Dylan knew what the outcome would be before the others even gave their response. Mickey had jumped to his feet, saying that, yes, they had to go on this hike.

When Lexi mentioned that Dylan didn't want to go, all heads turned to him. A part of Dylan believed that Lexi had brought up the topic in front of the others so that they could pressure him into going. And sure enough, that was exactly what had happened.

"Come on, bro. Are you afraid of the woods?" Mickey had asked in his strong Eastern European accent.

Dylan had made a meager excuse about wanting to be rested for his flight back, but his words were drowned out by Mickey's obnoxiously loud voice.

"Come on! What is the problem? You'll be leaving soon," Mickey had said, his short stature occupying the middle of the room due to how much he waved his arms. "Don't you want to do one last thing before you leave?"

He then flung an arm around Dylan's shoulders and pointed to Lexi. "Look at my sister. How can you resist those eyes? Can't say no to them, right? Right?"

Dylan could have tried giving more excuses about why he couldn't go, but he had gotten to know Mickey well enough during his stay here to confirm that everything Lexi had said about him was true. He was as stubborn as a mule, and he would not take no for an answer, no matter what Dylan had planned out.

So instead, Dylan agreed to go, much to Mickey's cheering and drinking. Dylan had exchanged a look with Lexi. She had offered a solicitous smile. He had offered one back, but unlike hers, it hadn't been genuine.

Dylan desperately needed some time alone so he could think, but he'd hardly had any privacy since he arrived. If it wasn't private time with Lexi, then it would be either her mom or Mickey showering Dylan with attention. He appreciated them being so hospitable to him, but he really wished he could grab some alone time.

He had been in Europe for less than two weeks, and already, he couldn't wait to go back to the U.S. He had come here hoping to find some answers, and find them he did, only he didn't get the ones he was hoping for.

He was not looking forward to this hike, especially since he was so distracted. But then again, maybe it would be good for him. Either way, after this trip, he would be flying home, and then he would finally be able to grab some time to think things through.

He gazed down the street left and right. It was empty and quiet, save for the occasional car or pedestrian passing by. Some of them waved to Mickey, and they exchanged a few words in their language.

"My head is fucking killing me," Mickey said, confirming Dylan's suspicion. The word "fucking" came out as "fah-keeng."

"When are Lexi and the others going to pick us up?" Dylan asked.

Mickey took his time inhaling the cigarette smoke and blowing it out before answering, "Should be in five minutes, bro. You miss my sister already, huh?" He grinned.

Dylan averted his gaze to the bakery across the street. He took out his phone to play with it and pass the time. Since he had no internet, he went into the gallery and mindlessly scrolled through the pictures. He didn't let his own problems cloud his perception. This country was beautiful despite its shortcomings.

In the past two weeks, Lexi had taken him sightseeing all over the city. It was Dylan's first time traveling abroad, and she had done her best to make him feel as comfortable as she could. The moment he landed, she'd been waiting for him at the airport, drove him home where her mother had prepared a meal worthy of a king, and she was generally considerate enough to ask him if he was okay going to this place or that one.

Really, Dylan couldn't have asked for a better welcome.

Over the course of the next few days, he and Lexi went to all the places she thought he might like. His phone was full of pictures that he'd taken of beautifully built churches, fountains, bridges, medieval fortresses, and so on.

Lexi's entire family was welcoming, too. Although her mother didn't speak English, Lexi was there to translate for them. She incessantly urged Dylan to eat and asked if everything was okay with the food. Dylan wondered if all the mothers in the country were so hospitable.

As for Mickey... he was a little too overbearing for Dylan's taste, but at least he accepted Lexi's new boyfriend, and that was good enough for him; worth the hassle of having to listen to Mickey's bullshit stories of triumph.

Dylan stopped at the picture of him and Lexi in front of a replica of a Game of Thrones throne. It was the first day of his arrival. Lexi had been so happy to finally see him that she could hardly separate from him. After seeing the city for the day, the two of them had gone back home where Lexi had told Dylan to wait while she got changed.

She had entered the room in sexy red lingerie and gave him a seductive glance. He had opened his mouth to ask about her mom and Mickey, but she beat him to it.

"Don't worry. They won't be back for hours," she had said before sitting in his lap.

His daydreaming was interrupted by a car stopping in front of him and Mickey. Dylan looked up just as the windows rolled down, revealing the interior. Local music boomed from the car.

"Hop on in," Lexi said from the driver's seat.

# CHAPTER 2

"Hey, babe." Lexi leaned across the seat and kissed Dylan.

He gave her a ghost of a smile before turning to face the road. A knot had been tied inside Lexi's gut since early morning. Every time she saw Dylan, a painful reminder that he was going home soon shot through her. Just two more days, and then they would have to go back to texting, voice messages, and late-night video calls.

The last two weeks had flown by too fast. If Lexi could go to the United States with him, she would. But she couldn't, and the only thing she could do was rely on him to come visit her, instead.

"Where are the others?" Mickey asked as he plopped onto the backseat.

"We'll pick them up on our way out of town," Lexi said.

She and her brother had made it a habit to talk in English when Dylan was around so that he wouldn't feel excluded. Mickey had complained about Dylan not wanting to learn their native language, but Lexi dismissed that remark by reminding him that Dylan was a guest; therefore, English would be the official language they used until he returned home.

*Which is in two days.*

"Do I need to put on my seatbelt?" Mickey asked.

"As far as I'm concerned, no," Lexi said.

Mickey took that in for a moment and then dragged the seatbelt across his chest and clipped it. "Last time, I had to pay a fine. The cop wouldn't even take a bribe. I'm not going to mess around this time."

"That's why I said, as far as *I'm* concerned, you don't need to put on your seatbelt."

"Fuck you," Mickey said.

Dylan let out a chuckle. Lexi's face snapped toward him, absorbing that laugh and that smile. There was something that made her feel all warm inside whenever she managed to evoke a smile out of Dylan, even if it was a weak one.

Lexi hadn't met a lot of Americans, but the ones she had spoken to were over-the-top perky and friendly, yet it was a condescending kind of friendliness that Lexi could see through right away. She was so glad that her Dylan wasn't like that even with strangers.

Lexi shifted into first gear and gently pressed the gas pedal.

***

"By the way, did you see what kind of a shifter we have here?" Mickey asked, pointing between the driver and passenger's seats.

Dylan's eyes turned to the shifter momentarily. "Yeah, I saw it."

"If we drove this car to America, we could leave it unlocked because Americans wouldn't know how to drive it." Mickey burst into a laughing fit.

A smile crept up on Lexi's face. She looked at Dylan to gauge whether he would be offended or not. The chortle he let out convinced her he was okay with the joke.

Ringing came from the backseat. Mickey answered his phone and spoke to the person in their native language. It was an exaggerated greeting, but then again, Mickey did that with all the people.

"So, who else is coming? Oscar and Hannah?" Dylan asked as Lexi turned right and sped toward the bridge.

Mickey raised his voice for a moment. Lexi waited until the car quieted down before responding to Dylan.

"Yeah." She nodded absent-mindedly. "This morning, they sent a message saying they were too hungover to go, but I convinced them to come."

She didn't really care much whether Oscar and Hannah tagged along, but she wanted Dylan to feel less alone as the only foreigner.

"Hm," Dylan said.

She continued listening to Mickey's conversation, trying to decipher who he was talking to. He mentioned going on a hike to the woods with his sister and her boyfriend and two German filmography students, and then uttered a series of "uh-huh" and "yeah."

"So, what's this place that we're visiting?" Dylan asked.

"Um, just a hiking trail in the forest. It has some kind of stories and legends to it."

"What kind of legends?"

"Stuff related to Slavic folklore, like fairies gathering to dance there, and witches, and devils, and so on."

"Sounds dangerous."

"Don't worry. My grandmother told me those stories all the time when Mickey and I were kids. I know exactly how to defend against those creatures if we run into any."

Mickey ended the call and put the phone back in his pocket. "Oh, by the way. Bogdan is also coming. Do you mind if we pick him up, too?"

Lexi scowled at Mickey's reflection in the rearview mirror. He must have noticed it because he shrugged and asked, "What?"

Lexi couldn't resist it. She switched to their language and asked, "You invited Bogdan on our trip?"

"Well, yeah. I mean, he asked where we were going, and I thought it was appropriate to ask him if he wanted to come."

Lexi continued shooting daggers at her brother.

"Oh, come on. He's going through a rough patch. His girlfriend recently broke up with him, and he could use some company." Mickey threw his hands up.

"You didn't even ask me and Dylan if we're okay with it. You do this every fucking time, Mickey."

"What are you talking about? Name one other situation when I did it."

"Okay. The four times you invited Momo to the family barbeque."

"He's our cousin!"

"He's annoying and obnoxious! And you didn't ask Mom if it's okay to invite him."

"Yes, I did."

"No, you didn't. You just told her to prepare another plate. Seriously, what the hell is wrong with you? Don't you have any consideration toward the rest of us and what we want? For fuck's sake!"

"What's going on?" Dylan asked, his eyes intermittently darting from Lexi to Mickey.

Lexi sighed just as they crossed the bridge and turned onto a street riddled with cars. "Mickey invited a friend to come with us."

"So? What's the big deal?" Dylan asked.

Lexi ran a hand through her hair and then looked at the rearview mirror again, where Mickey sat shrunken in his seat, a guilty look on his face.

"You'll see when you meet him," she said.

***

Five minutes later, Lexi pulled over at a bus stop where Hannah and Oscar were waiting. Oscar was wearing the same clothes as last night, Lexi noticed: a red, button-up shirt and swim shorts decorated with tropical trees. Hannah had torn jeans on and a purple blouse that accentuated her blonde hair. Both of them had large backpacks strapped to them.

"Come on," Lexi said, and then looked in the rearview mirror to see a bus approaching from behind. "Quickly."

"Are you allowed to park in the bus station like this?" Dylan asked.

"Probably not, but we'll only take a moment." Lexi shrugged.

He was in awe when Lexi first explained to him that the laws in this country didn't work like in America. Under the veil of the tourist-friendly country with smiling people and prospering businesses, a dark reality lurked, one that only the people who had grown up there would know.

There was no union to protect the employees, so workers were constantly exploited. Hell, Lexi herself worked in a betting shop for below minimum wage as an unregistered employee.

Cops could be easily bribed. The only time they didn't take bribes was when they were on camera.

Running your own business was pretty much impossible unless you had ties to the underground and could therefore prevent getting racketeered.

Elections were merely a formality, rigged so that the same political party would win every four years.

Dylan had asked her why she wasn't more angry about stuff like that happening. He went on to say that things like those in America would not be tolerated and that the people would overthrow the government. But he didn't understand.

He came from a country where you could say anything you wanted without repercussions. Over here, any attempt of an insurgence would be snuffed out before it properly bloomed.

So when he asked her why she wasn't more angry, she shrugged and said, "I learned to ignore it."

And that was the truth. Seeing the news did make Lexi angry, but there was nothing she could do about it, so she simply stopped watching TV and blocked all political outlets on social media. She had learned long ago that protests in this country did nothing to make the lives of the citizens better.

Hannah and Oscar squeezed in next to Mickey and shut the door.

"Hey, guys," Oscar said.

"Hi," Lexi said, still angry that they had one more person to pick up. "Mickey, where do you want me to pick up your friend?" She made sure to emphasize *your friend*. Why Mickey still hung out with Bogdan was beyond her.

"Turn right, and he should be at the movie theater," Mickey said.

The car lurched forward just as the bus approached.

# CHAPTER 3

Gerard sat on the bed, leafing through a fitness magazine that had been sitting on the nightstand ever since he arrived two months ago. His coworker James sat in front of the computer monitor, furiously clicking the mouse.

Occasionally, Gerard glanced up at him to see what the fuss was all about. Thirty minutes earlier, the two men were playing poker at the table in the middle of the room. A loud ping had come from the computer, and James's head had jerked toward the screen. He had muttered a barely coherent, "What the hell?" as his eyes widened at something. He had jumped off the chair, dropping his cards carelessly, revealing a hand that would have handed Gerard his ass back to him.

"What's up?" Gerard had asked, but James gave no answer.

He was already in front of the computer, furiously clicking something as his eyes darted to various corners of the monitor. Gerard had held onto his cards because he knew that James would be done with work as soon as he realized it was a false alarm.

Minutes passed, and Gerard's numerous questions yielded no answer from James, so he dropped his own cards and went to bed to give his spine a break from the hour-long sitting. Then, when he least expected it, James's voice tore through the room.

"It's picking up something," he said.

Gerard pried his eyes from the woman with chiseled abs on the page and looked at James. He was facing him, concern draped over his face.

"What?" Gerard asked.

"There's something close by. And I think it's what we've been stationed to look out for," James said.

Gerard lowered the magazine and studied James's face for a moment. "Really? How far away is it?"

"A couple of kilometers from here."

Gerard grinned. "Kilometers? Two months here, and you're already converting to the metric system."

"We need to check it out," James ignored his partner's remark.

"Okay, sure. Let's do it after lunch."

"No. We need to do it now."

Gerard scratched his chin. He didn't like the look of urgency on James's face. He also didn't like the idea of going out for a hike, looking for something that may or may not be out there. The equipment was still finnicky, and it often picked up big animals instead of what they were looking for.

In the end, he knew that James would not relent until they went to check it out. Technically speaking, Gerard could just let James go check it out on his own. Not like HQ was breathing down their necks. But if something were to happen—say, James got into some kind of trouble—then questions would be raised, and it wouldn't be long until they figured out that someone was slacking.

Gerard opened his mouth to ask if it could wait at least until he'd taken a shit, but he knew what James would answer before he even asked. "Okay, fine. Let's get ready and go then."

James was already up on his feet, putting on his boots and strapping equipment to his belt. Gerard was the one in charge of security, so he opened the weapons rack and retrieved his rifle. After so long of not using it, it felt heavy in his hands.

"Okay, ready when you are." He jutted his head toward the door.

James needed another minute to check if all of his equipment was in working order. He pulled each gadget out and fiddled with it for a moment before strapping it back to his tool belt. "Let's go," he finally said as he cinched his belt.

Gerard opened the heavy bulkhead door and allowed James to exit first. Once they were outside, Gerard closed the door and sealed it. From the outside, the small station where they worked was completely covered in ghillie nets, making it practically invisible. Passersby could walk mere feet past it and they wouldn't ever be able to tell that there was something hidden there.

"Which way?" Gerard asked.

The sonar device was in front of James. He swiveled left and right before breaking into a trek in a random direction. "Here."

Gerard took a final look over his shoulder at the hidden station, then at his wristwatch pinpointing his location and the location of the station. He took a firmer hold of his rifle and went after James.

***

Gerard's attempts at small talk were met with either silence or one-worded responses on James's end. Since his partner was so enthralled by whatever was on the sonar's screen, Gerard stopped talking and followed James in silence.

Occasionally, James would give a confused remark about something Gerard didn't understand. Gerard knew better than to ask him what was up. It was James just talking aloud to himself. Perhaps vocalizing the questions or the problems at hand helped him brainstorm solutions better. Either way,

Gerard didn't care. His role was to point and shoot if necessary. James was the one in charge of the logistics.

"There should be a clearing just past here," James said as he broke toward the tall undergrowth blocking their path.

No sooner did he dive into the foliage did he trip and fall on one knee.

"Careful," Gerard said, dragging his boots through the leaves and plants, carefully testing each step before planting his foot down firmly.

They jostled through the overgrown vegetation until it was gone out of nowhere. The two men stood in the middle of a beaten path that stretched in both directions as far as Gerard could see.

"There's a trail here? HQ never mentioned anything about that," he said.

"Yeah. There's not supposed to be one. I guess they didn't..." James trailed off.

"They didn't what? James, they didn't—" Gerard trailed, too, when he noticed the slab of brown and red in the middle of the trail not far from them.

Without a word, James looked at his sonar and then broke into a gait toward the piece of meat on the road. Gerard followed, his trigger finger just a little itchier. Something didn't feel right about it. He couldn't shake the feeling that they were not welcome here, but he couldn't tell why.

"Slow down, James," he called out.

But James wasn't listening. If anything, his pace quickened. When he was a few feet away from whatever was on the road, he clasped a hand over his mouth. Something that sounded like a gag escaped James's mouth. Gerard understood why the moment he approached.

Splayed in the middle of the road was a mutilated human torso. The head and limbs were gone, mangled stumps remaining instead of them. Long-since dried blood soaked the shirt and jeans beyond recognition. Flies nested and buzzed around the corpse, feeding on the rotten flesh.

The smell hit Gerard's nostrils hard. His throat constricted and refused to let him inhale any more air for a moment. "Jesus," he said.

Gerard walked past James and approached the body, careful not to step in any dried organs that spilled out of the eviscerated gut. It was safe to do an inspection since whatever had killed this person was probably long gone.

Gerard planted his heel on the side of the torso and flipped it over.

"It was a man," James said when he noticed the flat chest.

"Oh, yeah? How do we know it wasn't just some tomboy?" Gerard grinned.

"Look at that." James pointed to the large, gaping hole just above the chest, ignoring his partner's joke. "It looks as if someone drilled through his chest."

"Yeah, what is up with that? HQ was on to something when they said there was something wrong with these woods. We need to go back and report this. Not sure we'll want to stay out here with whatever did... that." James gestured to the mutilated body.

"What about the body?"

"What about it?"

"Shouldn't we take it back for the research teams to study it?"

"Do you want to be the one to carry it?"

Gerard shrugged. "Without its limbs, it's going to be pretty light. But I didn't bring any body bags with me."

"Leave it. Let the research crew worry about it."

"Whatever you say, boss."

James turned around and started down the way they came. He couldn't have done it in a bigger hurry.

Gerard squatted in front of the body, scrutinizing it. The smell was much stronger now. It was a mixture of iron, sweat, piss, shit, and rot.

Gerard had seen his share of dead bodies on this job, so he had grown somewhat accustomed to finding mangled remains. Mostly, it was just dead animals that he ran into, but from time to time, he'd find a dead human on the job.

He squinted at the torso. The shirt of the victim had been torn in steady lines. *Claw marks*, Gerard realized. He stared at the hole in the chest. Past the tunnel of sinew, broken bones, and cartilage, where the heart should have been, was a black hole.

He averted his gaze to the guts that spooled on the ground like a garden hose. The opening in the stomach was too wide and too deep. Gerard wondered if it was the cause of death. He hoped not. Then again, the idea of the person being alive while getting his arms and legs torn off was much worse.

Resolved not to worry about issues that weren't his own to worry about, Gerard stood up and turned to follow James.

But James was nowhere in sight.

He might have gone off the trail back to the station. Gerard made his way down the trail and then glanced at his wristwatch to see which way to go. With that, he turned to step into the undergro—

Blood on the ground caught his attention.

Not old, dried blood like they'd seen near the corpse. This was fresh. The crimson color of the droplets that mixed in with the dirt was testament to that. Gerard followed the droplets with his gaze. They led into the vegetation where they grew in abundance. Instead of droplets, it was now a wide trail of blood that swerved left and right, disappearing behind the trees.

*Shit.*

"James!" Gerard raised his rifle and took off the safety. "Fuck."

He was fucked. He was so fucked. He was wrong. Dead wrong. The thing that got the guy on the trail now got James. And now it was going to get him, too. Fuck.

"James!" he called out once more, unsure why he was even trying.

His instinct told him to bolt the hell out of there before whatever got his partner came back. He had to go back. He had to inform HQ that they'd run into something dangerous.

He kept his gun at the ready as he broke into a plod in the direction of the station. Whether it was a coincidence or something else, the trail slugged in the same direction. A part of Gerard—a selfish part of him—hoped that the trail of blood would lead elsewhere, anywhere away from him, so that he could go back to the station safely. The righteous part in him hoped to find his partner alive and well.

*Look at all this blood, Gerard. Do you really think James made it?*

One foot in front of the other. Gerard made good progress to the little dot on his wristwatch. Just a few hundred feet away. As much as he wanted to break into a sprint, a little voice told him not to lower his gun. Something was close by, and it was watching him. The silence of the forest was a testament to that.

A susurrus on Gerard's left caused him to snap in the direction of the sound. Something just slinked behind a big boulder. Conveniently, the blood led in that exact direction.

Check it out or run to the station?

After a moment of debating, he broke through the greenery toward his partner. His eyes and gun were trained on the trail of blood on the nettles disappearing behind the boulder. The entire time, something inside him screamed at him to turn around and make a beeline for the station, but he just couldn't. Not while there was a chance for James to be alive.

It wasn't until he got close to the boulder that he heard something coming from behind it. He couldn't tell what the sound was, but it was steady, constant, and barely above a whisper. Gerard resisted the urge to call out to his partner.

He sidestepped in front of the boulder, his gun trained on whatever he would find. His partner's feet stuck out from behind the rock, kicking and spasming. James's boots and shins were slick with fresh blood. Gerard took another sideways step, further revealing James. His entire body jerked spastically. He was drenched in blood. And his face...

Something hairy stood hunched over James's neck, buried in it, a cacophony of chomping and gurgling sounds filling the air. James's eyes flitted to Gerard in a silent plea for help. His lips were parted, blood gushing out of his mouth and trickling down the side of his face.

"Oh my God," Gerard said in a meek voice just as a loud crunch came from the thing hunched over James's neck.

It stopped chewing and slowly raised its head. It was him.

Despite having his finger on the trigger, Gerard spun on his heel and broke into a sprint in the opposite direction. A loud shriek came from behind him, one that made Gerard's blood run icy. Footsteps pattered behind him, catching up way too fast for his liking.

A hiss breathed at his heels, and then unimaginable pain exploded in his calf. Gerard stumbled headlong with a yelp. He rolled onto his back, pointed his gun in front of himself, and squeezed the trigger. Loud gunshots boomed in the air as he shot at...

Nothing.

Gerard looked around, but there was no one there. Just then, rustling and more footsteps came close by, from everywhere around him. Gerard's head swiveled, his gun pointed in various directions, but whatever was close by seemed to slink out of view just as he was about to catch it.

He had to keep moving.

He propped himself up on his palms and clambered to his feet using his good leg. His calf was on fire, and he was too afraid to look down to assess the damage.

*Safety first, first aid later.*

Gerard gave the area another scan, trying to pinpoint the source of the sound. The footsteps were still there, still taunting him, out of view whenever he looked at them but drawing closer with each passing second.

No use. Gerard turned around and dashed in the direction of the station. Not far now. His knee almost buckled when he put weight on the injured leg. He lumbered on, his eyes fixed on the spot behind the densely packed trees where the station was.

Whatever made those footsteps before was still behind him and still followed him, unrelenting. It could have caught up to him already, so why wasn't it tackling him?

Then it hit him. It was playing with him. It didn't want to kill him just yet. But why? He didn't care. He just wanted to get to safety.

*Come on, goddammit! Come on!*

The moment he slammed into the bulkhead door, he wanted to drop the rifle but didn't. It could determine whether he lived or died. Gerard grabbed the handle hidden behind the ghillie net and pushed it down hard. The lock opened with a metallic squeal.

*Yes!*

He rammed the door open with his shoulder and stumbled inside. He turned around and pushed the door to close it. Before the gap could disappear, something whipped through it and whacked Gerard in the face hard enough to make him fall on his back.

The side of his face throbbed with pain. Blood obscured his vision on that side. Gerard wiped the blood and felt that something was wrong under his fingers. Blood didn't obscure his eye. He was *missing* his eye.

The only thing that stopped him from screaming in pure terror at that realization was the clawed hand that wiggled itself into the gap and grabbed him by the foot.

"No!" Gerard shouted as he helplessly slid toward the door, away from safety.

He dug one heel into the wall while whatever was outside tugged at his foot. Then, that same foot exploded with pain unlike any Gerard had ever felt in his life. He threw his head back and screamed, a caterwaul that rang inside the room like a siren.

It felt like a dozen knives were slicing through his foot. And then, just like that, the grip on it was gone, and Gerard scooted deeper into the station, free from whatever had held onto him. A trail of crimson coated the floor where his foot should have been—where, instead, was a mangled stump just below the shin.

Gerard let out a petulant scream, or at least, he thought he did, but the ringing in his ears made it impossible to hear. He felt no pain, only horror at the mess of his leg and eye.

The clawed hand poked through the gap. It grabbed the edge of the heavy door. Gerard rolled onto his belly and soldier-crawled forward, just as the bulkhead screeched while the creature in front shoved it open.

Gerard was a dead man, there was no question of that. But there was one thing he needed to do before he died. One final act that would ensure this monster's death.

He crawled to the communications desk and wedged his fingers on the edge, pushing himself up. His hand slipped from the blood and he smashed his chin on the desk, his teeth clamping down painfully on his tongue. He could feel the creature standing just behind him. He could see its shadow rising across the wall.

With one final effort, Gerard slammed the big red button on the keyboard and allowed himself to fall down. He fell on his back, panting heavily, fear mixed with a sense of triumph.

A smile stretched his lips just as the creature lunged at him.

# CHAPTER 4

Dylan didn't want to probe Lexi with questions because he could see how pissed she was. Whoever this Bogdan guy was, Lexi didn't like him one bit, and she made sure to make it known.

A few minutes after picking up Hannah and Oscar, Lexi stopped in front of a movie theater and turned on the hazard lights. The traffic was pretty bad in this part of the town, and the driver behind honked in frustration. Mickey shouted something in their language and flipped off the driver.

An athletically built guy that had been staring around sheepishly made a step forward when his eyes fell on Lexi's car. He opened the door on Mickey's side and said something that was probably supposed to be "move over."

With four people in the backseat, Bogdan barely managed to shut the door. Considering his broad shoulders and being stuffed in the car with three other people, he looked like a gorilla in a cupboard that was too small. He said something, his eyes scanning everyone in the car before they fell on Dylan. He pointed a finger and asked Mickey something with an amused smile on his face.

"This is my boyfriend, Dylan. He's from America," Lexi said. "We speak English when he's around."

"Ooohhh." Bogdan threw his chin up, "America? Ohhh."

He proceeded to say something to Lexi in their language. The only word Dylan recognized in that sentence was Lexi's name. There was no doubt that Bogdan was saying something about Dylan, though.

"English," Lexi simply retorted, cold-faced.

"Uh... My English not so good. He not speak, uh..."

"No. English. Mickey can translate for you if you don't understand."

Lexi spoke English pretty well. The only thing that made it noticeable that she was not American was her accent, and even that was negligible save for some words where her native accent slipped. Everything else, though—even the pesky hard H and improper R that her countrymen struggled with—was perfectly pronounced.

"Okay, okay." Bogdan leaned forward and outstretched a hand. "Hi. I'm Bogdan."

Dylan craned and shook his hand. "Dylan. Nice to meet you."

Bogdan's grip was unnaturally strong. The way he squeezed his hand, the way his jaw clenched, and the way his eyes remained firmly fixed on Dylan made it clear that he was testing Dylan, trying to determine if he was man enough.

Dylan didn't understand what was up with the men in the country having such fragile egos that they constantly had to prove to others that they were as tough as they looked. Mickey was like that, too, and so were some other guys that Dylan met in the country. It must have been a cultural thing.

Even after Dylan loosened the grip, Bogdan kept his firm for a few seconds longer, just to clearly get the point across. Dylan didn't care about playing a petty macho game with this stranger. He averted his gaze and turned to face forward. He noticed Lexi giving him a stern stare.

"You okay?" He put a hand on her thigh.

She covered his hand with hers and squeezed back, nodded, and smiled.

After some silence, Bogdan asked something in their language, to which Lexi shot him a glower. Mickey cleared his throat. "Bogdan, let's speak English so that Dylan can understand us."

"Ah, okay, okay. Sorry. I forget we have American with us." He paused as if giving Dylan time to respond. When no response came, Bogdan continued, "I asked, where are we going?"

"*Vilinska Shuma*," Mickey answered. "There are good hiking trails over there."

"I bring nothing with me." Bogdan shrugged. "I have no food and water."

"You can share with Mickey. Right, Mickey?" Lexi grinned and looked over her shoulder at her brother. The corners of Dylan's lips stretched into a lopsided grin.

"Have you guys been there before?" Oscar leaned forward so that he could get a look at everyone. "Hannah and I read some stories online about it."

There was a momentary pause before Lexi answered that question. "Yeah, we went camping there for May Day a few times."

"Oh, those were good." Bogdan grinned. "We should do it this year, too. Your American boyfriend can join us. What do you say, American?"

He gave Dylan a tap on the shoulder, another reminder that he felt a desperate need to run the show.

"He goes home in two days," Lexi said.

"Oh, too bad," Bogdan said, but he didn't sound very sorrowful about it at all. "Maybe next year, yes?"

"Maybe," Dylan said in a clipped tone.

"So, what kind of stories did you read, Oscar?" Lexi asked, her chin momentarily raised toward the rearview mirror.

They had left the busy streets of the city and descended onto a badly maintained concrete road. The buildings on their left and right turned into old, sparsely-populated houses. Farm animals, stacks of hay, makeshift silos for corn, tractors, and fields of sunflowers populated the properties and fields. Most of the area was flat land, providing a view on every horizon. It was peaceful, but Dylan couldn't imagine living somewhere so far from town.

"Well, some of the stories we've read are myths," Oscar said. "Like the one about an evil witch in the woods, and that fairies gather around something called the Eye."

"Yeah. We'll go to the Eye if we can," Lexi said.

"Isn't Eye far away?" Bogdan interjected.

"Nope." Lexi offered no further explanation after the single word.

No one said anything for a moment. The only sound was the car's engine and the occasional skip as the tires went from one patch of the road to another.

"There are also true stories," Hannah said, breaking the silence. "People went missing in those woods, and no one knows what happened to them."

Dylan cocked an eyebrow. He wasn't too happy about going to a place where disappearances were known to have happened. He looked at Lexi, silently demanding an explanation. She noticed this, so she quickly said, "That was just a pair of hikers. And they disappeared because they didn't listen to the instructions and went down the trail that wasn't supposed to be used."

"They lived on the other side of the country, right?" Mickey asked.

"Yes." Bogdan nodded. "Strangers get lost in those woods often. You better watch out, American, or you might get lost there, too."

He and Mickey burst into a peal of laughter. Dylan didn't find the quip amusing. It was just another jab by Bogdan. Dylan was sure that if the situation were reversed, and he told him he would get lost in the Rockies, Bogdan would get offended.

No, actually, he wouldn't get offended. He would try to prove that he wouldn't get lost. Dylan didn't know how he knew that; he just did. Bogdan looked exactly like that type.

"So, they never found that couple?" Dylan asked.

"Nope. They did find a backpack, but they couldn't figure out what happened to them." Lexi stared at the road ahead.

"The official report said they were attacked by a bear," Oscar said.

"That's stupid." Mickey snorted. "There are no bears in the area. No dangerous animals at all. They must have been on drugs or something."

"Drugs?" Bogdan's eyes lit up as if it was the only word in Mickey's sentence that he understood. "I have some weed here." He patted his pocket as best as the tiny space allowed him to. "We can smoke in forest, yes?"

Silence draped the car. Bogdan was talking to the wrong audience. Dylan had never inhaled a whiff of anything smoke-producing in his life. Lexi had tried it a couple of times but claimed it was disgusting. Hannah and Oscar looked like they would cringe at something as innocent as jaywalking, let alone smoking weed. That only left one candidate to smoke with Bogdan: his pal, Mickey.

"Are you kidding?" Lexi asked. "You didn't bring anything for the hike, but you brought weed? If the cops pull us over, I'm not covering your ass."

"Relax, Alexa. Relax." Bogdan laughed. "We just have fun, no? No cops."

Lexi's nostrils expanded and contracted in suppressed anger. Obviously, she wanted to give Bogdan—and Mickey—a piece of her mind but was resisting the urge.

"Mickey, you and I smoke this, yes?" Bogdan asked.

Mickey looked at Lexi as if seeking approval. Noticing her stare, he said, "Maybe it's best if we leave it for another time."

"You guys not fun." Bogdan shook his head. "American, you're a good man. How about you?"

*You're a good man.* Of course he would try the amicable approach when no one else backed him up.

"No, thanks," Dylan retorted.

"Come on, it will be fun. Alexandra did it with us a few times, remember, Alexa?"

Dylan looked at Lexi, his expression silently asking what in the world she was thinking, smoking with a guy like Bogdan. Lexi scrunched her lips as if she had just tasted something sour.

"We're not smoking weed," she said with finality in her voice.

Dylan expected more pushing on Bogdan's side, but he shrugged instead and, without further complaints, said, "Okay."

The rest of the ride was somewhat silent, save for Mickey and Bogdan's talking in their language in the background. Lexi didn't remind them to speak English, and Dylan didn't care, either. He pulled out his phone a few times, a regular habit whenever he had nothing to do with his hands. No new notifications, so he put it back into his pocket.

His thoughts were elsewhere. As he stared out onto the crops that whizzed past them, he wondered what awaited him in life next.

He looked at Lexi, who was so intently focused on the road. Sometimes, he looked at her and couldn't believe how beautiful she was. She was the prettiest in those moments when she didn't know he was watching her. It was the most natural, unfiltered version of her. The version that Dylan had fallen in love with.

Other times, he would glance at her and feel absolutely nothing. He tried telling himself that it was completely normal to have bouts of affection and indifference, but something about that indifference toward Lexi had been bothering him lately.

He could go a while without missing her like he used to, whereas, she would be all emotional if they skipped just one day of video chat. He used to love everything about her: the way she mispronounced some words, the way her voice changed whenever she spoke in her language, the way she loved spending hours in the kitchen, cooking up all sorts of cuisine from her country.

Nowadays, he felt nothing about it. Moreover, it bothered him sometimes. He started to tell himself that he and Lexi had no future together. She lived an ocean away, and they were kind of different. He hated himself for feeling that way, but he couldn't help it.

All of that was enough for him to decide to visit Lexi before the agreed time. It was March, and he wasn't supposed to visit until June. But he had to come. He had to know how he would feel once he saw her.

A part of him believed that he would fall in love with her all over again once he saw her at the airport. Everything would be okay again. And if not? Then he would break up with her, as difficult as it was.

But that didn't happen. What he got instead was a mix of both. He was glad to see her, but the desire wasn't as strong as he expected it to be.

That left Dylan feeling even more confused than before. He felt like he couldn't give himself to her as much as she deserved, but he also couldn't bring himself to break up because, what if he realized that he'd made a mistake? Things would then never be the same between him and Lexi.

With everything going on in his life, he hoped to clear some of the confusion away, at least in the aspect related to his private life, but instead, he only had more questions—about everything.

He was studying biochemistry, and it didn't even interest him. He didn't really care what college he would go to after graduating high school. He just wanted those years of studying to be over so he could move on with his life and find a job. He wished that he'd thought things through more thoroughly before choosing biochemistry.

At the time, he looked at his grades and tried to determine what he would be good at. Chemistry was always an A, just like physics and English, and the rest were all B's or C's. So the choice was either English, physics, or chemistry. Physics was hard, so that was out of the question. English was easy, but what kind of a job would he have with literature? So, he opted for biochemistry.

The major hadn't bothered him during the first few years, but now that he was a senior, with the prospect of becoming an adult and getting a job closer than ever before, he contemplated the direction in which his life was going.

His poor choice for college and his inability to decide whether he still loved Lexi left him feeling like he was at a crossroads in life, with all the other trails as unclear as the one he was on right now.

"Oh, I've packed some of your favorite energy drinks from the store down the street," Lexi said.

Dylan smiled, warmth swaddling him.

"The ones that taste like raspberry?"

"Uh-huh." She nodded.

"Babe, you shouldn't have."

This was one of those moments when he loved her, when his emotions for her were so strong that he wanted to reel her in and kiss her until his lips hurt. She was so thoughtful. He honestly didn't deserve someone like her. She deserved someone who would love her unconditionally, and not look for flaws.

He reached across the shifter and took her hand into his. They interlocked their fingers and exchanged a warm glance with each other. Dylan could feel eyes on them. He looked at the backseat to see Bogdan ogling them. When his eyes met with Dylan's, he quickly looked back at Mickey, nodding at whatever he was saying.

"I'm going to miss this country's food when we go back to Germany," Oscar said.

He and Hannah were looking at something on their phones.

"Me too. But it's for the best. Otherwise, we would be one hundred kilograms by the time we go home," Hannah said. She looked at Lexi and asked, "Seriously, how do you manage to stay so slim with such good food?"

"You cry every day until you get used to it." Lexi shrugged.

"Not me. I eat whenever I want to eat." Mickey patted his ample beer belly.

How someone was able to be so skinny and still have a belly was beyond Dylan.

"So, did you guys get what you were looking for?" Dylan raised his chin.

Hannah and Oscar were Mickey's friends from back when he worked with his uncle in Germany during the summer. For their filmography school project, they traveled to the country to make a documentary about the culture and how it differed from the rest of the European Union countries.

"Yes!" Hannah exclaimed. "Not too much, but we did get enough for our project. Right, Oscar?"

"Yes. Everyone is so nice in this country. I thought we would have a lot more trouble getting information."

"Everybody here loves Germans," Mickey said. "Because everybody wants to go live in your country."

"You've been to Germany, Mickey. Why didn't you stay?" Oscar asked.

"I wanted to, but there was a delay in the papers I was supposed to get. I'll go back there this winter. Either there or Switzerland."

"What's in Switzerland?" Dylan asked.

"Money." Mickey grinned.

"When are you guys heading back?" Dylan craned his neck toward Oscar and Hannah.

"This Saturday," Oscar responded. "We would have stayed longer, but we have classes starting Monday."

"This is your third year, right?"

"Yes."

"And after that?"

Hannah and Oscar exchanged quizzical glances. They smiled at each other; loving looks that only they understood.

Oscar then looked at Dylan and said, "Well, the wedding is this summer. You guys are going to be there, right?"

Murmurs filled the car.

"Dylan, will you be able to join Lexi?" Hannah asked.

"Um..." Dylan hesitated. Summer seemed so far away, even if it was just a few months. Who knew where Dylan would be this summer? "I'm not sure, to be honest. I'll do my best, but I can't promise anything."

"Everything will be paid for, so you wouldn't need to worry about any costs," Oscar said.

"I appreciate that, guys."

"The offer stands, but we also understand that the United States is far away, so if you can't make it, no hard feelings."

"Thanks for understanding."

"If American can't join, it still plus one, yes?" Bogdan interjected. "Would be shame for invite to go to waste. I will be happy to go with Lexi."

Dylan pressed his lips into a thin line. What the fuck was this guy's problem? He had it in his mind to tell Bogdan right there that he *would* go to the wedding, just to spite him, but he didn't want to make any promises in anger that he wouldn't be able to keep.

Hannah cleared her throat and looked out the window. Oscar stirred. Nobody wanted to have someone like Bogdan at their wedding. Dylan knew the type all too well. He was the type to be the loudest at a party where there was a guest of honor. The type to binge drink and eat as much as he could just because it was free. The type to take slices of cake without asking if they were reserved for someone else.

Stereotypical? Maybe, but so far, Bogdan had fit the profile of every stereotype that Dylan disliked.

There was something else about him that Dylan didn't like, but he just couldn't put his finger on it. He dismissed it as Bogdan just being one of those people that he simply disliked because of his overbearing personality.

"So, what about after the wedding?" Lexi asked.

"We actually have a few job offers," Oscar said.

"Really?" Lexi raised her eyebrows.

"Yes," Hannah said. "A news company offered us a job, and there are also some other gigs that are interesting."

"Nice. How'd you get those offers?"

"We made a short horror movie and uploaded it to YouTube, and it just got noticed."

"That's really impressive." Dylan nodded.

"How much is pay?" Bogdan asked.

His question somehow knocked down the perky mood of the car's interior.

"We're not sure yet," Oscar said after a moment of hesitation. "The starting pay is around three thousand euros."

Bogdan let out something that sounded like a disappointed "ohhh," as if to say that the pay was too low for his standards.

The ride for the next fifteen minutes consisted of music on the local radio playing, a sheepish voice that howled imperceptible words. Mickey hummed along to some of them. The farmsteads were far behind them now, leaving them encased within rows of tall trees stretching along both sides of the road. The road ascended so gradually, that Dylan didn't realize how high up they were until he looked out the window at the roadside barriers and the steep, hilly drops beyond them. Pressure built in his ears, and he had to yawn to cause them to pop and restore proper hearing.

"How much longer do we have?" Dylan asked.

"Just twenty more minutes or something like that," Lexi said.

"Can we take break? I must piss." Bogdan leaned forward and scratched his shoulder, his bicep flexed just a little too hard, showing off the bulge and the thick vein that wormed down his arm.

"Hold it. We'll be there soon," Lexi said.

"Actually, I have to use the bathroom, too," Hannah said. A few heads turned to face her. "Sorry." She bit her lip. "Drank too much apple juice before we left."

"Okay, fine. Bathroom break, it is." Lexi sighed.

Since the road had widened, she was able to pull up to the side of it safely. Once the car came to a halt, she turned the key in the ignition, silencing the engine and the incessant howling of the singer on the radio.

"Take five, everyone," she said as she opened the door.

# CHAPTER 5

Bogdan's muscles were stiff from the ride, so he took a moment to stretch his arms and legs. He straightened his shirt and looked down at the muscles on his arms and chest. Mickey stood on the side of the road, a cigarette dangling from his mouth, a lighter brought to the tip as he struggled to flick it on. The others stepped out of the car, too, congregating into two small groups: Lexi and the American being one, the Germans being the other.

Bogdan stared at the American and Lexi for a moment. They weren't aware of him watching. He didn't like the way Lexi looked at the American. The way her eyes lit up whenever she talked to him, the way her smile refused to droop... It meant that the American was important, and Bogdan didn't like not being the important one.

He grimaced at the American's ridiculously perfect white teeth before sauntering across the road into the woods. He found a spot in the trees where the others wouldn't see him and took a leak. Not that he did mind if someone saw his tool, especially Lexi and the American. He was well-endowed, after all.

Despite his thick hair and well-packed muscles, Bogdan couldn't help but feel like he was still inadequate next to Lexi's boyfriend. Was it because he was from America? Americans did usually think they were better than the rest of the world. Or maybe it was his calm attitude that asserted confidence?

Or maybe it was the fact that they insisted on speaking English, despite not being in America. Everything centered around the American, and that made Bogdan angry.

Bogdan had worked hard on his body for years, until it had become a machine, and he dressed really well and wore only expensive colognes, but still, there was this guy, Dylan—what a stupid name—who looked like he hadn't done sports in his entire life, and Lexi was still falling all over him, not Bogdan. That made him angry, but no matter.

Bogdan finished taking a leak and zipped up his jeans. He returned to the car where the group talked about random nonsense.

"...parts of the year, the Eye is going to be almost completely drained, whereas, at other times, it'll be full enough to swim in it," Lexi explained.

In *English*, Bogdan noted.

"You talk about the Eye?" he asked just as he joined in.

He pretended to scratch his bicep, making sure to flex his muscles while doing so. Years ago, it had been a habit, something he used to do actively to show off his hard work to people. Now, it was merely a reflex. He noticed Lexi glancing briefly at him.

It was a start.

"Yeah," Mickey answered instead of Lexi.

"Going to Eye is dangerous. Very... how you say... high hills?"

"Steep hills?" the American corrected.

"Yes," Bogdan confirmed, even though he wasn't sure what *steep* meant. "And very long road. Maybe you not make it if you not used to walking."

"I'll be fine. I do plenty of hiking back home." The American smiled. It was one of those patronizing smiles that they offered to foreigners. Bogdan played along. He smiled back.

"So, you go back to America soon, yes? Lexi, will you go with him?"

Lexi crossed her arms and shook her head.

"She won't," the American said, casting a brusque glance in Lexi's direction.

The way Lexi suddenly turned slightly away from the group made Bogdan think she was uncomfortable. If there was one thing Bogdan was good at besides lifting weights, it was smelling crucial moments where something unsaid lingered between the lines; something that he could use to his advantage.

"Why not?" he asked as he stiffened his lips to push down the smile that tickled his mouth.

A moment of silence, and then the American said, "She couldn't get her visa."

"Ohhh, such shame." Bogdan looked at Lexi. In his mind, he was dancing. "Why not?"

Lexi's eyes were glued to her feet. The American gave her a somber look before turning back to Bogdan. "We don't know. They often deny people from here visas."

Bogdan, of course, knew about that. Lots of people applied for tourist visas to visit first-world countries like Canada and the Americas, and they got denied time after time after time. If they didn't have any proof that something bound them to their country of residence, their visa would be denied.

As if reading his mind, Mickey said, "They're afraid that she'll stay there illegally." He sucked on his cigarette and blew out a plume of smoke.

"And, would you?" Bogdan asked.

"Of course not!" Lexi was offended.

"I would." Mickey shrugged.

Bogdan expected the American to come to the defense of his country, just as all Americans do, but that never happened.

"Me too," Bogdan lied. He would never go to a pretentious country like America where people still acted like it was the Wild West. He loved his country, and he would never leave it even if it meant having to deal with corruption, low wages, and inflated prices.

"What?" Mickey asked when he noticed his sister's glower. "Lots of people I know went to live there illegally, and they're doing just fine. One guy who went to school with me was asked in his interview how long he planned on staying there. He said twenty days, and they gave him his visa for six months. He's been there for three years now, and he lives the American dream. Just like all the others who stayed there. They have a job, they earn more money than they ever would here..."

"And they live in fear," Lexi finished his sentence. "What if they get pulled over by a cop? What if their neighbor rats them out? What if they want to visit their family or their family wants to visit them?"

Mickey shrugged before inhaling some more nicotine.

"I have friend. He got denied five times before he got visa." Bogdan raised five fingers.

Lexi's eyes gleamed with hopefulness. Now she looked at Bogdan. Good. He liked that dependence in her eyes.

"How did he finally get it?" Lexi asked.

"He made fake documents about apartment he owns, and his friend hired him for company, but wasn't real job," Bogdan said, but he could see Lexi losing interest the moment he said the word *fake.* "I know you want to do things by rules, Lexi, but those visa officers don't give shit. You have to play dirty tricks."

"I'm not going to forge my documents. Do you realize what kind of trouble that could cause me? I could be blacklisted and never be able to enter the United States."

"Yeah, it's definitely not a good idea," said the German guy, who had been quiet the entire time.

"It's risky, but reward is good, no?" Bogdan asked Lexi, ignoring the German.

Bogdan failed to mentioned that the risks were pretty high, though. Lexi might get lucky like Bogdan's friend, and not have a thorough background check run on her, but if she gave the consular officers the forged papers and they decided to make just one phone call, it would all be over.

"We'll find another way," Lexi said.

"Like what?"

Lexi hesitated. "If Dylan marries me someday, then I'll have an easier time getting a visa."

The American looked elsewhere. Another one of those moments where something slithered between the lines, and then Bogdan understood with absolute clarity.

The American was questioning his relationship with Lexi. Bogdan ran a hand down his mouth to suppress another involuntary grin. "We should go, yes?" he asked.

Everyone silently agreed. Bogdan waited until most of the group was in the car. Just as the American opened the passenger's door, Bogdan grabbed him by the shoulder to get his attention. The American looked at him with a bemused stare.

"Hey, I'm bigger guy than you. I sit in front, okay?"

The American frowned, a clear indication that he didn't like the suggestion.

"Too tight on backseat." Bogdan hunched and pressed his elbows against his sides to indicate how squeezed he was in the backseat. "Very tight. I have problem sitting back, okay?"

"Um... yeah. Whatever, I guess." The American gave Bogdan a weird look as he stepped away from the door.

Complacent, Bogdan slumped into the passenger's seat next to Lexi just as she inserted the keys into the ignition.

"What are you doing?" she asked, her hand frozen on the keys.

"American say it okay for me to sit here with you." Bogdan gently patted her forearm. He hoped the American saw that, despite her moving her hand away.

Lexi looked at the backseat. The American shrugged with a "don't ask me" kind of look. "He says the backseat is too small for him."

"Huh," Lexi said with a nod. She let go of the keys and opened the door on her side. "Mickey, you drive the rest of the way. I'm feeling a little stiff."

Bogdan watched as Lexi and Mickey swapped places. Once she was in the backseat, she leaned her head on the American's shoulder and took his arm into hers. He gave her a peck on the forehead, his eyes briefly flitting to Bogdan as if mocking him.

Well, Bogdan's attempt at getting closer to Lexi in the car had been foiled, but it didn't matter. They had the whole day ahead of them. And if the American was having second thoughts about his relationship, then Bogdan would help him come to a decision faster.

# CHAPTER 6

Intervention Unit Officer Jackson was woken up by the door of the barracks bursting open and the light turning on. He couldn't tell what time it was except that it was the middle of the night.

"On your feet!" the familiar voice of the commander boomed.

Ten pairs of feet, including Jackson's, dropped out of their bunk beds and stood at attention. Years of working in this line of work made waking up from a deep sleep effortless for all the unit members.

The commander, a short, elderly man with droopy cheeks strode into the middle of the barracks, his hands folded behind his back. He observed every member under his frown, his boots reverberating in the silence of the barracks. Once he was in the middle of the room, he spun elegantly on his heel and paced in the opposite direction.

"Get dressed and haul your asses to the briefing room. We've got a new mission on our hands."

***

Not five minutes later, the unit was in the briefing room, seated behind desks while the commander and a woman in a uniform Jackson didn't recognize stood in front of the attendees. Someone whistled at her. Dixon, Jackson assumed.

"Keep it down," the commander said, exhaustion draped over his baggy eyes.

The old geezer was a legend back in his day, who should have retired long ago, but The Company refused to let someone like him go—and, he loved work way too much.

"Is everyone settled in?" the lady asked when the briefing room went quiet. "Good. Then we can start." She leaned on the desk and observed everyone in the room for a moment. "We don't have much time, so I'll spare you the details as well as I can," the lady said. "I'm Senior Logistics Officer Rivers, and I'm here to brief you for your next mission."

Jackson crossed his arms and shifted to a more comfortable position in the wooden seat. Another mission. It had been almost a whole year since the last time he'd seen some action, and he'd been itching for it for a while now. Hours that he spent daily at the shooting range and in the simulation chamber did nothing to make that itch go away.

The woman turned on the projector and pressed a button on the remote in her hand. The map of the world appeared on the whiteboard behind her.

"The Company has an outpost in this location right here," she clicked three more times, the picture zooming into a forest in Eastern Europe.

"What for?" someone in the room asked.

"There have been sightings of an anomaly of what we considered Code Orange for some time now. Our equipment picked up strange phenomena, but we haven't been able to confirm anything. Until tonight, that is."

She clicked the remote once more and assumed an akimbo stance, her eyes scanning the attendees. If she expected the briefing room to explode in awe, she was speaking to the wrong audience. Everyone in the room had already seen pretty much any kind of phenomena that The Company was dealing with, so the image from the projector showing a shadow among the trees didn't sway anyone.

"Charming," Hoover said.

"Two of the guards stationed there were killed earlier today. Before they died, they managed to send a distress signal to HQ."

"So, what the hell is it?" someone in the classroom asked.

"We don't know yet. Our data is limited, so we've classified it as Code Orange, Level Six until we're able to get more details. That's where you guys come in."

Rivers bit her lip, her eyes darting around the briefing room as if expecting the unit to complain. Had this been a classroom full of college students, the room would have exploded with groans and complaints. But this wasn't a room full of students. It was a room full of hardened veterans who followed their orders without question.

"You are to go to the location right now and investigate," Rivers said.

"Don't they have anyone closer there?" Dixon folded his hands behind his head.

"Afraid not. No one with your expertise, anyway."

"And we're supposed to do what, exactly?"

"Locate the target and tag it from a safe distance."

"That's it?"

"Yes, that's it. Until we figure out what we're dealing with, you are *not* to engage the creature. Is that understood?"

"I love a bossy woman," Dixon said, much to the roar of the briefing room.

Rivers remained stone-faced at that remark. The commander didn't bother shutting everyone up. Rivers inhaled, her shoulders tensing up before drooping. "Fat Guys Unit will be at the ready in case you need backup. Now, due to the secrecy of the mission, we will only be sending five unit members out in the field. Any volunteers?"

Hands rose in the air. Eight of them, Jackson counted. He didn't raise his own hand. The commander pointed to each member who volunteered and said, "Dixon. Trope. Berry. Hoover." His eyes fell on Jackson. "And Jackson."

Disappointed sighs boomed in the room, and heads turned to Jackson, giving him accusatory glances.

"Jackson, you'll be the designated team leader," the commander said.

Jackson raised a hand in frustration and let it fall by his side.

"You'll have Survivor leading the team?" Dixon grinned. "That's not good for us. Guess I better say my prayers."

The briefing room exploded in laughter, but Jackson—Survivor—found nothing about it funny. He didn't like his reputation as the only member to come out alive out of multiple missions.

"Everybody, calm down. This is just a recon mission. Tag the entity, get back to the LZ, and you're going home," the commander said. "You'll be briefed on the rest of the details on the plane. Now, get ready to leave."

In unison, all the chairs pushed back as the unit members stood up; the ones that weren't chosen for the mission a little more leisurely than the ones who were about to be deployed. Jackson followed his four mission companions out of the briefing room and toward the barracks.

"To tell you the truth, the only reason why I volunteered was because I saw that Survivor didn't," Berry said, giving Jackson a smirk.

"Well, I, for one, am looking forward to breaking Survivor's curse," Trope said. "When we are back from the mission alive and well, everyone will see that you're not cursed like everybody says, Jackson. It's just mindless superstition."

But Jackson didn't respond. His mind was already on the mission, on the plans for how to keep his unit alive. He knew that the mission was supposed to be simple. Locate the target, tag it, and get out of there. No need to engage it.

But despite the simplicity of the task in front of them, he couldn't shake the feeling that the mission that awaited his unit would end in another bloodbath.

And he was bracing himself for it.

# CHAPTER 7

The forest was mesmerizing. Dylan stared up at the trees reaching high in the sky. Despite the bevy of canopies, the foliage still provided more than enough sunlight to peer through while giving adequate shade to the group.

Dylan pulled out his phone and snapped a few photos here and there. Hannah and Oscar did the same with their camcorders. Mickey and Bogdan stood at the back, chatting while Mickey smoked.

No matter what setting or angle Dylan used with his phone, the photographs never did justice to what his eyes were able to see.

"What do you think?" Lexi stopped next to him. "We may not have tall skyscrapers like in America, but our nature is something else."

"It sure is. And it's pretty close to your home. Where I live, it's just endless deserts and rocks," Dylan said. "But if you go West, you can find redwood forests in California. Have you ever seen those trees?"

Lexi shook her head.

"They're huge. Like a giant. It would take, like, twenty people to wrap their arms around one."

Lexi smiled, but her eyes looked sad."

"What's wrong, Lex?" He brushed a bang behind her ear.

"Nothing." Lexi shook her head, her eyebrows raised in a "what are you talking about" manner.

"Come on, babe. I know you. What's up?"

He rubbed her shoulders. She pursed her lips and looked down before raising her gaze up to Dylan. "I'm sorry."

"For what?"

"For not getting my visa."

"What are you talking about? So what if you didn't get it?"

Lexi sighed. "I really wanted to visit you in the States. I wanted to see all the places that mean so much to you, like where you grew up and where you go for fun, and what your college is like..." She wiped her eyes now glistening with tears. "I'm sorry."

Dylan pulled her in, wrapped his arms around her, and caressed the back of her head. "You did everything you could, Lexi. It's not your fault."

She hugged him around the waist. "I'm just afraid that you'll love me less because of it." She looked up at him.

"No. Of course not. Why would I love you less because of a stupid visa?"

"Well, because you're over there, and I'm here, and... I just feel like you might realize that we have no future together."

Dylan slightly detached from Lexi, just so she wouldn't be able to notice his increased heart rate. "No. Of course not. Listen, when the time comes, we'll find a way to get you to the United States."

"What if we don't?"

"We will."

"But what if we don't?"

"Then... we'll live somewhere else."

But even Dylan didn't believe his own words. He and Lexi had met on a trip to Italy, and what a coincidence it had been. Dylan had come with a group of friends. He and Lexi had stayed in the same hotel, on the same floor, so they'd seen each other every morning when they went down to breakfast.

Dylan had been immediately mesmerized by Lexi's beauty. He hadn't recognized the language that she spoke to her girlfriends, but it sounded like Russian or Polish. His friends egged him on to approach her, but he was too embarrassed with all the other girls around.

It had been three days before his departure that he ran into her in the lobby in front of the vending machine. He knew that it was probably the only chance he would get to talk to her alone. Despite being nervous as hell, he approached her with a simple, "Hi."

That was the beginning of their relationship.

They'd spent the next three days inseparable—in the hotel room, in restaurants, walking around the place, riding the gondolas—until the moment Dylan had his flight back to the States. By then, Dylan thought this would be a one-time adventure and that there was no way anything more would come out of his time with Lexi.

But they continued chatting over text when he returned to the States, then video chatting, and then he visited her where she lived. Dylan knew back then, without a shred of doubt, that he loved Lexi and that he would love nothing more than to spend the rest of his life with her.

"Listen, we'll find a way, okay?" Dylan said. "If we get married, you'll have an easier time getting your visa."

Lexi nodded. "I love you."

Dylan couldn't bring himself to say it. So, he smiled instead and kissed her on the forehead.

Footsteps from the other group members approached them, breaking the meager moment of privacy that Dylan and Lexi had. As he pulled away from her, he spaced out when Oscar started talking about how he and Hannah should have brought their more expensive cameras to record stuff in the woods. All he could think was: What if Lexi was right and he started to realize that they had no future together?

A strong voice broke him out of his thoughts.

"So, how is life in America?" Bogdan asked. He had somehow appeared right next to Dylan, his hands on his hips, elbows wide to occupy more space, his arms tensed hard. "You have job there?"

"No, not yet. I go to college," Dylan said.

"College? You not work while going college?"

"No. It takes up most of my time."

"When I go college, I study and work at the same time. Fourteen hours a day."

"Sure."

"Ask Lexi if you not believe me."

Dylan's eyes fell on Lexi. She was talking to Hannah and Oscar about something, oblivious to Dylan's gaze.

"You guys hung out a lot?" he asked.

"Oh, yes. We hang out very much." Bogdan flashed a shit-eating grin. "We, uh... how you say... very close friends."

He gave Dylan a pat on the back and, without further explanation, sauntered to the others.

*That motherfucker.*

Dylan's blood boiled. Was that what the whole deal was? Was that why Lexi got so angry over Mickey inviting Bogdan?

Of course it was. How could Dylan have been so stupid? How could he not see the obvious signs? Then his anger careened from Bogdan to Lexi.

*How could Lexi not tell me the truth?*

Lexi was done talking about whatever story she was sharing, and Bogdan had started speaking, a hand on Lexi's shoulder. He threw a not-so-subtle glance in Dylan's direction as if to make sure he was watching. Dylan's hands closed into fists. Ex or not, Dylan wanted to walk up to the son of a bitch, shove him, and tell him to get his hand off his girl.

*No. Calm down. Don't make an unnecessary scene.*

Either way, Lexi took two steps forward, just enough to get Bogdan's hand off of her. Bogdan continued talking in his obnoxiously loud voice without paying attention to Lexi. By the time he was done with his story, he and Mickey were laughing loudly while Oscar and Hannah offered forced, courteous chuckles. Dylan and Lexi's facial expressions remained reticent.

"We should get going. The Eye is pretty far away." Lexi tucked a small bottle of water into her backpack and hoisted it over her shoulders.

She walked past Dylan with a curt "come on, babe." She spun around as if remembering something and asked, "Oh, you want that energy drink I bought for you? I picked a cold one, but it won't stay that way for long in this heat."

"No, I'm good. Thanks," Dylan said.

"Everything okay?" she asked, caution veiling her face.

"Yeah. Lead the way."

Lexi smiled and brushed his hand in passing, something she always did whenever she wanted them to hold hands. Dylan ignored that remarked and continued walking behind her.

The trail awaited them.

# CHAPTER 8

Guilt loomed above Mickey like a mosquito that refused to go away no matter how much he flailed. He wished that he had thought before speaking. But he didn't, and he once again found himself in a situation where someone suffered because of it.

His sister and his exes always told him the same thing: Mickey, you need to take your time and really consider whether what you want to say is a smart thing to say.

And so, Mickey did that most of the time. He refrained from cracking jokes in large groups because he knew they might not be to everyone's liking. He took his time, nodding to questions before answering, because he wanted to be sure the answer wouldn't be stupid.

Still, words sometimes involuntarily spilled out of him in the heat of the moment. Just like with Bogdan. He hadn't intended on inviting him on this trip; it just felt like the right thing to do. In hindsight, he really shouldn't have done it because, literally, nobody in the group wanted Bogdan on this trip—Lexi least of all.

Mickey was okay with him, but it was evident that Bogdan didn't sit well with the others. Dylan had a hard time hiding his annoyance with the muscle man. Hannah and Oscar avoided communication with him altogether like he had headlice.

Truth be told, Mickey had realized his mistake the moment the words left his mouth on the phone call, but it was too late to take them back. Since he had already dug a hole for himself, he told the others and hoped they would just dismiss it as, "Okay, no problem, just another member joining us. Cool."

Oh, was he wrong.

He'd seen that scowl on his older sister's face only a few times in his life. The first time was when she'd caught him going through her diary. The second time was when she had a couple of friends for a sleepover and he kissed Stella on the mouth before running away. Mickey still cringed at that memory. The third time was when he'd gotten back with an ex who he previously trash-talked with his sister to kingdom come. The fourth time was today.

She refused to look at him, and every time their eyes did meet, which was after an unsavory joke made by Bogdan, Lexi's look said, *You really don't pick who you're going to hang out with, do you?*

But since it was Mickey's fuck-up, it would also be up to him to resolve the situation. He would keep Bogdan as busy as he could so that others wouldn't need to. Besides, Mickey enjoyed his company despite his antics. The two of them had known each other since childhood, and after knowing someone for years, a person gets used to the other person's quirks. Bogdan was a little... specific, but he was still Mickey's friend, and he was a good guy.

"Is there anything else interesting on this trail?" Oscar asked, his camera pointed at a chartreuse hill off the trail.

"They say there used to be a village somewhere around here, but I think those are just stories," Mickey said. "Or maybe not."

"So, this Eye? What is it, exactly?" Dylan asked.

"A natural rock formation. It's like this deep crater where there's always water. During summer, the water pretty much drains, leaving only a puddle, during fall and spring, it fills until it's like a pool, and during winter, it freezes. It's called the eye because when you look at it while it's somewhat drained, it looks like an eye."

"Maybe we can swim," Bogdan said.

"We didn't bring our swimwear." Hannah bit her lip.

"So what?" Bogdan shrugged. "We swim naked."

He winked at Hannah and then focused intently on Lexi's ass, his tongue stuck out like a dog awaiting his treat. Mickey really wished that Bogdan would stop with the subtle flirtatious remarks directed toward his sister. He knew that Bogdan was only joking, but others might not know that. And if they did, they would not appreciate Bogdan's remarks.

Luckily, Dylan was in front, walking beside Lexi, so he didn't catch Bogdan ogling his girlfriend like a tender steak.

"Swimming is probably a bad idea," Mickey interjected. "The water is dirty."

He expected Bogdan to provide a counter-argument to that sentence, but he simply shrugged and lumbered on.

***

Lexi was not having fun on this trip. Not one bit. This was supposed to be a fun trip with her boyfriend; a final outdoors thing they would enjoy doing together. Instead, that moment of joy was encroached on by Bogdan. He was a ubiquitous presence that no one wanted here, that no one could stand.

Lexi carefully monitored Dylan, to make sure he wasn't too annoyed. For the past twenty minutes, ever since they left the car, he'd been quiet, distant, as if he was deep in thoughts that he wasn't sharing. Maybe he'd just had enough of hanging out with people. He was an introvert and couldn't stand spending too much time in large groups, especially ones that had loudmouths as obnoxious as Bogdan.

If things became too unbearable for him, Lexi would grab him by the hand, and the two of them would double back. There wasn't a bus station too far away, and walking some extra distance was a small price to pay to separate from Bogdan and her brother, who fucked up by inviting him.

Lexi remembered that they would reach a crossroads soon. From there, they could pretty much take any trail they wanted and would still end up at the Eye. Perhaps she and Dylan would take a detour. There were some nice places to see on the old road, like the abandoned wheelbarrow, a creek that followed the trail, and so on.

But if they separated from the others, that would mean that Hannah and Oscar would have to be with Mickey and Bogdan, and Lexi couldn't do that to them. In that case, she would simply pull Mickey aside and tell him to take Bogdan down the other way.

That way, everyone would get at least half an hour of rest from Mickey's friend.

***

Walking on the trail was easy at first because it was flat and wide. But then it gradually tapered and snaked in various directions, leading the group between the maze of trees that surrounded them.

Tiny bugs flew around, congregated at certain spots, sticking to Mickey's shirt and sweaty face. He was so annoyed that he ended up smoking more than usual. When he went to pull out another cigarette, his eyes fell on the two that remained in the pack. They wouldn't be back for at least a few hours, so Mickey had to make them last. He returned the pack to his pocket and continued flailing his arms at the insects that buzzed persistently around him.

At one point, Lexi slinked next to Mickey and gently pulled him until they were at the back of the group. Mickey knew it could mean only one thing: trouble.

"Look, I'm sorry. Okay?" he justified before she even said anything. "But seriously, he's not so bad, come on."

"He's a fucking menace. He's ruining everybody's experience here, Mickey. What the fuck?"

"I said I was sorry."

"Okay, look. We're going to reach the crossroads soon. You're going to convince your buddy to go with you in one direction, and the rest of us will go in another."

"Are you serious?"

"Yes. Dead serious. You're the one who invited him here."

Mickey wanted to argue against that, but in the end, Lexi was right. He silently nodded. Lexi's glower morphed into a smile.

"Thanks, little brother," she said before breaking to the front of the group again.

Sometime later, they crossed an old wooden bridge above a creek. They stopped for a moment, giving Dylan, Hannah, and Oscar time to take in the place. For Mickey and Lexi, the bridge and the creek had long since lost their charm. One could see something only so many times before it became boring.

Mickey leaned his back on the bridge, his hand instinctively digging through his pocket for a cigarette. It was a habit—you stop somewhere even for a moment, it means you're having a smoke break. He pulled the hand out, mentally giving it a slap on the wrist.

"Peaceful, isn't it?" Lexi asked Dylan as he pointed the camera of his phone down the creek.

He murmured something in agreement. Lexi was trying so hard to make Dylan comfortable. Just like Mickey, she was a people pleaser but a different kind. She was kind to strangers, gave all of herself to the people she loved, and gave nothing to the people who had wronged her.

Mickey hoped that Dylan wouldn't fall into that final batch in the future. With Lexi, one could never know.

"This place is really nice," Oscar said. "Hannah, I think I found our new hobby."

"Yeah." Hannah slowly swept the camcorder across the treeline. "Too bad we don't have places like—"

A small scream erupted from her mouth. Mickey's eyes had been fixed on her when she spoke that last sentence, so he noticed how violently her camera jerked upward.

Heads turned in her direction, some with concern on their faces. Not Mickey. Probably an insect that buzzed around her or something.

"What's wrong, honey?" Oscar asked.

Hannah's camera was lowered, her eyes wide in fixation at the treeline far ahead. Oscar was by her side, scrutinizing her face and then the place where she was staring. Dylan and Lexi's shuffling and exchange of baffled stares instilled a sense of urgency in Mickey. It made him feel like he, too, should have been worried about Hannah.

"I think I saw something out there." Hannah pointed a wobbly finger in the direction she was staring.

"What did you see?" Oscar asked.

"Someone stood there."

"Someone?" Lexi asked.

"Yes."

"Probably some other hikers." Mickey shrugged.

Hannah's face grew rigid in sudden realization. She raised her camcorder and said, "I think I caught it on camera!"

Before long, most of the people were gathered around Hannah, staring intently at her camcorder. Mickey rolled his eyes at the needless drama and approached as well. Since he was shorter than the others, he needed to stand on his toes and hold Bogdan and Lexi by the shoulders to take a peek.

Hannah's video played on the camcorder's screen. The video showed the trees moving aside as the camera swiveled. Hannah's voice said something in the background, and then the camera jerked, followed by a piercing scream.

"I didn't see anything," Oscar said.

Mickey didn't see anything either. It was just trees.

"No. It was there. Let's look again," Hannah said as she pressed a button to rewind the video.

The view of the trees appeared on the screen again. Hannah's voice, then the scream and the jerk of the camera. Hannah paused, rewound a few seconds, and played again.

"There's nothing there, Hannah," Oscar said.

"There is, and I saw it!" Hannah hissed.

She rewound once more and then slowed down the video. The camera moved frame by frame, scanning the blurry trees. The frame panned up, then Hannah rewound again and paused the video.

"There!" she victoriously pointed at the camera.

No one said anything. Mickey squinted, trying to make out what she was showing to everybody. Aside from the trees, he didn't see anything that would strike him as strange.

"Where?" Oscar asked.

"Right there. Don't you see it?"

"Uh... no?"

"This shadow right here. Look!"

Hannah's voice conveyed annoyance. If Mickey were in Oscar's shoes, he would have agreed with Hannah just because women could be like ticking bombs sometimes in his experience.

Mickey stared intently at the screen, as much as he could see given the angle and the fact that Hannah constantly moved the camcorder. A slightly darker shadow merged with the surrounding ones in the frame.

*Just a tree,* Mickey thought.

"There's nothing there, babe," Oscar said.

Hannah pressed a button to move the frame. The shadow now stood in the center of the camera, partially behind a tree. It was too blurry. Hannah pressed the button once more. The blurry image cleared up somewhat.

"Whoa," Dylan exclaimed.

Lexi gasped.

That was definitely not just a shadow. In the camera frame stood a dark silhouette among the trees, almost fully merged with the surrounding shadows and obscured by the branches in front. The shape of the head, the arms, and the legs that protruded from it were unmistakable.

The person in the woods looked like they were staring at the camera. The hairs on Mickey's forearms prickled.

"Is that a bear?" Oscar asked.

"Impossible. There are no bears in the region," Lexi said.

Mickey nodded in agreement. But the more he stared at the shadowy thing in the camera, the more he realized it could be both. It was standing upright, just as bears sometimes did, but due to the blur, it was impossible to tell how thick, thin, or tall the silhouette was.

"That looks like a person," Dylan said.

"I think it's a bear. It looks like a bear," Oscar stuck to his guns.

Hannah pressed the button to move the frame again. The camera swiveled a little, and the silhouette moved. It went from facing the camera to hunching sideways.

"See? It's a bear," Oscar said.

"How can you tell?" Hannah asked.

"Because it's bending down to get on all fours."

But Mickey wasn't convinced. And based on the facial expressions that the others conveyed, neither were they. Even Lexi, who knew very well the forest harbored no bears, looked skeptical. Bogdan and Dylan were the only ones whose facial expressions conveyed indifference; boredom even.

Hannah moved the frame several more times, but the image was too blurry to see anything. She rewound to the frame of the figure standing upright, staring at it intently, probably trying to decipher what she was looking at. Oscar's plea for her to let it go fell on deaf ears.

Hannah then lowered the camera and looked toward the trees where she'd caught the silhouette. "Guys, this is kind of creepy."

"I'll admit it, I'm not very happy about hiking in an area with bears, either," Oscar said.

"Don't be pussies," Bogdan said. He'd been awfully quiet in the past few minutes. "We walk or not?"

"Yeah, you guys are being ridiculous." Mickey rubbed his forearms to calm down the hairs that still stood upright. "We'll be okay."

"I don't know, guys." Hannah bit her lip, scanning the faces of the other group members.

Bogdan was already across the bridge, striding down the trail.

"We'll just make sure to cause a lot of noise, and the bear will know to steer clear," Dylan said.

"Yeah. These trails are safe, Hannah." Lexi smiled, but her eyes looked worried.

Mickey knew that it wasn't bears that she was worried about. She was far more terrified by the notion that some weirdo was stalking them in the woods.

"And if it's someone messing with us, we'll kick his ass," Dylan added.

Hannah still looked skeptical. It was Oscar who intervened by putting an arm around her and saying, "Don't worry, honey. I'll be here to protect you from big bad bears."

Hannah looked embarrassed at that, but it was enough to convince her.

Without another word, the group continued down the trail.

***

Nestled among the trees, something watched the group walking deeper, satisfied and restless at the prey that headed into its trap.

# CHAPTER 9

Jackson leaned on the seat and closed his eyes. The smooth flying of the chopper allowed him to detach from his surroundings. Just because he was appointed as the team leader didn't mean he had to break his routine of relaxing before the mission. His squad was a group of self-sufficient adults who knew what they were doing. Jackson wouldn't need to babysit them.

"I always wanted to go to Europe. Just didn't think I'd go like this," Berry said as he rubbed the desert eagle in his hand with a small rag. "My wife would be jealous as shit if she found out."

"What did you tell her?" Trope asked.

"Just told her I'm going on a mission." He shrugged. "She understands I can't disclose any details."

"That's not what I tell my wife," Dixon jumped into the discussion. "Whenever I go, I tell her I want to see warm dinner on the kitchen table when I come back home, and her naked upstairs in the bedroom."

The squad laughed.

"If I told my wife that, the only thing I'd get would be a slap on the face and some extra blankets to sleep in the living room," Berry said. "Does that approach ever work for you?"

"Let me tell you something, Berry." Dixon leaned forward. "It doesn't matter how confident you are or what you say, or how many chores you do, or how rich or pretty you are. The only thing that matters is your wife's mood. And if your wife ain't in the mood, there ain't a god in this world that's going to make her spread her legs for you."

The chopper roared in laughter. Jackson opened his eyes, observing the group under his eyebrows.

"I don't know, man," Berry said. "My wife loves it when I do the chores around the house. I get laid even when I don't want to."

"How long you been married for?"

"A year."

Dixon pursed his lips and let out an "oof" sound. "Wait 'til you've been married for twenty. You'll see pussy once in a Halley's Comet." He slapped Berry on the knee.

More laughter in the chopper.

"If he stays married for that long," Trope said. "I have three ex-wives behind me. This job isn't kind to marriages."

"You sure it's the job, and not you?" Hoover joked.

"Oh, fuck off," Trope retorted just as another wave of laughter exploded.

Berry wasn't laughing, though. Jackson could see worry on his face. Berry was young, only in his mid-twenties. All the other squad members were in their late thirties and forties.

"Any kids?" Jackson asked.

Everyone turned their heads to face Jackson, surprised at his unexpected question. Berry looked taken aback for a moment. "Um... my wife's pregnant. Six months in. Girl."

"Congratulations." Dixon patted him on the back. "My advice? Use your vacation days before the kid comes along because, when you become a dad, you can kiss that peace and quiet goodbye."

One thing that Jackson appreciated about being an Intervention Unit officer was that the unit always looked out for each other, especially the rookies. They roasted each other as a form of camaraderie, and when it came to fighting back-to-back, they bled for each other.

A smile crept up on Jackson's face at the knowledge that the squad would do everything they could to get Berry alive and well back to his wife and unborn child.

"ETA twenty minutes!" the pilot shouted.

"Gear check." Jackson shot up to his feet.

The others did so without a word, too. They double-checked to make sure everything on their suits was functional and strapped in well then retrieved their weapons from the racks. Jackson's preferred firearm of choice was the Heckler and Koch MP5. As for the sidearm, he usually went with a Glock 19 with an extended mag, but this time, he opted for a modified Colt M1911 with grips, a compensator, and flashlight. Since the mission was more of a recon than assault, Jackson attached a suppressor to the MP5.

The Intervention Unit was free to use whatever weapons they liked as long as they were compatible with the nature of their mission. It was also important for the team to be diverse, just in case the need for it arose.

Once they were all set, they sat back in their seats. The mood of the unit when the pilot announced the ETA could vary. Jackson was unfortunate enough to see a lot of team changes, and he'd seen two basic patterns: Either the group continued joking as if they were blue-collar workers on a lunch break, or the air would become heavy with anticipation as they discussed the mission details.

Today, it was the former.

Dixon continued cracking jokes, and the group followed with laughter. Jackson zoned out again. Since he had nothing outside his work, nothing was what he thought about. It was as Trope had said. This job was not kind to personal lives.

Jackson was okay with that. He'd come to terms with it a long time ago. No wife, no children, no living family members. The only thing that existed for him was his sense of duty as a security officer of the Intervention Unit.

And right now, only the mission.

"Ten minutes!" the pilot shouted.

Jackson could easily fall asleep if he wanted to. The twenty hours long ride to the base in Europe, and then another hour in the chopper, took their toll on him.

"Five minutes!" the pilot announced.

That was their cue to stop joking and get serious. Dixon made one final misogynistic joke before shutting up. Jackson gripped the MP5 and leaned forward. "All right. Listen up. Once we're at the drop-off point, we head North to the guard station. We scope out the situation, inform HQ, and look for the target. Dixon, you'll tag the target."

"Roger that." Dixon nodded just as he shoved the tag gun into his holster.

"The rest of you, stick close. Radios have known to become jammed in the area."

"All right, we're here!" the pilot shouted.

Everyone was already on his feet. Hoover slid open the chopper doors. The gust and noise of the rotor blades were deafening. Whatever talking the unit wanted to do, it would have to wait until they were on the ground.

Hoover dropped the rope out and ushered each team member out. Berry gripped the rope and smoothly slid down. Next came Dixon, then Jackson, then Trope. Hoover was last. As soon as they touched the ground, their firearms were raised, securing the wooded area. Once the final member touched down, the chopper ascended, the noise and the massive winds caused by the blades receding in the distance until the only thing that surrounded the unit was the chirping of the birds under the noon sun.

"Let's move," Jackson commanded.

# CHAPTER 10

The sinuous hills were exhausting. A thin line of annoying sweat covered the back of Lexi's shirt. She was out of breath. She'd overestimated her hiking stamina when she suggested this trip. The last time she'd been in these woods was years ago, but back then, she weighed six pounds less and worked out consistently three times a week.

The others weren't looking too cool, either. Everyone except Bogdan and Mickey was out of breath. Bogdan had taken the lead and was striding down the trail with ease. He'd put enough distance from the group to turn around and shoot judgmental glares at them, his face silently urging them to stop being weaklings and catch up.

It was his way of trying to assert dominance in the group. Yet another reason why Lexi hated being around him.

Hannah occasionally looked over her shoulder or snapped her head in the direction of a distant sound, her eyes wide in fearful expectation. She was still on edge because of the video she'd recorded earlier.

Lexi had been worried about that, too. She'd watched too many horror movies of girls being stalked by creeps in the woods. She knew that things like that didn't happen often around these parts, but one could never know. She then remembered that their group was big, so only a moron would dare mess with them.

"How about we... take a break?" Oscar said between pants.

"You tired already?" Bogdan spread his arms.

"I just need... a short break," Oscar replied.

Lexi wouldn't have responded to Bogdan's juvenile provocation, but Oscar was polite, and he was trying not to antagonize anyone, she supposed.

"A break sounds like a good idea," Dylan said.

"There's a gazebo down this trail. We can rest there," Lexi said.

Lexi grabbed Dylan's hand and held onto it as they walked. The grip on his hand was loose the entire time, as if he couldn't wait for Lexi to let him go. Sure enough, once she relaxed her squeeze, his hand drooped out of her clutch. He didn't look at her the entire time. As much as Lexi wanted to pull Dylan aside to ask him what was wrong, now was not the time. She'd ask him when they were back home, alone in her room.

It was the visa. The stupid visa. She was sure of it. She replayed the interview with the consular officer so many times in her head that it was ridiculous. She pondered what she could have said differently, and how that might have convinced the officer that she had no intention to stay in the United States.

But the officer had only asked her two questions.

*Why do you want to visit the United States at this time?*

*Do you have a job or any property on your name?*

The first question was easy enough. The second one was the issue. She knew well what the officer was trying to find out: whether there was anything in Lexi's country binding her to her home. Lexi could see the consular officer's demeanor changing the moment she gave her answer to the second question, and it was at that moment that she knew the response she would get even before the officer said, "Your visa is denied."

Once those words were spoken, it was all over. There wasn't a thing Lexi could do to change the outcome of the situation. Two questions, and her visa status was concluded.

*Your visa is denied.*

He had said it so coldly, so... robotically.

Those words had rung out in her head like a gong when she made her way through the security lanes and back outside the embassy. After the dust had settled, the only thing that remained was a sense of defeat.

She cried that night on the call with Dylan, and when they ended the call, the interview played out in her mind over and over until she wanted to pound her head with her fists. She tried telling herself that it was just bad luck; she just happened to run into a consular officer who got the wrong impression about her. That still didn't change the bitter taste of rejection in her mouth.

But Lexi would do better next time. She would find a company that would vouch for her, she would buy a small apartment, and if that wasn't enough... no, she didn't want to think in that direction.

The gazebo came into view soon enough, an old structure sitting by the side of the trail, somehow untarnished by the other hikers. Mickey was the first one to plop into the seat under the gazebo. As soon as he did so, he pulled out a cigarette and lit it, his head thrown back like he was in some sort of trance.

Hannah and Oscar were next. They groaned in relief when their asses slumped into the seats. Bogdan sat next to Mickey, and Dylan took up a seat near the edge of the seat next to Oscar. He then looked up at Lexi and squeezed sideways, giving her room.

"I'm gonna go use the ladies' room." Lexi hooked a thumb over her shoulder.

Bogdan perked up his chest. "I must go, too."

Lexi turned around and sauntered into the stalks of grass. The trees in this part of the woods were sparse, and every time she turned around to see if the gazebo was in sight, it was. She ended up putting a lot of distance from the group before she finally broke the line of sight with them.

She didn't think she'd need to use nature as her bathroom, but she'd drunk too much water, and it had now finally caught up to her. She pulled down her jeans and panties, ducked down, and did her business. The stream seemed endless.

It only stopped abruptly when a branch nearby snapped.

Lexi's head whipped around, trying to locate the source of the sound. Something rustled somewhere. Suddenly feeling uneasy, Lexi stood and pulled up her clothes. No sooner had she stepped out from behind the tree did she bump into whatever was stalking her.

***

Dylan couldn't focus on the conversation of the group. Mickey, Oscar, and Hannah were talking about something related to healthcare in Germany, but Dylan's mind was somewhere else.

He stared intently at the spot where Lexi had gone to pee. One moment, she was slinking between the trees, and in the next, gone. It was so easy to lose sight of people in woods like these. He wasn't worried about her getting lost, though. He was worried because she'd been gone a while. It must have been at least five minutes, which was way too long to pee.

Dylan hadn't realized that his foot tapped on the wooden floor of the gazebo until Mickey called out to him. "Hey, you okay, brother? You look a little nervous."

"Yeah." He continued staring at the treeline.

"Don't worry. They'll be back any minute now," Mickey said nonchalantly as he sucked in smoke from his cigarette and expelled it from his mouth.

But Dylan couldn't stop worrying. Something about the tall trees bothered him. Something about the way they could easily provide someone with a view on the group while they, themselves would need to scan the trees fervently to spot anything incongruous to them.

He would give Lexi one minute, and then he would go after her.

***

"What the fuck are you doing here?" Lexi asked.

Bogdan stood in front of her, a grin plastered to his face. "Sorry, didn't mean to scare you."

"Have you been stalking me?" She crossed her arms.

"No, of course not. Do you think I'm some sort of a creep or something?"

*Yes,* she wanted to say but refrained from doing so.

"The others are waiting," she said as she stiffly started forward.

Bogdan stepped in front of her, blocking her way. The look of amusement refused to leave his face. Lexi shook her head as if to ask him what the hell he was doing.

"Your boyfriend, the American, he's a really interesting guy," he said. His eyes gleamed with something Lexi didn't like.

She didn't say anything to his remark. How would one respond to it, anyway? Instead, her eyes fell behind Bogdan. The gazebo was nowhere in sight.

It then hit her.

*The gazebo was nowhere in sight.*

She and Bogdan were alone in the woods, away from the group, and he was blocking her way. He was taller, stronger, and he'd be able to overpower her easily, probably before she'd even be able to scream. But Dylan and the others were right there, just barely out of sight. The thought of Bogdan doing something to her so close to safety made Lexi shiver despite the warm rays of sun. Her eyes scanned the treeline behind Bogdan once more, desperately looking for the gazebo.

Bogdan noticed this because he looked at what caught Lexi's attention. She could push him and hope she managed to disorient him enough to run back to the others. But he would probably be faster.

Bogdan turned back to face her, not budging from his spot. He stood close enough for her to smell the sweat that clung to his wife-beater shirt. "You want to go back?"

"Yes."

Bogdan squinted at Lexi as if considering whether he was going to allow her to do that.

"Okay." He finally stepped aside, gesturing in the general direction of the gazebo. "After you."

Lexi hesitated. A part of her believed that Bogdan was waiting for her to turn her back to him so that he could do something to her while she didn't expect it. That smile that said Lexi was a part of a prank that Bogdan knew about bothered her a lot.

"Well, are we going? Or do you want to stare at this a little longer?" he asked as he flexed his pecs.

Lexi let out a groan as she walked past him. She tried not to quicken her pace, no matter how much she wanted to put some distance from Bogdan. Her walk felt stilted and unbalanced.

"I'm glad you found someone," Bogdan said. "You deserve it. Even if it's an American."

Lexi ignored him.

"You seem really happy. I wonder how long he'll stay with you."

She didn't want to stop and turn around, and yet, for some reason, she did. When she looked at Bogdan, he was no longer smiling, but the corner of his lip danced ever so slightly.

"What's that supposed to mean?" she asked.

"I didn't mean anything." Bogdan shook his head with an incredulous stare.

"No, go ahead. Say what you wanted to say," Lexi said.

"No, I really didn't—"

"Hey, you opened this can of worms, so why don't you say what you want to say?"

*Since it's what you want to do.*

Bogdan huffed, seemingly annoyed that he had to cave in, confirming Lexi's suspicions. "Well, I mean. He's American."

"Okay, so? What's wrong with that?"

"There's nothing wrong with that. It's just that... he lives in America. Okay?"

"Yeah, so?"

"You live here. And they denied you your visa. This is, what? The second time?"

*Third time, actually,* but Lexi didn't want to give Bogdan the satisfaction of being right.

"The more times they deny your visa, the harder it is to get it. Right? It's like looking at a restaurant with bad reviews."

Lexi put her hands on her hips and chewed on her lip. The heat of her body rose, and she was sure it had nothing to do with the weather. "That's not going to stop us from being together."

"I mean, I get that. But, this isn't a romantic movie, Alexa. It's real life. And things sometimes just don't work out how we want them to." He shrugged. "For all the time you've been together, you've only seen each other for a total of...what...three weeks?"

Bogdan upturned his palms and intermittently raised and lowered them as if weighing something in his hands. "Long-distance relationships get cold after a while. People fall out of love. It happens. And I see the way you look at him." He raised one palm then lowered the other. "And I see the way he looks at you. You know?"

A painful pang shot through Lexi's chest. She opened her mouth then closed it.

"You don't know shit about me and Dylan." She turned around, refusing to entertain the topic. She was afraid because Bogdan's words were getting to her. Because he was right, about everything.

"Hey, Lexi. Lexi."

Lexi quickened her pace.

"Lexi!" Bogdan's hand wrapped around her wrist, stopping her in her tracks.

She snapped at him. He was inches from her, his lips sucked into his mouth. "Look. Sorry if what I said is hurtful.

But you asked me, and I'm just trying to be honest. It's sometimes hard to see things right when you're directly involved in the problem, but the rest of us see it. Okay? And sometimes, it's hard for us to see the truth even when it's right in front of us. So we pretend not to see it and live in an illusion that everything is okay, waiting for something to change. You don't deserve to wait, Lexi."

His grip went slack, his fingers brushing her hand as he retreated.

"Come on, let's go back. The others are probably already worried," he said.

Lexi couldn't move for a while. All she could do was stare at her feet while the thoughts swirled in her head. As they cleared, she came to realizations; truths that she'd been blind to, just like Bogdan said.

Dylan's demeanor toward Lexi *had* changed. It had just been so gradual that she failed to see it. No, she *refused* to see it. And now, it might be too late.

As she broke into a reluctant stride back to the group, she was left with only one thought—the realization that her love for Dylan might not be enough to save their relationship.

# CHAPTER 11

Dylan was relieved to see Lexi approaching the gazebo. That feeling only lasted for a moment when he realized who she was walking with. Bogdan was in front of her, strangely quiet. Lexi's head hung down—guilt washed over her face even at this distance.

Why?

"Did you see anything out there?" Hannah asked when they returned.

"Oh, yes. Many bears. Big bears," Bogdan joked, but no one except Mickey laughed.

"Be serious. Anything?"

"No. It safe."

"What's up with you, Lexi? You looked like you got pissed on." Mickey laughed.

Lexi gave him a brief, impassive look before averting her gaze. She didn't need to say anything for Dylan to know that something was wrong with her. But instead of focusing on her, he looked at Bogdan. A complacent smile tugged his mouth as he stretched his arms, making sure to flex hard in the process.

Dylan was inches away from getting up onto his feet and telling the others that he was going back. He wouldn't even dignify his action with a proper response. He'd just turn around, leave the woods, and go straight to the airport.

It was just a passing, momentary thought. If he did that, he would look like a tantrum-throwing five-year-old. Bogdan would have the satisfaction of knowing he managed to get the American to leave. And Dylan didn't want to let him have that kind of satisfaction.

"All right, let's go." Dylan stood. He tried to do it as casually as he could because he knew Lexi would notice that something was wrong otherwise.

The others slowly got up, too. Mickey was the one who led the way this time. The mood in the group seemed to drop significantly. No one said a word as they walked for a while. Dylan fished his phone out for the hundredth time since the trip started. He had no signal.

At one point, a faint, distant sound interrupted the silence.

"Do you guys hear that?" Mickey asked.

Dylan couldn't tell what it was at first, but as it grew closer, a distinct *whup-whup-whup-whup* filled the woods.

"A helicopter," Lexi said at the same time when Dylan realized what it was.

The engine grew louder and louder until it boomed right above them. Everyone looked up at the black chopper that flew overhead before disappearing out of sight.

"Cool," Oscar said.

"What's a chopper doing here? I've never seen one around these parts." Lexi looked at the others.

"Maybe someone needs rescuing." Mickey shrugged.

"Really?" Hannah asked.

"Probably not," Lexi replied.

"It's possible," Mickey said, his words overlapping with Lexi's. "These woods are huge. I mean, gigantic. If you started walking in the wrong direction, you could wander for days or weeks before someone finds you. But you'd probably be dead long before then, anyway."

"Why?" Hannah asked.

"Starvation, dehydration, wolves..."

"Wolves?! You said there were no wild animals?"

"Well, not here. but I don't know what's deeper in the woods. It could be fucking Bigfoot for all I know."

The topic changed slightly at that point to Mickey talking about ways of surviving in the woods. Dylan had tuned out after Mickey started explaining how to make a makeshift tent and snares for animals.

The only reason he was jerked back to reality was because of Bogdan loudly yelling, "Boo!" as he jabbed Hannah in the hip with a finger from behind. Hannah screamed, flailed her arms, and dashed away from him a few steps before realizing the source of the scare.

Bogdan and Mickey were the only ones laughing at that. Hannah's face was ruddy with embarrassment. Oscar made an awkward grimace.

"Your face was funny," Bogdan pointed at Hannah through laughter.

"That's not funny," she sternly said.

"Oh, come on. I just joke little."

When he realized that he and Mickey were the only ones who found the joke amusing, he stopped laughing.

It wasn't long before they finally reached the crossroads that Mickey had mentioned at one point. The trail forked in three other directions, each one not differing from the others. Dylan stopped in the middle of the crossing trails and spun in a circle. The only reason why he knew which way was back was because his companions stood on that trail. How did people not get lost in this place?

"Uh, I'm not sure if I want to go further," Hannah said. "What if we get lost?"

Dylan's eyes fell on Hannah. Worry draped her face. He happened to look at Bogdan, who stood nearby. His gaze was fixated on Hannah, a look of amusement on his face. Dylan had grown to hate that look even if he'd only known Bogdan for a very short time.

"No way to get lost here," Mickey said. "All trails merge eventually. You couldn't get lost even if you wanted to. There used to be signposts over here, but I guess somebody ripped them out."

"Speaking of which," Lexi said theatrically, "the Eye is this way. We can also reach it using this trail, but it's longer. But, there are plenty of nice things to see there. Mickey, you said you always wanted to go that way and see what it's like. Right?" She enunciated the last word.

"Nope. What are you talking about?" Mickey frowned.

When Lexi's intent stare refused to move away from her little brother, Mickey nodded fervently, his eyebrows raised high, as if he had just remembered something. "Oh, right. Yes. You're right. I always wanted to go down that path. Uh, Bogdan? You wanna come with me?"

"Why?" Bogdan asked.

"Because the trail is nice. Come on, what do you say?"

Bogdan's deadpan stare conveyed no amusement at Mickey's suggestion. But then, he simply shrugged and said, "Sure. Why not?"

This seemed to make Mickey happy, and a smile appeared on his face. "Cool. Let's go then. We'll meet you guys at the next crossroads."

Mickey started down the middle trail while the others went after Lexi toward the left path.

"Wait. No one else coming?" Bogdan asked. "Hannah? You not want come?"

"I... think I'll stick with the shorter path." Hannah flashed him an awkward smile.

"So, only Mickey and me?" Bogdan turned to the others, and when he seemingly realized that no one else was going to join him, he shrugged. "Okay."

Without another word, he and Mickey strode down the path, taking with them an invisible weight that loomed in the air ever since Bogdan first entered the car.

"Fi-na-lly!" Lexi let out an exasperated sigh of relief once Mickey and Bogdan were some distance away. "Now we can finally rest our brains a little." She turned to Dylan. "Babe, I'm so sorry. He wasn't supposed to be here. I swear to God, this is like, the fifth time Mickey pulled shit like this."

"It's fine." Dylan smiled. Even that insincere gesture took a lot of effort. Lexi eyeballed him for a moment as if considering his response.

"Well, let's go." She pulled at the straps of her backpack.

She spun on the balls of her shoes and started down the designated path. Hannah and Oscar followed. Oscar recorded stuff with his camcorder. Hannah did not. Not since the incident at the bridge.

Dylan followed them, tempted to take the third path where he would walk alone.

*Boris Bacic*

# CHAPTER 12

"You said the trail was nice. I don't see anything nice here," Bogdan said.

On their left was a sheer rock wall. On their right, the ground descended into a barren valley. There were no trees here to provide them with shade. Lately, Bogdan couldn't stand the sun. Ever since he started going to the gym and packing the insane amount of muscle mass, he'd become less resistant to heat. During summer, he could go outside just to take out the trash, and the back of his shirt would already be drenched in a patina of sweat.

"It *is* nice. We'll get to the nice parts soon," Mickey said.

But Bogdan knew that Mickey was bullshitting him. Bogdan wasn't stupid. He knew that the only reason Mickey was so desperate to get him on this trail was to give the others privacy.

Bogdan had seen how the others looked at him. He knew those looks of annoyance like the back of his hand. He'd learned to ignore them. For a long time, he'd tried fitting in with people, but wherever he went, he seemed to stick out like a sore thumb.

People always looked at him like he was a menace, a nuisance, even though he tried being nice. Bogdan was a good guy, and he knew it. But people refused to see it. They didn't even want to give him a chance. It took him a while to realize that the reason why they didn't actually like him was because they were jealous of him.

And why wouldn't they be? He was smart, funny, handsome, and had a chiseled body that would get every woman's waterworks running. So, he stopped trying to fit in because, in the end, it should be they who should want to fit in with him and not the other way around.

"So, how do you like the American?" Bogdan asked.

"He's everything I hoped he'd be," Mickey said. "I was skeptical at first before meeting him because you know how Americans can be loud and annoying, but Dylan is okay. Really polite and considerate, too."

"Okay." Bogdan grimaced.

*It's a shame the American won't stick around for long in your sister's life,* he wanted to say but refrained from doing so. His conversation with Lexi in the woods was still in his head. He had told the others he needed to take a leak, which was a lie. He just wanted to get close to Lexi so that he could speak to her.

He hadn't expected to get a view of her bare ass while he snuck up on her. It was a nice bonus. The real treat was the actual conversation, though.

The way she looked at him with fear in her eyes, like she was about to start screaming, crying, pleading with him. It made Bogdan's crotch ache pleasantly. And then the way her face vacillated between dread, confusion, and anger when Bogdan installed the little worm of doubt in her mind...

It was beautiful. And he would now just need to let her simmer in her own thoughts for a while, let Lexi reach her own conclusion, figure out that the American was not a good fit for her.

Bogdan was doing her a favor. Lexi could spend years in an unhappy relationship with the American, who, frankly, wouldn't care what his European girlfriend was going through. Bogdan had seen what years of toxic relationships could do. The couples would go back and forth, break up and make up, always vow to be better, only for the cycle to repeat.

Then, when they finally did end the relationship, they were so broken and carried so much baggage that they were incapable of starting their life with someone new without comparing them to the old partner. It was either that, or they stayed long enough for the woman to get pregnant.

Then, the kid that would come along would work as a temporary Band-Aid for the already fucked-up marriage. The couple would be too busy with their new baby to worry about anything else, and by the time their child grew up, the marriage would go back to the way it was before the pregnancy—and it would be too late to separate without hurting their kid.

That's why Bogdan was helping Lexi fast forward to the inevitable conclusion. He was a good guy, and Lexi deserved better.

"Yeah, the American is okay. But something bothers me about him," Bogdan said.

"Yeah? What?" Mickey asked.

"I don't know. You haven't noticed anything?"

"No? What was I supposed to notice?"

"I don't know. It's hard to put my finger on it. But... something about the way he looks at Lexi."

Mickey's pace slowed down a little. "What do you mean?"

"Nothing. I'm probably just imagining things. Forget it." Bogdan dismissively waved and continued sauntering.

"No, no. I want to know. What did you see?"

Bogdan grinned from the front where Mickey couldn't see him. He made a serious expression before craning his neck to face Mickey. "Okay. It's just... he's kind of cold, you know?"

Mickey frowned.

"It's like I can see how he means the world to Lexi. She's glowing with the love she has for him, and that's visible. But when you look at him..."

"Well, speak up. What is it?"

Bogdan got his attention, good.

"I think he's hiding something," he said.

"What could Dylan possibly be hiding?"

"Like I said, maybe I'm just imagining things. It's stupid. It's just the way he looks at Lexi that bothers me. It was the same way Peter looked at Myra toward the end of their relationship before they broke up. Remember that?"

"Yeah. I guess."

"These things are visible. Especially if it's disparate like it is with Lexi and the American."

Mickey stared at the ground for a while before finally shaking his head. "No. Don't be ridiculous. Dylan is probably just sad that he's leaving soon."

"Yeah. You're probably right. There's just one other thing that bothers me."

Mickey's eyes locked with Bogdan's for a moment. He kicked a pebble on the trail, which rolled off of it and tumbled down the slope on their right.

"I've seen him checking his phone a lot. And I mean, *a lot*. And I know you're going to say that it's no big deal, but I've seen him smiling at his phone. And I know that look, man."

Mickey stopped. Bogdan mimicked him. They were facing each other. Bogdan's face went rigid with how hard he was trying not to smile. He couldn't help but be proud of his clever manipulation.

"You think Dylan is cheating on my sister?" Mickey asked.

"You're the one who said it. Think hard. Has he always been like this? Maybe it's just the way he is."

Mickey looked down at his feet. "No, I don't think he's like that. Not that I remember."

Bogdan had to play his cards right. If he pushed too much, the plan could backfire. If he was too mellow, his words would be forgotten. He sensed that now was the right time to back down since he'd made his point clear.

"You know what, I don't want to cause relationship problems for Lexi. It's stupid. Let's just forget the whole thing, okay?"

He turned around to continue down the trail when Mickey called out to him. "Hold on a second."

Bogdan stopped and faced his friend.

"If Dylan really is hiding something, then we have to find out what it is. It's my sister we're talking about," Mickey said.

*Bingo.*

"Well, what do you plan to do?"

"I'm going to ask Dylan."

"No, don't do that."

"Why not?"

"Because he'll never tell you. He'll just become defensive."

"What do you propose then?"

"Talk to Lexi."

Mickey blinked in a comically furious way. "To Lexi?"

"Just hear me out. Don't tell her you think Dylan is cheating on her. That'll cause all sorts of problems. Just tell her to keep an eye on him because he seems distant. Say it in a way that it sounds like you care about the American's wellbeing, like he might be going through something he's not talking about."

"Yeah. That's a good idea. Thanks, bro."

"Just one thing. Please, don't tell her that I said anything. She might think I'm trying to sabotage her relationship, and I don't want to be involved in this in any way. I'm just telling you as a friend what I see."

"I know. And I really appreciate it. Don't worry. I won't tell Lexi we had this conversation."

As soon as he'd said that, a scream erupted in the valley. Both Mickey and Bogdan jerked their heads in the direction of the sound. Bogdan's heart thumped in his chest. The scream sounded like a woman was being flayed alive.

"What was that?" Mickey asked, his voice shaky.

"It sounded like a woman," Bogdan said, scanning the valley. For once, he was grateful that there were no trees in the valley because they had a clear view on the land below.

"It sounded like a cougar," Mickey said.

"A cougar?"

"Yeah. Have you ever heard them screaming?"

"No."

"Well, they sound exactly like that."

"They sound like a screaming woman?"

"Yes. I'm not even joking."

Bogdan's eyes refused to scrutinize the valley and the treeline beyond. He didn't see any cougars around.

"Okay. Well, if there's a cougar close by, we should probably move."

"Good idea."

They broke into a hurried gait, their heads diligently scanning the valley for any wild animals. A few minutes later, the excitement dissipated, and Bogdan could relax once more.

Standing behind Mickey, he allowed his mouth to stretch into a wide Cheshire cat grin, happy with the way his operation was going. Now, Mickey would need to talk to Lexi, confirming the suspicions that Bogdan had already planted in her head. Then, the waiting game would start.

And if things moved too slow, then Bogdan would move on to manipulating the American. He'd seen his facial expression when Bogdan and Lexi exited the trees together. It was doubt. Fanning the flames a little more wouldn't hurt.

One day, they would all look back and realize how well it worked out. Bogdan would receive no credit for it, though. He was like a ninja who struck from the shadows.

But Bogdan needed no credit because he was a good guy.

# CHAPTER 13

The squad progressed well through the forest. No signs of hostiles yet. Intel they received from HQ said that the entity was more active at night, but that didn't mean they could let their guards down.

They needed to steer clear of any potential trails, too, because the last thing they wanted was to run into civilians. Warning them to leave the woods was a no-go. That would only raise a lot of questions.

With today's technologies, it would only take a few photos for the mysterious unit of armed soldiers to go viral, which would raise a lot of questions from the public. The Company did a pretty good job cleaning up any evidence left behind, but it was still a hassle.

HQ had informed the Intervention Unit that they closed all the roads leading into and out of the zone of the sighting, but they couldn't sweep the area for any civilians who might have already entered. Hopefully, they would stay on the trail without encountering anything strange, and on their way out, the personnel posing as the local cops would let them leave, informing them that there was a wildfire in the forest, hence the need for a roadblock. That always worked like a charm, and no questions were raised.

"Station should be just around here," said Hoover, who was the point man.

"Eyes open," Jackson commanded.

The building was well hidden. The ghillie nets that draped it blended in really well with the woods, and since it was so out of the way of any nearby trails, the chances of someone running into it were close to non-existent.

Only two things were amiss about it, though. The first one was the tiny, vertical crack of silver that fell down the middle of the building. The second was the dried blood on the door and the ground outside.

"Door's open," Hoover said as the team took up positions in front of the crack.

Berry opened the door, then Hoover, Trope, and Dixon rushed inside, leaving Jackson to cover their six.

"Clear!" Hoover shouted from the room a moment later.

"Go," Jackson urged Berry, and then he himself followed.

The interior of the building was bathed in a hue of gray that the walls were made of. The windows were designed in a way that the people inside could see outside, but whoever was outside wouldn't be able to see anything. In terms of spaciousness, the place wasn't large. Two beds, a table with cards messily splayed on it, a communications desk, a kitchenette, a TV, a small bathroom, and...

A lot of blood.

The floor was painted in a streak of red that went from the door to the desk where more of it was smeared around the wooden surface and the big button on the keyboard. Under the table was a foot.

"Damn. These guys didn't have a fun time, huh?" Dixon asked.

"Check for a news feed," Jackson ordered.

Trope laid his weapon on the desk and began clacking away on the keyboard. While doing so, Jackson scanned the rest of the room for any clues. He tried to reconstruct in his mind what had happened here.

The most blood was near the entrance and close to the desk, which meant that the victim lingered on those spots for a little bit. The dried pool was wider near the desk, so that must have been where the guard sustained lethal injuries. The foot must have been severed near the entrance.

Gazing at the stump, Jackson tried to determine what kind of weapon could have caused such damage. The stump was a mangled, bulbous mess of flesh and splintered bone, so whatever had done that to the guard probably had sharp teeth, but not a big enough jaw to chomp down the foot in one bite like a shark.

"Nothing. They don't have cameras," Trope said.

Dixon scoffed. "No cameras for a place like this? The Company's starting to cut corners, I see."

"Okay, now what?" Berry shrugged.

"Anything else useful on that computer, Trope?" Jackson asked.

"Hold on. I'm checking." Trope typed some more on the keyboard. "Nothing."

"We follow the trail. Head to the zone of the sighting," Jackson said. "Locate the target, tag it, and head back to the LZ."

The others nodded.

Since there was nothing more to do in the building, they exited. They made sure to seal the door just in case someone did happen to wander inside. From there, they followed the trail. It was easy at first because blood streaked the grass.

They stopped when they reached something in the middle of the clearing.

"It's the guard," Hoover said as he approached the mass on the ground.

The guard, or whatever was left of him, was a mess. A deep scar ran down his face, right across the eye, the eyelid and the eyeball split in half in a perfect slice. Dark blood drenched his uniform. His right arm had been torn from the elbow, one foot missing. A crater sat in the middle of his chest, exposing a broken ribcage and shriveled lungs.

"What the fuck?" Dixon leaned to take a better look at the mess. "Look at the hole in his chest. And his heart is missing."

"His heart?" Berry asked.

"Yeah."

Jackson gave the body another once over. Dixon was right. Where the heart should have been was instead a pile of broken ribs and mangled flesh.

"What the hell are we dealing with over here?" Hoover asked.

Jackson pressed the PTT button on his shoulder, "This is Team Alpha. Do you copy?"

"Loud and clear, Alpha. What's your situation?" the pilot asked.

"We found the guard. KIA. The other one's still missing. We're headed to the sighting zone."

"Copy that, Alpha. Keep your guard up."

"Move out," Jackson commanded.

Hoover led the team where the trail followed. Although Jackson knew how to track targets in the wilderness, it wasn't his expertise. Hoover had a keen eye, especially for this sort of thing, so with his tracking skills, the team would be able to cover a lot of ground fast.

Every few minutes, Hoover would stop and take a closer look at the ground before deciding which way to continue. Not ten minutes after finding the dead guard, Hoover raised a hand in a stop sign to the team. He raised two fingers to his eyes then pointed at the blood-smeared boulder ahead.

The team sneaked around the boulder, taking up positions to ambush the target if it was still there. When they jumped in front of the boulder with their arms raised, the other guard's dead body came into view. Just like the first one, this one had a hole in his chest, the heart missing.

"Okay, I guess we can agree that whatever we're hunting is on a special heart-based diet." Dixon patted his chest. "You think it'll be able to rip a hole in these vests?"

"Let's hope we don't need to find out," Jackson said. "Keep going."

After following the trail some more, Hoover stopped, turned his head to face the others, and said, "It's headed away from the zone."

He pointed at the dark and dense treeline ahead.

"Keep your eyes open. Could be an ambush," Jackson said.

The beams of sunlight hardly penetrated through the canopies of the trees in this part of the woods. Jackson was tempted to use flashlights, but visibility wasn't that bad, and he didn't want to scare off the target in case they ran into it.

"Tracks are pretty fresh," Hoover said. "At this pace, we should be able to bag the target fast."

"You point, and I'll shoot these fancy transmitters at the fucker," Dixon said.

"Quiet," Jackson commanded.

"Don't worry," Hoover said. "We're not that close yet anyway. Still gotta—"

But Hoover never managed to finish his sentence. Jackson had seen it too late. A wash of dark flesh emerged from behind a tree and flanked Hoover, a terrifyingly quick swipe of a clawed hand in the air before it scurried off into the trees again with rapid steps.

Hoover's scream erupted in the forest. Then gunshots blazed and boomed.

"Shit! I don't see it!" Dixon shouted as the team assumed a defensive formation around Hoover, who was on the ground, groaning in pain.

The distinct smell of blood was already in the air, but Jackson couldn't look down. Not when every second counted. Footsteps stomped perpendicular to Jackson, merely twenty feet away. He squeezed the trigger, aiming to shoot the legs of the creature. The others opened fire, too.

He couldn't tell if they hit anything.

"Hoover's bleeding! We need to get him out of here!" Trope said.

Jackson's gun remained trained on the spot where he'd last seen the silhouette merging with the trees. He was waiting for it to come out of its cover because it had nowhere to go.

But he underestimated its speed.

By the time he fired again, the creature was already behind the next tree, farther from the team. From there, it continued running in the opposite direction. It was safe now to take a look at Hoover.

Jackson looked down but refused to lower his gun. Three even gashes ran down Hoover's shoulder and neck. Berry was kneeling in front of him, his hand pressed on Hoover's neck.

"Lights!" Jackson shouted.

The team turned on the torches installed on their weapons, bright cones of light cutting through the darkness of the forest. The creature was nowhere in sight.

"Survivor, we need to patch him up!" Dixon shouted.

He could hear the anger in his teammates' voices. They were accusing Jackson for not letting them take care of Hoover. But it was still too dangerous. The creature might still be nearby, and it might be waiting for them to turn their backs so that it could strike.

"All right, pull him out. Pull him!" Jackson shouted.

Berry grabbed Hoover by the locker loop and dragged him backward while keeping his gun pointed in the general direction of the threat. Hoover howled in pain. The rest of the team followed, their guns still trained at the woods in front.

A rapid patter of footsteps tore through the woods, followed by the same silhouette dashing right at Jackson. But it wasn't coming from the front.

It was coming from his left.

By the time Jackson turned his gun on the creature, the claws were already too close.

# CHAPTER 14

"Do you guys hear that?" Dylan asked.

It sounded like distant popping sounds.

"Woodpeckers, maybe?" Lexi shrugged.

"Maybe," Dylan hesitantly agreed.

The murmuring of the creek followed them. It was on their left, flowing over the rocky ditch, winding under hills and continuing on the other side. It was serene, but Dylan still couldn't stop thinking about Bogdan being Lexi's ex.

*And the way they exited the woods together.*

"How long do you think we have until we reach the Eye?" Hannah asked. "We need to be ready for a trip back, too."

"Maybe fifteen minutes or something like that," Lexi responded.

"How long until those two catch up?" Oscar joined them after recording the creek.

"At least twenty-five minutes or something like that, so we have some breathing space until then. Guys, I'm really sorry about Bogdan. If I'd known that Mickey was going to invite him, we would have gone without him."

"It's fine." Oscar waved. "He's not a pain to deal with." Hannah and Lexi shot Oscar incredulous stares, so he quickly corrected that sentence into, "Okay, he's a pain maybe a little."

"He's just not my type to hang out with," Hannah said. "I'm sure he's a nice guy, I just don't see myself spending time with him."

"Mickey doesn't choose his friends, huh?" Oscar asked.

Lexi laughed. It was a well-known fact among everyone that Mickey hung out with everyone, everywhere, at all times.

Lexi had told Dylan many times about Mickey's busy social schedule. At five, it was a drink with a guy he'd met at a game of soccer. At six, a house party at his former classmate's place. At eight, a meet-up with a guy who was his coworker for one month at the mechanic's shop.

Being an introvert, Dylan not only avoided hanging out with people as much as he could, but the ones he did hang out with he chose very carefully. He only had so many hours to dedicate to socializing, and he didn't want to dedicate them to the wrong people.

"Yeah, that's Mickey," Lexi said. "I can't even keep track of all his so-called friends."

"He was like that in Germany, too," Hannah chirped. "Oscar and I agreed to invite him over more because we thought he was lonely as a foreigner and all, but he was so busy with the people he'd met that we ended up needing to schedule appointments with him."

Lexi rolled her eyes, a groan escaping her mouth.

It wasn't long before the trees became sparse and the greenery was replaced by jagged, rocky surfaces. The trail tapered, which effectively forced the group to walk in a row. Lexi confidently led the way, knowing where each turn was before they even saw it.

An arduous, steep climb later, the Eye came into view below them.

***

For a while, Mickey didn't let Bogdan's words bother him. But then, like a boomerang that came back at full force, thoughts started to run rampant in his head. He refused to believe that Dylan was cheating on Lexi. No way. Dylan and Lexi were the perfect couple, and everybody knew that. No way would he do something like that to Lexi, right?

But Mickey knew all too well that people revealed their true colors after *years* sometimes.

Bogdan looked behind every now and again, probably to make sure the cougar they'd heard earlier wasn't following them—if it was a cougar. But he didn't tell Bogdan that cougars didn't let you see them. They saw you long before you had enough time to react, and by then, defending yourself would be pretty much impossible.

But there were no cougars in this area. Right?

"How long does this trail go for?" Bogdan asked.

"Not much longer. We should catch up with the others soon."

"That German girl, Hannah... she gets scared easily, huh?"

"Um, I don't know. I guess?" Mickey shrugged.

"Did you see how scared she looked when she recorded that bear in the woods?"

"It *was* kind of creepy."

"It was just a bear. No reason to get so frightened over it. But did you see how she reacted when I startled her?"

"Yeah, that was kind of funny."

"Yeah."

Bogdan was smiling to himself. Mickey knew that facial expression well. It usually meant he was plotting something.

"What's on your mind?" Mickey asked.

"Nothing." Bogdan shrugged, but the smile refused to abate.

"It's not nothing. Come on, spit it out."

"Wouldn't it be funny if we pranked the others?"

"Pranked them how?"

"I don't know. Do something when we catch up to them."

"Okay?"

But before they could finish that conversation, something rustled in the bushes right next to them.

***

The Eye was pretty much how Dylan had envisioned it in his mind's eye. A wide crater sat in the middle of the rocky surface as if a meteor had fallen into it. Ledges and jagged rocks protruded inward, creating natural stairs that led directly down to the seemingly small puddle of emerald water in the shape of a human eye.

"Here it is," Lexi said, turning to the others, waiting for their reaction.

Hannah and Oscar's camcorders were already pointed at the bottom of the hole, words of awe coming from them. Dylan wanted to spend a moment taking it all in with his own eyes before he took out the camera.

It was an impressive sight. The bottom of the crater was about fifty feet below them. Dylan wanted to take a closer look at the actual eye.

"Can we get down there?" he asked.

"Sure." Lexi nodded.

She turned around and made her way down the path that seemed the safest: wide and with lots of ledges just under.

"You're going down?" Hannah asked, concern in her voice.

Lexi stopped just as she took a step down. She turned around and looked up at Hannah. "Well, yeah. That's the whole point of coming here. You gotta take a closer look at the Eye. Come on, guys."

"It doesn't really look that safe," Hannah said.

Dylan was already making his way after Lexi.

"It's fine!" Lexi shouted back just as she stepped farther down. "Look, it's like a staircase. I've been down here a dozen times!"

*With Bogdan?* Dylan wanted to ask. He clenched his jaw at that thought as he hopped down the ledge.

"Come on, Hannah. We can take pictures over there." Oscar took Hannah's hand. Reluctantly, she went after him.

The descent was not all that difficult, but climbing back up would take some effort. Some of the "steps" were way too high, which meant that the group would need to use their hands as well as their feet to climb out. Dylan was too mesmerized by the Eye to worry about that.

He could see movement in the water, shades of orange and silver that slinked here and there. Only when they got closer did he realize those were fish.

"The fish are able to survive in that small puddle?" he asked, out of breath from the descend.

They'd reached the lowest point they could and stopped in front of the Eye. From that point of view, it looked like just a puddle of water, but it was clear enough for Dylan to see that it went very deep.

"Yeah." Lexi nodded. "It's not always like this for them since the Eye constantly shrinks and grows because of the rain and so on."

"And what's the story of this place?"

"Not really much of a story, just a legend. They say that fairies gather here on certain nights to dance. People have been coming here for years, trying to catch a glimpse of the fairies."

"Has anyone managed to catch them on camera?"

"Not that I know of. Unless you count the one where one of Mickey's numerous friends took a blurry picture of the Eye and circled the little shapes around it, claiming those were fairies.”

Dylan chuckled.

“The worst thing is a lot of people believed him,” Lexi said.

Hannah and Oscar only just then arrived. They were out of breath.

“Okay, I have no idea how we’re going to climb back out,” Hannah said. “But either way, I can’t worry about that now.”

She raised her camcorder and slowly swiveled it around the place. Dylan spun around, glancing up at the surrounding formation that looked like a giant rock coral. His eyes fell on the figure at the top that disappeared out of view the moment he looked at it.

It was subtle. Fast. It all happened in the blink of an eye, enough for Dylan to question whether he’d really seen it. But the tiny pebble that tumbled down the ledges with a loud clacking noise was evidence enough that someone *was* up there.

Bogdan and Mickey, maybe?

“What’s up?” Lexi asked.

Dylan must have been staring for a while, he realized. He raised a finger and then brought it down. “Nothing. I think I saw someone up there is all.”

Lexi looked toward the top of the crater. “Mickey and Bogdan?”

“I don’t know. I couldn’t see clearly.”

“I think it’ll be a while until they catch up to us. It was probably nothing.”

“Yeah, probably,” Dylan agreed, unconvinced.

Noticing the serious expression on his face, Lexi cleared her throat, turned to the German couple, and said, "All right. How about we get climbing? It's a long way up."

Oscar and Hannah were taking a selfie on the rim of the Eye, oblivious to Lexi and Dylan's conversation. Oscar lowered his phone and nodded. "Okay. Let's go."

Dylan took one final look at the Eye. He imagined a group of small, beautiful women with translucent wings and pointy ears holding hands and dancing around the Eye under the full moon, singing songs in a language long forgotten. He was suddenly more interested in Slavic folklore.

This time, it was Hannah and Oscar who went first. Oscar and Lexi assisted Hannah with the particularly high ledges. None of them were high enough that one would need to do a pull-up to get on top, but Hannah just seemed to become clumsy whenever she needed to climb. Overthinking caused fear to control her, but luckily, her friends were there to assist her.

Dylan was at the rear of the group, waiting patiently while they got Hannah on ledge after ledge. By the time they reached the top again, they were all out of breath.

"Hoo, that was exhausting." Oscar collapsed on the grass.

Just then, a scream erupted mere feet from them in the nearby thicket.

# CHAPTER 15

Lexi gasped when her eyes fell on Mickey covered in blood, staggering toward them. His hand was on his belly, the fingers and shirt drenched in red.

"He... help!" Mickey whimpered.

Another scream exploded, this one from Hannah. It was a scream of pure terror.

Mickey fell to one knee then collapsed sideways into the grass, moaning in pain. Up until that point, Lexi's brain had refused to process the visuals in front of her. Only when Mickey collapsed did it spur her into action.

*He's hurt. He's been attacked.*

Lexi's heart hammered in her chest as she broke toward her brother, his name on her lips, but she couldn't be sure if she'd actually said it aloud or not. She skidded on her knees in front of him and took his hand, tears of panic blurring her vision. Within seconds, Mickey was surrounded by the group—everyone except Hannah, who kept her distance.

"It attacked us... it... it's still close," Mickey said, his voice wheezy.

"Don't talk," Lexi said. "We need to get you patched up. We need to—"

Her hand trailed to his stomach. Her fingers touched the blood. She froze.

A loud, guttural roar ripped through the air, and then a feminine scream joined in. Everyone turned their heads to see Hannah held in the arms of a bulky figure, raised in the air as she bucked and screamed. And then...

The figure started laughing.

Mickey started laughing.

Lexi stared at Bogdan, who brought a terrified Hannah down. She fell on all fours and scooted away from him, shaking like a leaf in the wind. Lexi looked at Mickey, whose face of pain had morphed into a grimace of laughter. All the eyes were fixed on Mickey in confusion.

"Got you, bitches!" Bogdan shouted then continued cackling, a hyena-like sound that echoed around them.

"It's just berries," Mickey said, showing the pink on his fingers.

The laughter continued. Lexi was convinced that the only reason why nobody else had said anything was because they were too frazzled by the stupid stunt Mickey and Bogdan had pulled off.

Lexi's hand flew toward Mickey's face on a whim. The slap cracked in the air, instantly silencing not just his laughter but also Bogdan's.

"Oh, shit," Lexi heard Bogdan murmuring in the background.

"Are you out of your fucking minds?!" Lexi clambered up to her feet, her eyes glued to Mickey.

Her brother's hand was pressed on his red cheek, a look of hurt on his face.

"Seriously! What the fuck is wrong with you two?!"

"Are you out of your minds, pulling a stunt like this one? What the hell is wrong with you?" Dylan stood in front of Bogdan, arms spread confrontationally.

"We just joke. Relax, American. No need take joke like dick." Bogdan waved a hand and put it on his hip, tensing his muscles.

"You think this is funny, asshole?"

Bogdan's face went rigid at that. His hands dropped and his shoulders tensed up. That was when Lexi realized that this prank gone wrong could turn into a fistfight between Bogdan and Dylan.

"All right, enough!" Lexi strode to Dylan and tugged his hand.

He didn't budge.

"Listen to your woman, American," Bogdan said, a sly grin appearing on his face.

For a second, Lexi was sure that Dylan was going to lunge at Bogdan. Instead, he pulled his hand free of hers, turned around, and paced in the opposite direction. Bogdan's smile stretched wider at the seemingly hollow victory he'd just attained over Dylan.

"Ow," Mickey yowled as he stood up, his hand still on his cheek. "I can't believe you slapped me."

"Think, Mickey. *Think* before you do something stupid like this." Lexi jabbed her temple with a finger. "Whose idea was this? Was it your idea?"

She turned to Bogdan.

"It was mine," Mickey said.

Lexi looked at him, considering for a moment whether to believe him or not. No, this wasn't Mickey's idea, she was sure of it. Bogdan had probably suggested it, and Mickey played along because he was like that. He went along with whatever the flow in the group was. And now he was covering for his friend because he knew what Lexi's reaction would be and he wanted to stop the situation from exacerbating.

Oscar was on one knee by Hannah's side, holding her hand and stroking her hair. Hannah was still distraught, her eyes wide in terror, her chest violently heaving up and down.

"Why everyone so stiff?" Bogdan asked. "It just joke. It funny."

"It's not funny," Dylan retorted.

"Pranks are never funny." Oscar helped Hannah up onto her feet.

"Okay, sorry. All right?" Mickey said. His face, hands, knees, and shirt were smeared in pink. Lexi couldn't believe that her idiot brother went through such trouble—even going as far as to ruin one perfectly good t-shirt—to pull a prank on them, and not even a good one, at that.

But they scared them out of their wits, and that was the whole point of the prank, which meant it *was* good. But Lexi wouldn't admit that to Mickey. Especially not in front of Bogdan. She didn't want to encourage them to pull shit like that again.

"Okay, where we go next?" Bogdan asked.

"Don't you want to at least look at the Eye?" Mickey pointed to the crater.

Bogdan shrugged. "Nothing special. We come all this way for that?" He let out something that sounded like a cough and chuckle.

"The trail leads on," Lexi said. "There's a vista nearby."

"Okay. Let's go, then," Mickey said.

"Actually, I'm done," a small voice said.

Everyone turned to face Hannah. She was somewhat composed now, but the way her nostrils expanded gave away her residual fear from the jumpscare.

"I'm done. I've had enough of the woods. Enough of the walking. Enough of..." she trailed off.

*Enough of Bogdan,* Lexi completed Hannah's sentence in her head.

"I just want to go home," Hannah said. "Okay? I'm leaving."

With that, she waved everyone off and started down the trail.

"Honey, wait!" Oscar called out, but she didn't listen. "Come on, Hannah. Don't go just yet!"

"I'll see you back in town." Hannah wasn't having it. She spun in a circle to give Oscar an aloof glance.

"But how will you go back?" Lexi asked.

"I'll... I'll walk." Hannah shrugged.

"It's too far, Hannah," Dylan joined in on the game of "convince Hannah to stay."

"I don't care," she said.

"Hannah, come on. You can't go alone. The town is too far for walking."

"You guys can just pick me up on the way back."

"There is bus station when we drive here," Bogdan said.

Everyone looked at him in an accusatory manner for not helping the case.

"See? I'll use the bus!" Hannah said.

"Hannah, wait!" Oscar took a step after her and touched her shoulder.

"Stop, okay?" Hannah whirled around. She looked like she was holding back her anger. Oscar seemingly noticed this because the hand that touched her flew up in a surrendering sign as if to tell her he wasn't going to come any closer.

"I told you earlier that I wanted to go back," Hannah said. "You didn't listen. So, just leave me alone now, okay? I'll see you back at the apartment."

And with that, she spun right around and hurriedly walked away, ignoring the pleas of her friends.

***

For a while, silence veiled the air. Everyone stared at the path where Hannah had left. Dylan felt like something more should be said. Not about Hannah but about Bogdan and Mickey. They were the reason Hannah had left.

"Well, nice work, Mickey," Lexi finally spoke up.

Her words were directed at Mickey, but she equally blamed Bogdan.

"Come on, guys. We were just joking!" Mickey upturned his palms, guilt written all over his face.

He was, at least, apologetic enough. Bogdan's reticent stare conveyed indifference—amusement even. For him, the prank was fun. The drama was the cherry on top of the sundae. No matter what the others told him, he wouldn't accept their blame. To him, there was no harm done, and at the end of the day, he would laugh it off even if it was the cause of Oscar and Hannah sleeping in separate beds that night.

More silence followed before Dylan said, "We should probably go after her."

"No," Oscar disagreed. "Not right now. She needs to cool off. She might come back."

"But what if she doesn't?" Lexi asked.

"Then I'll go after her." Oscar shrugged. "Oh, come on. Don't give me those looks, guys. You heard her. She wants to be left alone. So, let's leave her the fuck alone."

His jittery movement revealed how upset he was, but no one wanted to address that because they were afraid of Oscar's reaction.

"She will be okay," Bogdan said.

Dylan shot daggers at him. That motherfucker had no say in any of the matter.

"Uh... okay." Lexi scratched her arm. "The trail leads on this way. I guess we can follow it a little more, and then we should really turn back."

"Okay, let's go!" Bogdan clapped his hands together and spun to lead the way.

Oscar was the first one who moved after him. Lexi, Mickey, and Dylan cast furtive glances at Oscar, afraid to meet his eyes because he might understand why they were eyeballing him that way. He was acting like an unstable runaway patient from an insane asylum.

Silently, the group broke into a harmonious stride.

***

Hannah wiped the tears that wouldn't stop pouring out of her eyes. She was angry at everyone in the group. At Bogdan and Mickey for pulling such a stupid prank, at Dylan for not hitting Bogdan right in his smug face, at Lexi for not having Hannah's side more, at Oscar for not coming after her.

Hannah had looked behind a few times in hopes that her fiancé was coming after her. Maybe he was on his way right now. She would hear his voice. He would catch up and tell her how sorry he was and how the others could go fuck themselves, and then the two of them would go home together. Hannah would still be angry at him, but she would be slightly less angry than she was now.

But Oscar wasn't there, no matter how much she slowed down her pace and how many times she turned around. He was not coming. That only made her more indignant. She wiped the remaining tears from her face and hurried along. If Oscar changed his mind and decided to come after her, then let him worry about Hannah.

It was a long way back, though. Hannah's feet were killing her, and it took a while until she reached the crossroads. She froze in front of the intersection, staring down each path, trying to remember which one they'd taken when they came here. All of them looked the same, but Hannah was fairly certain that it was the one that curved to the right a little.

*Impossible to get lost here,* Mickey had told her.

Getting lost didn't worry her so much. What worried her was running in circles. Annoyed at the heat, the insects, the pain in the soles of her feet, Hannah collapsed into a sitting position in the middle of the trail. She shuddered, but no more tears came out. Her eyelids stung from the excess rubbing.

She hung her head down and closed her eyes, suddenly feeling extremely tired. She inhaled—it came out as a sobbing hiccup—and blew the air out of her lungs. She opened her eyes and looked up at the canopies of the trees where the chirping was coming from.

A distant sound on the trail behind her droned in her ears—the distinct sound of dirt crunching under shoes. Finally, Oscar was coming for her, she realized. As much as she didn't want him to find her sitting in the middle of the trail like an abandoned puppy, she was relieved beyond words that she would not be alone in the woods anymore.

The footsteps seemed to approach forever, the sound growing nearer and nearer. When they were a few feet behind her, they stopped.

"What? Changed your mind?" Hannah asked, her gaze fixed on her hands in her lap.

Oscar didn't say anything.

"Why are you even he—"

When Hannah turned around, there was no one there. Hannah's eyes darted around the trail. "Oscar?"

Something off the trail rustled the undergrowth, close enough for her to see. A twig snapped nearby. Hannah's gaze was fixed on the general direction of the sound. The heat drained from her hands and feet. The hairs on the nape of her neck stood straight.

Suddenly, she couldn't help but remember the one thing she'd tried so hard to suppress in the past hour or so—the recording of the silhouette among the trees. And with that came a terrible, terrible realization.

She shouldn't have left the group.

*They're just pranking you. That's all they're doing. It's Bogdan, and he's back to play another prank.*

But she didn't believe her own words. She opened her mouth in an attempt to call out to whoever was out there, tell them this wasn't funny anymore and had long since stopped being so.

The bushes stopped rustling, and the footsteps migrated, circling, slinking to the side, behind Hannah. They were trying to get the drop on her. And still, even as they inched closer to the trail, the rustling and crunching louder with each passing second, Hannah couldn't move.

She didn't truly believe that she was in danger. Not until the moment she heard the groan emanating from the foliage. Not until she saw a pair of eyes staring back at her from the darkness.

Hannah didn't let out a scream. She wanted to, but her vocal cords refused to cooperate. Her legs did work, though.

She spun on her heel and bolted into the trees. She thought she heard the thing behind her, stampeding after her, but if that was the case, the sound was too drowned out by her heavy panting and whimpering. Branches abraded her cheeks and hands as she jostled through them, her sprint reduced to a shuffle as her shoes sank into the soft ground.

She made the mistake of looking back. That split second of inattention was enough for mother nature to trip her, causing her to fall headlong. Hannah put her hands out in front of herself, the grass cushioning her blow.

She rolled onto her rear and scanned the treeline. A big, black silhouette stood far behind her—the same one from the video—dwarfing the surrounding trees. No, there was no one there. Her panicked mind just conjured shapes where they didn't exist.

Hannah should have breathed a sigh of relief that she managed to run away from the thing that stalked her, but she couldn't. Something wouldn't let her.

Her gasping sounded too loud, so she forced herself to calm down. A plethora of thoughts ran rampant in her mind.

What was that thing, and why was it chasing her?

What did it want with her?

Where was she?

How would she go back to the trail?

Hannah's eyes burned with oncoming tears, but before they could fill her eyes, a snap nearby gave her pause. It was still close. Hannah crawled to the closest tree and pressed her back against it, her knees brought to her chin. Her hands clamped over her mouth in a desperate attempt to stop her breathing from giving away her location.

Silence. Dead silence. An unnatural muteness that shouldn't have been possible in the woods. And yet it was.

Hannah listened as the soft steps sank into the dirt somewhere behind the tree she used as cover. They grew closer, then receded, then grew closer again, until they were mere feet from her. Tears streamed down Hannah's face. She squeezed her eyes shut, praying for the footsteps to go away.

Insects tickled her lower back and ankles. She resisted the urge to shrug them off.

Her prayers were answered because, in moments, the stalker's crunching steps receded in the distance, step by step, a slow and agonizing departure. When Hannah could no longer hear anything, she lowered the hands from her mouth and sighed in relief and exasperation.

Timidly, she peeked around the tree, scanning the forest for any movement. Only the trunks of the trees greeted her back. Hannah took her time scrutinizing the horizon once more, just to make sure she wasn't missing anything.

She breathed another sigh of relief and slowly stood up, her hand never letting go of the tree. It was her safety, a pillar that provided cover from whatever was in here with her. The persistent tickle on her lower back reminded her that she still had insects crawling all over her. She swatted at herself, her eyes still diligently surveying the forest.

She didn't have much time. She had to find the trail and return to the group. Panic overwhelmed her at the thought that she might be lost. *You could end up wandering the woods for days or weeks,* Mickey's words rang in her head.

*I shouldn't have left. I shouldn't have left. I really shouldn't have—*

Something in the corner of her vision caught her attention. Even before she turned her head, she knew that it was something that didn't belong in the woods—or rather did belong there and belonged so perfectly. The shape was too bulbous, too incongruous to the surroundings to be a tree.

Hannah was stuck in a frozen moment that seemed to last an eternity. As long as she didn't look at it, she would be fine, a ridiculous thought told her. But she couldn't not look. It was like telling someone not to think about oranges after mentioning oranges.

She barely had enough time to turn her head when the shape lunged at her. As Hannah clawed at the ground, breaking her fingernails in a desperate attempt to get away, shrill screams ceasing only when she needed to draw breath, she knew pain like never before.

And as her strength waned and her body and throat gave out, reduced to a mere sluggish resistance, the pain replaced by a lingering numbness and the sound of gnashing teeth and slurping, Hannah came to terms with the fact that she wasn't going to leave these woods alive.

*I hope Oscar doesn't come for me,* was her final thought before her vision went dark.

# CHAPTER 16

The group was quiet on the trek along the trail. Even Bogdan, ever the loudmouth, stopped talking after a while when the group failed to respond to his remarks. The tension in the air was palpable. Dylan could almost feel what everyone in the group thought in that moment.

He and Oscar were pissed at Bogdan.

Lexi was worried about Hannah.

Mickey was cautious about a fight breaking out.

And Bogdan? Dylan swore he could feel pride emanating from the guy. It was either that or indifference. If he was sorry in any way about the prank, then he didn't show it.

A few times, Dylan opened his mouth to suggest to Oscar to go back for Hannah, but he still looked pissed over the prank, so Dylan refrained from saying anything that might aggravate the situation further. Maybe when he calmed down a little.

"It just trail. Just trees. Boring," Bogdan broke the silence.

"Well, we were at the Eye, and you didn't even peek at it," Mickey said.

"Boring. There nothing else in forest?"

No one gave him an answer. They continued plodding in silence, heads hung down. Then at one point, Bogdan pointed at the ground and said, "Look. Something die here."

He was pointing at the dark liquid on the dirt.

"Damn. Must have been a wild animal," Mickey said.

"I thought there weren't any wild animals here?" Oscar asked.

"I thought so, too. But, I think we were wrong," Mickey said. "Maybe they're just migrating. Bogdan and I heard something back on the trail, too."

"What?" Lexi asked.

"I don't know." Mickey shrugged.

"Mickey say it sound like cougar," Bogdan added.

"A *cougar?*" Lexi asked. "And you didn't think to share this information with the rest of us?"

"I'm sure it was nothing," Mickey said, another wave of panic swaddling his face.

Luckily, his sister didn't have another outburst. Mickey's cheek was still red from where she slapped him. Dylan's mouth contorted into a smile at the sight of that. He had it coming. Bogdan should have gotten slapped, too. Dylan had seriously considered punching him in the face. He didn't know what stopped him from doing so.

If one thing was for certain, though, it was that Bogdan's big muscles didn't scare Dylan.

Oscar checked his phone once in a while; a momentary glance at the screen before shoving it back into his pocket. Expecting a message or missed call from Hannah, undoubtedly.

The distinct popping sounds came from somewhere in the woods again, just like the ones they'd heard earlier, only they were a little closer, Dylan thought.

*Woodpeckers*, the word entered his mind.

But it didn't sound like woodpeckers. Woodpeckers made a different sound. Not a *popopopop*, but rather a fluid *trrrrrt*. And these sounds were too uneven, too overlapping, each clack too slow for a woodpecker, but fast enough for...

*For a gun*, Dylan thought.

He'd only once heard the sound of guns going off in the distance like that, and they usually sounded like fireworks, depending on the gun, the distance, the spaciousness in which the bullets were fired, and so on.

"I think we should turn back," Dylan said.

Lexi looked at him, agreement on her face. Oscar's face communicated uncertainty. Mickey's expression was draped with concern directed to the others. Bogdan didn't even turn around.

"How about we go a little longer, and then go home?" Mickey suggested.

"A few more minutes. There's nothing else ahead," Lexi said.

"Yes, there is," Bogdan said.

He had stopped walking and was staring at something off the trail. Dylan couldn't see anything past the sun-bathed foliage in front of Bogdan until he got closer.

*Whoa*, the word formed in his mind at the houses that stretched below.

***

"I think we found our mystical village," Lexi said.

She refused to blink, a part of her believing that either the village would disappear if she did so, or that she would lose sight of it, since everything about the houses was so congruously brown and green, just like the surroundings.

"There's a village. There's actually a village," Mickey perkily exclaimed. "I knew it. Grandma's stories were true all along, I knew it."

"What stories are those? She never told me stories." Lexi ogled Mickey.

Mickey mumbled something about a village from the Middle Ages, the sentence blended into a long, incoherent word. He was already breaking toward the slope leading down. His exuberance seemed to spur the others into action as well, and soon, everyone was trekking down the gradient.

On the way down, Lexi wondered how such a place could have gone unnoticed. It seemed to sprout out of nowhere, she realized. She thought back to the last time she visited this place. Had she used this trail? Had she walked past the village without even seeing it?

Not possible.

The nettles burned Lexi's ankles, but there was no way around them. They were too widespread, and she didn't have the luxury of going around to look for a safer way down. Up until they reached the bottom, Lexi had been convinced that the houses they'd seen from the trail would turn out to be just weirdly shaped trees.

Those doubts were rinsed away the moment she gazed at the numerous, dilapidated structures placed around the cobblestone street.

On cue, Mickey let out a triumphant, effeminate cry that echoed in the village. He broke into a hasty stride across the undergrowth, sagging branches, and saplings along the way, not caring that they would sling back to the person behind him—the person in question was Bogdan.

Only when Lexi's foot touched the hard surface of the cobblestone did she fully become convinced that the village was actually, really there, and not an illusion or an optical trick. She found herself spinning in circles, mesmerized by the sight, her mouth agape in wordless awe.

"This is so fucking cool!" Mickey shouted, his voice once more booming in the village.

Dylan's eyes flitted from house to house, too much to absorb at once, too many things to look at. Even Bogdan, who couldn't care less about some historical place, looked slightly impressed, his eyes wide with caution and wonder.

"Holy shit," Lexi heard Dylan muttering next to her.

When she looked at him, the phone was in his hand, but not pointed at anything yet, just ready to snap pictures once his eyes had had their turn at taking in the view. Lexi gawked at each individual building that stretched alongside the path, wondering what it might have been used for.

Most houses looked like small homes, but as they walked farther along the street, they came across a smithy with an anvil in front and rusted tools scattered around, and a church with a broken rooftop. Most of the structures had been battered by time and weather and mother nature that crept in to reclaim its territory, but enough of them remained for Lexi to imagine what daily life must have been like for the villagers.

The houses largely resembled the ones she'd seen in Ethno Villages, which were places built after the model of the old country villages, which served the sole purpose of letting people visualize the history of their country while also enjoying historical food and drinks in the taverns.

"This is insane," she said, staring into the smithy.

Everyone went their own way, exploring the place. Lexi entered a two-story house that she assumed might have belonged to the richest person in the village. When she turned around to see where Dylan was, her eyes fell on him disappearing through the collapsed door of the rundown house down the street.

***

Dylan had never been one for urban exploration, but this was something else. Unlike those famous YouTubers who went in search of haunted mental institutions and abandoned prisons, Dylan enjoyed the sight of places that were more serene; like this ancient village.

Its ramshackle houses, scattered tools, and minimalistic furniture told a story of their own: of how the villagers used to live back in the day, of how they didn't have much, but it was something they could call theirs, of how every villager had their own function that would help in keeping the place alive and running.

The house Dylan was in was mostly empty, save the collapsed wooden roof that pinned down the old table and the rocking chair. The entire house consisted of a single room. Dylan imagined a family living there centuries ago: a husband and wife, and their two children, perhaps a daughter and son.

The father would be out all day, tending to the animals—if they had any—or forging something at the smithy. The wife would prepare meals and take care of the children, just as tradition dictated back in those days. The children might go to school if a school existed in the village. If not, they might either be homeschooled or would need to help their parents, trained from an early age to take over one day.

It was a tough life. People back then had no luxury of worrying about trivial matters like wondering if they would be accepted into college or land a position in a company, or eat gluten-free food. They had only one concern—surviving day to day.

"Ugly house. Very ugly," Bogdan's gruff voice broke the silence.

Dylan turned to see the buff man standing in the doorway, ogling the house with a wrinkled nose.

"They didn't really get to choose back in the day. I bet they had to build their homes with their own hands," Dylan said.

Bogdan didn't seem impressed by this in the slightest. He walked inside and scrutinized the table under the wooden beam.

"How you like in this country, American?" he asked before turning to Dylan.

"It's good," Dylan said.

"Good?" Bogdan raised an eyebrow.

Dylan couldn't tell if the gesture meant he was surprised by the positive response or if he expected something above the answer of "good."

"Yeah. Good," Dylan repeated.

"You would live here?"

Dylan froze. He considered himself stupid for not realizing right away that this was a game to Bogdan. A test to see whether the American was fit to be Lexi's new boyfriend.

"Of course you wouldn't." Bogdan flashed him a complacent smile. "I see on your face. You like America better."

Dylan didn't respond to that remark. It was a taunt, and he wasn't going to fall for it.

"Lexi will be sad when you leave her," Bogdan said. Dylan scowled at Bogdan. "When you go home, I mean," Bogdan added belatedly as if he'd just remembered to clarify, which, Dylan was sure, was all a part of his trick.

"Don't worry about Lexi," Dylan said.

"I don't. She a good person. Very strong."

"You sound like you know her well."

"Oh, yes. Like I said, we close friends."

"Funny, she never mentioned you before."

Bogdan pressed his lips tightly together, which gave him the appearance of stifling a laugh. Dylan took a step closer to Bogdan until the two of them were inches from each other. Dylan's hand squeezed into a fist, but he only vaguely became aware of that.

"Level with me," he said. "What's Lexi to you?"

Bogdan stared a Dylan a while longer with that same, tight-lipped expression, and then made a popping sound with his mouth as if he'd come to a decision on what to say. He walked past Dylan, a hand on the American's shoulder. "Forget past, American. It is always full of pain."

He strode outside, leaving Dylan fuming. Dylan bet that if he stepped in front of Bogdan, he'd see a wide grin on his face.

Minutes passed, and Dylan refused to leave the house until he calmed down. He didn't want anyone to see him like this. He especially didn't want Bogdan to have the pleasure of seeing that his words had an impact on him because it wasn't just anger that he felt.

It was hurt: hurt over being lied to by Lexi. Hurt that his girlfriend would be with a douchebag like Bogdan. After his thoughts cleared up, he was surprised to learn how okay he was with the whole thing. Not entirely, but more than he thought he would be.

He walked outside just as he'd heard Lexi shouting his name.

***

Bogdan, Oscar, and Mickey had gone their own way, exploring the other side of the place, while Dylan and Lexi stuck together on their end. She was glad to be able to grab a moment alone with him.

"I don't see any trash or whatever. You think the place is guarded by someone?" Dylan asked.

"It could be. I mean, I'm sure we're not the first ones who found it, so maybe someone comes here from time to time to clean it up or something."

They walked up to the church, contemplating how to enter, but the vegetation that blocked the entrance was too thick. Lexi didn't let that dissuade her, though.

She took off her backpack and dug through it to find the knife that she'd brought. Her fingers brushed against the somehow still cold can of an energy drink, so she took that out first. "Would you like another one?"

Dylan shook his head. Lexi returned the drink to the backpack and continued rummaging until she found the knife. When she approached the foliage to slice through it, Dylan's hand fell on her shoulder. "Let me do it, okay?"

As much as she wanted the pleasure of massacring the wooden limbs, she let Dylan have the knife. He worked pretty good and fast with it. Branch after branch was chopped off and tossed aside, weeds pulled from the ground, until the passage up the concrete stairs was clear enough.

The ancient double doors that served as the church entrance were entangled in persistent roots that merged with the structure. One side of the massive door was slightly ajar, revealing a dark interior with a musty smell.

Cutting through the thick branches here would prove to be impossible, so Dylan shoved the ajar door with his shoulder, instead. Even with that effort, the door barely budged, the bottom stuck firmly to the swollen ground. It took a few rams, but the crack was finally wide enough for both him and Lexi to step through.

He poked his head through the crack for a moment then leaned back and returned Lexi's knife to her. He gestured with his head for Lexi to follow him and disappeared through the door. Lexi held on to the knife, just in case they still needed it, and sidled into the church after Dylan.

Momentarily, a sour smell that came with old buildings and dampness invaded her nostrils. It was a lot colder inside. Lexi's eyes adjusted to the darkened interior, and then she gasped.

Most of the pews were broken and rotted. The floor was littered with leaves, dirt, and murky puddles of water. Far above, a ray of gray light peered through the tiny hole in the roof. It cast barely any light into the interior compared to the stained glass windows depicting saints riding and fighting beasts that glowed from the light outside.

Lexi watched in astonishment at the flaking walls where remnants of painted artwork still remained, the faded and battered altar, the cross that still stood firmly above.

The need to be quiet overcame Lexi. She was in a church, and there were rules that needed to be followed in such a place. She'd already broken one by not crossing herself before entering. Even in its abandonment and decay, the place filled Lexi with a profound sense of protection and tranquility.

"Wow," she finally said, her voice hollow in the spaciousness of the vast interior.

"I've never seen anything like this." Dylan's head slowly scanned the tall ceiling.

Lexi was glad to be here alone with Dylan. There was no one she'd rather share this moment with. Her fingers looked for his, and she squeezed his hand. Their eyes met. A smile formed on Dylan's lips, and as she studied him, no uncertainty lingered on his face. He looked at Lexi with the same affectionate stare that he'd given her the first time they'd kissed, and she knew without an ounce of doubt that he loved her and would never let her go.

*I'm here for you, and I'm here with you. Forever,* that look said.

They inched closer for a momentous kiss when an ape-like voice boomed outside, freezing them in place.

It was Bogdan shouting something and then bursting into laughter.

The emotions on Dylan's face sagged. The moment was over. Lexi bit her lip, disappointed but also furious at Bogdan for ruining the moment.

"Bogdan is the last person I wanted on this trip. It was supposed to be the last outdoor activity we did together before you leave. I'm sorry," she said.

Dylan shook his head, not saying anything. He licked his lips and turned away from her, his eyes falling on the ruined altar. She sensed resistance in his hand, so she let it go.

"Why do you dislike Bogdan so much? What's up with that?" Dylan asked.

Lexi blinked sheepishly. "What?"

"I mean, you seem to have a huge problem with him. Is there something you're... maybe not telling me?"

He was trying to make those words sound amicable, she realized, but he was failing miserably. The accusation in his voice was palpable. That caused a twinge in Lexi's chest. For a moment, she felt like she was staring at a stranger interrogating her, and not her boyfriend.

She gave her head a swift shake, closed her eyes firmly, and upon opening them asked, "What?"

Dylan sighed, his face going stiff. He opened his mouth to speak, but then another scream erupted outside. This one wasn't Bogdan's. Both Lexi and Dylan jerked their heads to the door. Silence took over, and then a shrill, feminine voice shouted a single word that sucked the heat out of Lexi's body.

"Help!"

# CHAPTER 17

Just when the creature's claws were about to connect with Jackson's face, a series of rapid gunshots staggered it, causing it to retreat into the darkness once again.

"No eyes on the hostile!" Trope exclaimed.

His and Dixon's rifles were pointed in front of them, providing cover to the team while they patched up Hoover. The bleeding wasn't as terrible as Jackson originally thought. Hoover would be okay as long as they evacuated him soon.

"Dixon, tell me you tagged that fucker," Jackson said.

"Sorry, man," Dixon said. "It was too fucking fast."

"Shit."

"What's the plan, Survivor?" Berry asked.

Jackson didn't like that Berry had jumped on the bandwagon of calling him by his infamous nickname, but it was inevitable. Nicknames in units stuck like well-cooked pasta to the wall.

"Hoover, can you stand?" Jackson asked.

"Yeah." Hoover nodded.

He raised a hand, and Berry took it, helping him up onto his feet. Hoover groaned a little then blinked furiously a few times. "Feeling a little woozy, dammit."

"It's the meds. Just take it easy," Berry said.

"I can't fucking take it easy. Didn't you see what we're after?" Hoover snapped.

"All right, enough," Jackson interrupted. "We're going back. Dixon, get the tag ready."

"We're going back there?" Berry asked, his eyes wide.

For a moment, he looked like a boy, and that was exactly what he was in the face of the life-threatening danger that loomed above them. Jackson had seen his fair share of Intervention Unit officers becoming skittish boys when faced with the impossible horrors on the missions. In situations when that happened, they were pretty much already dead because years of training gave way to panic.

"I need you to stay focused, Berry," Jackson said. Because it was the only thing that came to his mind. "We still have a mission to complete. We find the target, tag it, and get the fuck back to the LZ. Got it?"

But Berry's eyes flitted to something behind Jackson, his focus on the leader broken. It was a look that said, *We don't need to look for the target.*

"Contact! Twelve o'clock!" Dixon shouted and then gunshots exploded.

Everyone was at the ready, their guns scanning the treeline.

"Shit, where is it?!" Trope shouted.

It all happened way too fast. Something hung down from the tree, mere inches from Jackson. He pointed his gun upward and fired. He hit the creature, which let out a hissy scream just as its enormous hands wrapped around Trope and pulled him up like he weighed no more than a feather.

More gunshots, but the creature was gone along with Trope, whose screams came from the trees. The team pointed at the canopies, unloading there, but it was futile. They couldn't see what they were shooting.

"Cease fire!" Jackson shouted.

Instantly, the shooting stopped, but the remaining team members never took their aims off the trees. Trope's screams were distant, a caterwaul of pure pain. Three loud cracks came from above. Trope was using his handgun, Jackson realized. The screams continued louder before turning into gurgling.

"It's killing him!" Dixon shouted.

"Hold!" Jackson commanded.

They couldn't move. Not yet. The creature would get the drop on them if they did so.

The gurgling went on a little longer, mixed with painful gasps and squelching. Then, something heavy plopped from a nearby tree with a loud *thud*.

"Shit! Trope!" Dixon broke into a dash toward the body.

"Don't move!" Jackson shouted, but his words fell on deaf ears.

Dixon was already in front of Trope's motionless body, his gun scrutinizing the treetops. Jackson, Berry, and Hoover didn't move from their spots. Jackson had his crosshairs aligned near Dixon, in case the target went for another attack.

"Shit, he's dead!" Dixon said when he knelt to inspect Trope's body. "His fucking heart has been gouged out!"

Those were the last words Dixon would ever utter. Despite being ready, Jackson couldn't stop what happened next.

The target emerged from behind one of the trees, an elegant and lightning-fast sidestep that closed the distance to Dixon in the blink of an eye. Jackson had already opened fire on the target. Dixon, who must have seen it at the corner of his vision, pulled out the tag gun and turned it on the creature.

But before he could fire, the target thrust a hand with elongated claws at Dixon's face. The fired shots that illuminated the area briefly allowed Jackson to see the unnatural fingers piercing Dixon's eyes and knocking him on his back, the tag weapon flying upward.

The gunshots were mixed with Dixon's bloodcurdling screams as his hands closed around the fingers stuck in his eyes, trying to get them out. Blood abundantly gushed out of his sockets and down his face. Jackson knew right then and there that, even if they saved Dixon, he was still a dead man.

The creature raised the other clawed hand high up in the air and then brought it down on Dixon's throat, turning his screaming into hollow gasps and burbles. Even as the bullets tore at the monster's body, it continued clawing at Dixon's head and chest while letting out high-pitched screams.

Dixon's face was a cavernous mess of holes, gashes, and mangled flesh. His eyes were holes filled with blood. Blood came out in spurts from the wounds, drenching his face in red entirely. The corner of his lip had been torn all the way to his ear, revealing the rows of bloodied teeth, his jaw hanging loose and disjointed. His neck had been sliced halfway through, almost completely to the neck bone.

And even then, he was still alive, twitching violently, gurgling as if blowing through a straw.

Jackson aimed at the creature's head and fired. The bullet grazed the top of the hairy skull, and that, finally, made it fall back to the ground. The barrage of bullets did not stop. The creature was riddled with red holes, and still, it refused to die. Its clawed hand raked the ground, snatching Dixon by his limp hand, and then, just like that, it was gone among the trees along with Dixon's body.

The whole thing—the moment between the creature emerging and running off with Dixon's corpse—couldn't have lasted more than a few seconds.

In those few seconds, Jackson had finally caught a clear look at the creature, but he had no time to consider its features. He was more focused on the practical side, and now that he knew what they were up against, he realized how utterly fucked they were.

"Fuck!" Hoover shouted. "Where the fuck is it?!"

"Survivor, what do we do?" Berry asked.

Jackson's MP5 was still trained on the woods where they'd last seen the creature. They could take it down. They'd managed to hurt it. All it would take is one well-placed shot to the head.

"Survivor?" Hoover echoed.

Survivor's eyes fell on Dixon's tag gun nestled on top of the pine needle-riddled ground.

They could stay here and try to take the target down, but with their numbers reduced from five to three, the odds were highly stacked against them. The creature knew what it was doing. The Intervention Unit was on its territory where they stood no chance against it. They had to retreat to a place where they would recover and prep adequately.

Survivor bent down and picked up the tag gun, his eyes never flitting to the ground because he knew what one second of distraction could do.

Once Dixon's weapon was strapped to his holster, he backpedaled. "Fall back. Fall back now."

# CHAPTER 18

"Help!" the single word that cracked in the village street startled Bogdan.

For a moment, he was absolutely sure that the voice belonged to Hannah because who else could it possibly belong to? But when he turned his head to face the source of the sound, he saw not Hannah but an unfamiliar woman stumbling down the street.

He couldn't see her well at this distance. She looked and sounded young, was slim, and her clothes were torn and covered in layers of dirt.

"What the fuck?" Mickey said aloud.

The woman fell onto her hands and knees, her disheveled hair hanging down her head like wet spaghetti noodles. Bogdan remained frozen in one spot. Instinctively, he thought that this might be a junkie, and he didn't want to get close to those kinds of people. But Mickey and Oscar were already jogging toward the woman. Lexi and the American had exited the church and were striding toward her as well. Not wanting to be the odd one out, Bogdan broke into a casual walk toward the mysterious person.

She threw her head up when the others approached her and scanned each face above her with dreary, fear-stricken eyes. Bogdan took a better look at her now that he was closer.

Although she couldn't have been older than him, the crags on her skull-shaped, simian face and the dirt that covered her from head to toe made her look ten years older. The strands of her long hair were either frayed or stuck together. Her front teeth were chipped. Her clothes looked like they hadn't been taken off in weeks. Cuts and bruises were visible in the missing patches where her clothes had been torn. Bogdan detected a faint whiff of old sweat mixed with dirt.

"Are you okay?!" Lexi asked in their native language as she knelt in front of the girl.

She winced and recoiled at Lexi's touch like a scared animal.

"It's okay. We're not going to hurt you," Lexi said. "What happened to you?"

The girl slumped on her rear and planted a palm on the ground. Her bony elbow quivered violently as if unable to hold the weight of her own body. Her head slumped down, her eyes fluttering, her lower lip drooping. She suddenly looked like she was dead tired.

"What happened to you?" the American asked in English.

The girl looked up at Lexi and then at the American. Her lips moved, forming wordless shapes with her mouth. Bogdan recognized only two words before the girl fell sideways unconscious.

*Baba. Dangerous.*

"Oh, shit. Shit, shit. What the fuck is going on?" Mickey asked. "We need to get her to a hospital."

"We need to get out of here is what we need to do," Bogdan interjected.

The American's eyes darted from person to person in confusion at the language he didn't understand. He was not the focus of attention anymore.

"Guys, what's going on?" he asked.

"We have to leave," Lexi said, switching to English.

"Why? What did she say?" the American asked.

"I didn't understand a word." Lexi shook her head.

"She said something about danger. And *baba*. Which translates to grandmother in English," Mickey said.

"Danger? What kind of danger?" Oscar asked.

"Who cares. Let's leave." Bogdan shrugged.

Lexi was on her knees in front of the girl, her hand touching her forehead and neck. "We can't risk moving her like this."

"Then leave her be. We'll find help and send them back for her," Bogdan said in their language, not caring whether the American understood or not.

Lexi shot him a hateful look. "We're not leaving her behind, Bogdan," she said in English, emphasizing every word of the sentence, probably for her American boyfriend to understand.

"I not carry her." Bogdan pointed at himself.

"Nobody asked you to," the American rebutted.

"Shit. Hannah," Oscar said. It sounded like he was thinking aloud. He pulled out his phone and fiddled with it for a moment before swearing something in German. When he brought his phone down, he looked at the group and said, "I have to find her."

"Wait, you're leaving right now?" Lexi asked.

"What choice do I have? She could be in danger. I mean, look at her!" He gestured to the unconscious woman.

"He's right. Now is not the time for Hannah to be alone out there," the American said.

"We can't go splitting up now. It's too dangerous. Who knows what's out there," Lexi said.

"I'm not fucking waiting until whatever attacked her gets to Hannah!" Oscar exclaimed, by the inflection of his timbre, sounding offended.

"We'll all go back together, okay? Let's just wait until the girl's up."

"She could be unconscious for hours. Hannah must be miles away by now. I can't sit and do nothing."

"Everyone, calm down," Mickey said.

"Fuck this. I'm leaving." Oscar turned around and started down the street.

"Oscar, wait!" Lexi called out. "Someone, go with him. We can't go separating now."

The street went mute as the group exchanged glances, wondering who the volunteer was going to be.

"Bogdan should go," Lexi said after a long moment of silence.

"What? Why me?" Bogdan frowned.

"Because your prank was the reason Hannah stormed off." Lexi didn't wait for Bogdan to give a counterargument before she turned to the unconscious girl.

Bogdan inflated his lungs, ready to disagree, but then he noticed the accusatory stares from the others: from the American, which was expected. From Oscar, whose eyes harbored something even deeper, something akin to hate. Even Mickey's facial expression silently communicated agreement with the rest of the group.

Bogdan didn't care what they thought. There weren't any official laws in the group. If they had to draw straws over who was going to be sacrificed, and Bogdan got the shortest straw, he would still refuse the sacrifice because the voting system was total bullshit—unless it worked in his favor.

But going back to fetch Hannah also meant getting closer to the forest's exit. Whatever predator lurked in the woods, Bogdan didn't want to stay with it.

"Okay, fine," he said, groaning to feign disappointment.

"Good," Lexi said. "When you find her, call for help. We'll catch up as soon as we can."

"We need car keys to find help," Bogdan said, outstretching a hand to Mickey, who he knew had the keys on him.

Mickey dug into his pocket.

"*Call* for help using your phones," Lexi said sternly, interrupting Mickey's action.

*I won't let you drive off without us,* the sentence between Lexi's lines said, but she gave no voice to those thoughts.

"What if phone not work?" Bogdan asked.

"It will. There's signal in the area."

Bogdan nodded and smiled. He looked at the unconscious woman. He was glad that he didn't need to be the one dealing with dead weight. He gave Oscar a firm pat on the shoulder and said, "Okay, friend. Let's look for Hannah."

# CHAPTER 19

Dylan's thoughts swam in and out of focus. A part of him couldn't shake the feeling that this was all just another elaborate prank. He *hoped* it was because the thought of actually being in danger didn't sit well with him.

As he stared at the battered, unconscious woman on the ground, scrutinizing the old and new bruises and scars all over her face and body, Dylan knew that this was no prank. It was real, and that meant that the danger was real, too.

"What the heck happened to her?" Lexi asked as she clambered up to her feet.

Dylan paced down the street, his eyes fixed on Bogdan and Oscar, who were plodding through the undergrowth toward the slope leading back to the trail. In his head, he calculated how long it would take them to get back to the car.

*Hours,* he realized.

He hoped Hannah didn't put too much distance between herself and the group so that Oscar and Bogdan could catch up with her.

"Hey," Mickey said.

He had somehow appeared next to Dylan without him noticing. With his small stature, he moved "like a wraith" as Lexi would often say.

"Hi," Dylan said back.

"You okay, brother?" Mickey asked.

"Yeah. You?"

"I guess."

Mickey pulled out the cigarette pack from his pocket and opened it. One sad-looking cigarette sat in there. Mickey brought the pack to his mouth and pulled the cigarette out with his lips. He crumpled the pack and stuffed it back into his pocket. Dylan respected that Mickey had enough respect for this ancient place not to litter.

"What a fucked up day, huh?" Mickey asked as he lit up the cigarette.

"Yeah. I just hope Hannah's okay."

"Me too."

"She's sleeping," Lexi said.

She, too, had somehow snuck up on Dylan. Dylan craned his neck toward the girl on the cobblestone. She seemed peaceful from here. He couldn't bear to stare at her because he was afraid of what would happen if he saw her waking up.

He already dreaded it. Would she scream? Thrash? Attack the group because she would think she's in danger?

"I don't think she's hurt bad. Just scared shitless," Lexi said.

"What could scare her like that?" Mickey asked, puffing his cigarette.

"Did you see the wounds she has? She looks like she's been in the woods for days. Actually, it could have been weeks easily. Even *months*." She put the stress on the last word and raised her eyebrows.

"Okay?" Mickey frowned and then opened his mouth when realization draped his face. Dylan understood what Lexi was trying to say, too.

"The thing is, I inspected her thoroughly, and there's no doubt about it," Lexi said. "She's the hiker who went missing a while ago."

"Shit," Dylan proclaimed.

Mickey huffed the smoke out.

"I'm surprised she survived for so long," Dylan said.

"Me too." Lexi bit her lip. "There's hardly enough food in the woods to survive for a few days, let alone months. She must have some amazing survival skills."

"Or a lot of luck." Mickey's head tilted.

"Whatever it is, she's alive, but she might not have a lot of time left," Dylan said. "We need to get her to safety before it's too late."

"She'll be too weak to move." Lexi shook her head.

"By the time rescue comes, it could be too late. I'll carry her."

"It's a long way back."

Dylan shrugged. "We'll take breaks if necessary. If we sit here, it could be hours, maybe even a whole day, until rescue arrives. She doesn't have that long."

"Uh, guys?" Mickey called out.

Dylan and Lexi had been focused on each other so intently that they didn't notice Mickey staring back at the cobblestone where the girl was lying. Or rather, where she *had* been lying.

Because when the group looked at the spot, she was gone.

***

Bogdan was bored. He hated cardio. Nothing more annoying than taking step after step, seeing the same trees over and over, counting the kilometers. He was okay with physically difficult exercises. That way, his mind was at least occupied with something. But this? It was just a boring hike in the woods where everything looked the same.

The thought of losing precious muscle mass from the extensive walking he did today bothered him. He knew the atrophy wouldn't come so fast, but he would need to compensate for it by eating a big meal when he returned home. Perhaps a family-sized pizza? It had enough nutrients, and after today, he'd earned the cheat meal, as unplanned as it was.

Oscar's stride was fast and confident. From time to time, he pulled out his phone, probably to check the bars on it, before shoving it back into his pocket with almost frustrated jitteriness.

"Relax, friend. Your girlfriend is fine," Bogdan said matter-of-factly.

Oscar glowered at him for a moment as if to say *this is all your fucking fault*. Whether he was too focused on looking for his woman or afraid to start a conflict with Bogdan, he didn't say anything. Good. Frustrated or not, Bogdan would be damned if he'd let some asshole foreigner take out his anger on him.

"We have to hurry." Oscar leaned forward to gain momentum.

They were past the Eye and close to the crossroads. It took them well over forty minutes to reach the place, and they still had a long way to go.

"I hate to say this," Bogdan said. "But your woman probably out of woods now."

Oscar shot a look at Bogdan. "I sure hope so. But I'm not stopping until I find her, even if it's out of the woods."

"No need panic," Bogdan said. "Everything okay."

"*Okay! Okay?* Did you see that woman back there?!" Oscar slightly raised his voice.

Bogdan was ready to tell him to watch his tone, but he decided not to do it just yet. He would wait a little longer, see if the situation escalated. Then, he would threaten the German to shut up.

"She was scared, yes. But nothing to be scared of." Bogdan shrugged.

Oscar didn't respond. He didn't even dignify Bogdan's words with a look. His initial focus and angered expression instantaneously drooped, replaced by anxiety and concern. Bogdan immediately noticed what the German was seeing.

Fresh blood, right in the middle of the trail.

"Oh, shit." Oscar broke into a run toward the blood.

When he halted in front of the streak, a hand clamped over his mouth, his eyes wide, the corners of his eyebrows arched upward as if he was about to start crying. When Bogdan caught up, he realized why Oscar was so upset.

In the middle of the drying blood was a shoe. Even Bogdan immediately recognized it as Hannah's shoe. The two of them stared at the ground for a little while, too shocked to move or say anything. Then Oscar pointed to the right.

"There. The blood leads there," he said with a shaky voice.

"You're going after it?" Bogdan asked.

"Yes. Hannah could be hurt."

*Hurt? Look at all this blood. She is probably dead.*

"Okay," Bogdan simply said, not wanting to be the bearer of any bad news, no matter how obvious the signs were.

The trail was easy enough to follow. The blood that soaked the mossy ground and grass lay in abundance like a trail of its own. Bogdan kept scanning the area because he knew that whatever got Hannah might still be close by.

He thought back to the cougar scream he'd heard with Mickey. As a precaution, his eyes darted around the ground in search for a stick big enough to defend himself.

"Hannah!" Oscar shouted, his voice booming between the trees, startling Bogdan.

"Quiet, fool!" Bogdan warned him, observing the surroundings a little more fervently.

"Hannah, where are you?!" Oscar ignored him.

Bogdan gritted his teeth. If Oscar's yelling reeled in the predator that took Hannah, Bogdan wouldn't stick around. Oscar would be on his own.

"Shit!" Oscar shouted in a petulant voice.

It wasn't until they were close to a clearing that Bogdan saw it.

"Stop!" He put a firm hand on Oscar's shoulder and brought both of them to the ground on their stomachs.

"What are you—" Oscar started and then followed where Bogdan's finger was pointing.

The trail of blood ended in the middle of the clearing, right where Hannah lay. She was splayed on her side, facing away from the two, curled into a fetal position.

"Oh, shit. Hannah!" Oscar planted his palms on the ground to propel himself up, but Bogdan's hand was on his shoulder again, stopping him from doing so.

Oscar gave him a venomous look.

"No." Bogdan shook his head. "It could be trap."

"I'm not leaving her there."

"Look at blood, my friend. She's already dead."

Oscar jerked free from Bogdan's grip and stood up, "Fuck you," he said as he sprinted into the clearing after Hannah. Bogdan pressed harder against the ground, refusing to move, his head swiveling left and right in search of any movement other than Oscar's.

***

"Hannah!" Oscar knelt in front of his fiancé, both relief and dread washing over him.

He grabbed her by the shoulder and rolled her limp body onto her back. The feeling of relief vanished. The dread intensified.

Hannah's wide eyes stared vacantly at the sky. Her lips were slightly parted, emphasizing a trickle of dried blood crusted at the corner of her mouth. Oscar hadn't noticed the rest of the gruesome details until his hand touched her chest, his fingers coming in contact with something wet and slippery.

When he looked down, a hole adorned Hannah's chest, deep enough for Oscar to stick his entire hand into. And even though the sight in front of him was clear as the sun that shone above, Oscar's mind refused to *understand* what he was looking at; that the person he was holding, who he cherished so dearly, was no longer with him.

But before the shock and the pain could even poke their heads out, a scream in the clearing interrupted him.

***

"Oh!" Bogdan slapped a hand over his mouth to stop himself from screaming.

He watched as another person walked into the clearing from the other side of the treeline. He thought of it as a *person* because he couldn't find a better description. *Animal* didn't quite fit, either.

What ran into the clearing right at a frozen Oscar resembled an old woman but was too lanky for any human. Her limbs were too long and thin, her hands and feet too big. The elongated fingers tapered into sharp claws. The few strands of hair that remained on her head were gray and frayed like an old broom. Her mottled face was riddled with wrinkles of old age and saggy skin. Her crooked nose was so long that it almost fell into her mouth.

The face itself was what seemed the most natural about her. It was the face of an old woman, and yet, something was wrong even there. It was as if she was either missing some features that would make her look more human or that she had too many features that made her look less so.

The sack she wore fell loosely against her body all the way to the ankles, but Bogdan could just barely make out the outline of two tear-shaped tits that sagged to her stomach.

Oscar never moved from his spot. His gaze had been fixed on the old woman the entire time as she screamed and dashed toward him at incredible speed, each large foot closing the distance to the German. Even as she drew a hand back, the clawed fingers contracted, he didn't move. Even as the claw swiped at Oscar's throat, he didn't move until impact.

And then, Oscar was on the ground next to Hannah, fresh blood coming from him, but Bogdan couldn't see the source of the injury. Oscar got onto his back, placing a hand on his throat as he scooted backward with his heels, the other hand raised in front of him in a stop sign.

Another swipe had Oscar finally letting out a scream. It took Bogdan a moment to understand that what remained of Oscar's hand was a fingerless stump. He stared at his mutilated hand and shrieked in terror while the old woman stood above him, her impossibly long fingers dancing with anticipation.

Oscar rolled onto his stomach and began crawling—directly toward Bogdan!

*No, you fool! You'll get us both killed!*

Oscar's injured hand reached forward in a futile attempt toward Bogdan, and their eyes locked. Those eyes pleaded with Bogdan, begged him to help him, but Bogdan was no fool. If he moved from cover, they would both be dead men.

The old woman straddled Oscar, one hand on his scalp, the other on his chin. Her fingers somehow seemed to shrink until they were almost normal-sized. The pointed tips seemed to disappear, too.

"N-no!" Oscar bucked against the woman.

Then, his hands started clawing at the woman's, the stumps of his fingers smearing blood over his head in a desperate attempt to get her grip to release. He screamed a bloodcurdling scream, one that Bogdan imagined a person would let out when being burned alive.

Oscar's jaw pried open violently, and then it continued unhinging, more and more. A sickening snap came from his jaw as his mouth opened to a size not possible for any human alive. And still, it continued opening under the old woman's tug, her fingers digging into the German's scalp and chin until they drew blood.

Oscar's scream's never let up, even as a series of snaps came from his jaw, even as the corners of his lips tore like pieces of paper all the way to his ears. Then, he went limp. The woman still held on to the scalp, but the hand she used to unhinge his jaw let go. Oscar's jaw dangled loosely, his uvula and all his lower teeth visible, even the barely poking molars at the back of the rows. His tongue comically lolled out of his ruined mouth, a rain of blood dripping from his upper jaw.

His eyes fluttered open. He was still alive!

The old woman let Oscar drop to the ground and then turned him over on his back. Bogdan felt like vomiting at the sight of Oscar's lower jaw dangling like a loose ball sack. The woman's fingers grew again. It was such a subtle action that Bogdan convinced himself he was imagining the whole thing.

Oscar's mangled hand rose feebly then fell. After all this, he was still alive somehow. The woman sat on Oscar's stomach, and with one swift motion, dug the clawed fingers into his chest. Oscar let out one final sound—something between a gurgle and a hiss. The rest of his remaining life was spent twitching silently as the woman dug through his chest, and the sounds of squelching blood and crunching bones filled the air.

Bogdan knew that the right thing to do would be to look away, but he couldn't. Something was forcing him to stare, and it wasn't just the fact that the creature in front of him was something new, something inconceivable, and that he couldn't pry his eyes from it. It was the fascination with the violence. As much as it made him sick, he also couldn't stop watching.

He'd heard about it in the past. People who went to the dark web in search of snuff videos and videos of fatal, violent accidents always went back looking for more, always in search of a death more violent than the previous one, to satisfy their craving for gore.

Oscar had stopped moving after a while, long after the woman's hand was buried inside his chest wrist-deep. When she pulled her hand out, Oscar's still-beating heart was in her hand. She stared at it with lust in her milky eyes, a tongue licking her retracted mouth. It was a very human look, Bogdan realized.

Before he knew it, the woman had bit into the heart. Bite after bite, she tore chunks of it while letting out wild, guttural sounds between chewing. The heart was gone in just a few bites, the only evidence remaining that it was ever in her hands being the blood that drenched her mouth.

With that, the old woman stood up and wiped her mouth with her forearm. Her eyes flittered to Bogdan. Bogdan let out a whimper. He was next. She was going to kill him just as she had killed Oscar.

Bogdan planted his hands on the ground, bracing himself for an explosive push-up, already considering the route he should take. Would he even stand a chance against her? This *thing* looked like an old woman, but it moved so fast.

The old woman turned around and sauntered back into the woods that she'd come from, her long, orangutan-like arms swaying next to her body. Just as she entered the darkness of the treeline, she turned around one last time, and that's when Bogdan saw it.

He blinked multiple times, convinced that the sight in front of him was just a trick of the eye. Whatever it was, the woman was already gone.

# CHAPTER 20

"Fuck. Where did she go?" Lexi asked.

She couldn't understand how the unconscious woman had managed to disappear on them like that. One moment, she was there—weak, barely able to speak, let alone move—and then, no trace remained that she ever existed.

"Hey! Lady!" Dylan shouted.

His voice was loud enough to echo in the village, but no response came back to him. Lexi bit her lip. The woman must have been scared after being lost in the woods for weeks. She might have considered the group a threat, too.

Lexi and Mickey shouted after the girl in the local language, yelling that they meant no harm and were just trying to help her.

"Dammit. It's no use," Dylan said. "She's gone. We need to go back right now and inform the authorities while she's still close."

Lexi surveyed the village once more. The girl could be anyone. Inside any of the buildings, behind any tree. Or, she could be far away by now, running through the woods, putting more and more distance to the village with each passing second.

"Lexi?" Dylan called out.

Lexi put a hand on her forehead then lowered it. "Okay, you're right. Let's call for help before it's too late."

They gave a light jog to the slope where they'd come from. The climb was easy enough, but they were all tired from the hike, which made the ascent more difficult. As soon as they were back on the trail, Lexi whipped out her phone to check for a signal.

No bars, of course.

Throughout the walk, Lexi took her phone out over and over, hoping to make the call go through, but it did no good.

"I can't believe we let her slip away like that. How could I be so reckless?" Lexi whined.

"It's not your fault, Lexi. I mean, she's delusional," Dylan said.

"Yes," Mickey agreed with a nod.

"And who knows? If we had tried to stop her from leaving, she might have become violent. We don't have the expertise to handle rescue victims."

"I guess," Lexi said. "But it still feels so wrong. We should have kept a closer eye on her. Shit."

Dylan gave her a dolorous stare. "Let's just get out of here. The sooner we call for help, the sooner they can rescue her."

But doubt swirled in Lexi's mind. It would take them hours to get out of the woods, and by then, the girl could be anywhere. Lexi was on the fence about turning around and going back to look for her, but then she realized how futile it would be.

The forest was *enormous*. Even if the girl stayed in the village, which Lexi doubted she did, playing hide and seek just in that one particular spot would make the job of finding her extremely difficult. Add kilometers and kilometers of densely packed trees into the equation, and the task would become not only close to impossible but also dangerous.

Lexi's gaze was fixated on the ground in front of her. She was tired from the walk. Her feet were killing her. Whenever she became aware of the ache in her neck, she'd pull her shoulders back and realize how much she was slouching.

Then, as if her prayers had been answered, when she raised her head to stretch her neck, she saw the woman.

"Look." Lexi's eyes widened as she pointed forward.

The girl from before was seated in the middle of the trail, facing sideways. Almost as soon as Lexi pointed to her, the girl's head turned to the group. Her mouth opened in shock, and she clumsily scrambled to her feet, kicking the dirt behind her.

"Wait!" Lexi shouted.

But the girl was already lost between the trees.

Lexi, Dylan, and Mickey broke into a run after her.

"Stop!" Dylan shouted.

He and Lexi were already among the trees, going after the girl. She was tottering from tree to tree, her legs weaving over each other as she stumbled.

"Guys, wait!" Mickey shouted from behind. "*Wait!*"

Lexi stopped and spun around to see what her brother was so bothered with. Mickey was staring at something rustling on the other side of the trail. Lexi's mouth dropped open.

Then, Bogdan emerged from the bushes, red in the face, out of breath.

"We have to get out of here," he uttered in the local language in one clipped sentence.

"What happened? Where's Oscar?" Dylan asked.

Lexi turned around to see where the girl was. She was already at least a hundred meters away. How did she manage to gain that much distance from them in such a short time?

"Dead." Bogdan's word cut the air. "He... is dead."

The air went mute with shock and tension until Dylan broke it. "What the hell are you talking about? What do you mean, dead?" What happened to him?!"

"Dylan, there's no time. The girl's getting away!" Lexi's head intermittently darted from the group to the girl, who was now disappearing and appearing behind trees.

"Monster," Bogdan said.

Everyone looked at him. Bogdan wasn't joking this time. The fear that seeped out of his eyes was so real, so tangible, that Lexi fully believed that the threat in question really was a monster.

"Monster," Bogdan repeated. "Old woman. Big nails. She..." He took a few deep breaths before continuing, "She take out Oscar's heart."

"What?! Is this a joke?!" Dylan hissed.

Lexi looked back at the girl. She would be gone soon. Lexi couldn't wait any longer.

"I'm going after her!"

"No! We must leave, now! Monster is close!" Bogdan groaned, his nostrils flaring with fear and frustration that the others weren't listening. The gesture seemed so out of his character. Whatever Bogdan had seen, it must have been terrifying.

"Wait for me!" Lexi shouted and, without waiting for the others to respond, spun around and beelined after the girl.

She ignored Mickey and Bogdan's shouts warning her that she was going to get lost and die. Only a minute into running did she realize that Dylan was by her side. She realized then and there she loved him even more because he was with her despite the possible danger they were facing.

They were closing distance to the woman. She was scared. Every now and again, she looked back at her pursuers, and her face contorted into a rictus.

"Please, wait! We're not going to hurt you!" Lexi shouted.

But the girl refused to stop. How she had so much stamina after being so battered was beyond Lexi. Adrenaline was one hell of a thing. For a brief moment, she looked back in the direction of the trail.

She couldn't see anything past the rows and rows of trees.

***

"Fuck. Oh, fuck. Fuck!" Mickey grabbed his head with his hands as he watched the trees—no sign of his sister or Dylan.

He needed a cigarette right now, but he was all out. Shit. He was torn between running after them or waiting. Getting swallowed by the trees could only cause more trouble. They'd be all scattered, unable to find each other, in more danger than they already were.

"What the hell do we do? Shit, what should we do?" Mickey moaned aloud, his feet itching to break into a dash toward the woods.

"We have to leave, Mickey," Bogdan said. His voice was still electrified, on edge. "We have to leave right now."

Mickey inhaled deeply. The fresh air did him no good. He needed *smoke*. *Nicotine*. "What happened to Oscar?"

Bogdan looked over his shoulder as if he expected someone to be standing just behind him. When he made sure they were alone, he looked at Mickey and said, "It killed him. It..." He raised a hand to his chin, then lowered it.

"What did?" Mickey upturned his palms.

"It was a woman."

"A woman?"

"Yes." Bogdan nodded fervently. "An old woman."

Mickey raised his eyebrows.

"Don't look at me like that. I'm not crazy. I know what I saw. The old woman... she ripped Oscar's jaw off clean. Hannah is dead, too."

"Shit."

Mickey had a hard time believing Bogdan's words. It wasn't that he didn't believe his account; it was just that his brain had difficulty accepting such an outlandish story. Two people dead—and they were people he knew, people he'd seen just minutes ago!

Bogdan had to be wrong. He had to. Mickey feigned a sorrowful grimace and looked back to the woods where Dylan and Lexi had gone.

"You don't believe me," Bogdan said.

Mickey turned to face him. Sometimes, Bogdan was too smart for his own good. He wasn't smart for academics, but the intellect he possessed was far more useful, Mickey thought.

"I'm not fucking around, man. That girl said it, too, when we found her. She said "dangerous." Don't you remember?"

Mickey nodded. "Okay, but... an old woman killed Oscar and Hannah?"

"You want me to show you their bodies?" Bogdan asked, his voice dancing on the edge of fury.

"No," Mickey timidly said.

"If you saw what I saw, you would have pissed your pants! You would have run off screaming like a little girl!"

Mickey went mute at the sudden barrage of insults. Bogdan's reaction was so unexpected that Mickey couldn't find the words to respond to him.

In the next moment, a high-pitched scream crashed through the woods, followed by a distant but heavy pattering of footsteps.

"Who's that?" Mickey asked, his eyes scanning the woods relentlessly.

The footsteps came again, then the scream, this time from a different direction, Mickey thought.

"Shit. It's back. We have to go!" Bogdan said.

"But Lexi and Dylan—"

"We have to go *right now!*" Bogdan pulled Mickey just as a third scream, a much closer one, erupted somewhere.

And then, the two of them were running.

***

Dylan and Lexi were catching up to the girl. She had somehow gained speed when they closed the distance between them. She whimpered, cried, and uttered words in the country's local language that Dylan couldn't understand. He assumed they were words of plea.

Lexi shouted something back at her, most likely asking her to stop. It was no use. They could go on chasing each other for hours until they collapsed. Dylan would have to be firm with her.

He jackknifed into a dash and quickly closed the last few steps between himself and the girl. She let out a shrill yelp when his hand closed around her wrist. Unable to break free, she turned around and hit him over the head with the side of her fist.

"Calm down!" Dylan shouted before the next hit landed directly on his nose, sending a painful surge through his nostrils, his eyes watering. Unreasonable anger flooded him. He wanted to slap the girl, but it was only a momentary thought.

He sidestepped behind her and wrapped his arms around her. She screamed and thrashed and kicked against him while he shouted at her to calm down. Meanwhile, Lexi stopped in front and uttered her own warnings until all three voices were too meshed together.

Dylan held the woman firmly in the bear hug, focused on not careening along with her while her feet thrashed in the air. Then, just like that, the screaming wound down to a whimper, which then reduced to heavy panting. The kicking had stopped. Whatever Lexi was saying, it was working.

Dylan still refused to ease the grip on her, his gaze trained on Lexi. Lexi's eyes flittered to him, and she gave him a nod of approval. "It's okay. You can let her go."

Skeptically, Dylan gradually loosened his grip on the woman. She didn't try to fight back. Instead, she drooped in his arms, and he barely held on to her as she slid into a sitting position on the ground. Dylan knelt next to her, one hand on her back, the other on her shoulder.

Lexi knelt, too. She said something in her language. The intonation told Dylan it was a question. The woman expelled a couple of timid words. Lexi asked her something again, and they went back and forth a few times with questions and answers. Concern washed over Lexi's face.

"What's going on?" Dylan asked. By then, he was no longer holding onto the girl.

Lexi ignored him and continued talking to the girl, whose words came as gasps and sighs between breaths. The conversation was interrupted when a feminine cry tore through the air.

It lasted for a long time. Dylan couldn't tell how long, but he knew it was long because he considered when the person who let out that scream would run out of breath.

All three raised their heads, all senses alert.

"What was that?" Dylan asked.

The woman then spoke in a quick, quavering manner, her nails digging into the soft ground. Lexi asked her something.

"What's going on?" Dylan asked, frustration slowly replaced by a growing sense of fear.

This time, the girl looked directly at him. For the first time, they understood each other. It was a look that said, *We're all in terrible danger, and you and I both know it.* She inhaled, pressed her lips together, and then, just before a second scream, a single word left her mouth.

"*Baba.*"

# CHAPTER 21

"Shit," Dylan muttered when the third scream erupted.

His blood ran cold at that sound. That was no cougar. He couldn't tell how he knew that; he just did. His brain quickly came to the conclusion that the creature that stalked them in the woods and attacked this woman was something that rivaled the legends they had back in the United States: Wendigo, the Skinwalker, Bigfoot...

Whatever was here in Europe was no different than those mythical creatures.

*But those were just sightings. Blurry images captured on cameras. No one has ever confirmed the existence of Bigfoot, or Wendigo, or the Skinwalker, or UFOs.*

But the legends had to have come from something, even if it was just a bedtime story. Hundreds of thousands of miles of forests remained unexplored on earth. It would be foolish to think that a new species couldn't exist, even if it was as improbable as the Skinwalker.

Dylan shook those thoughts out of his head. On a normal day, he wouldn't even entertain the notion of a monster being more than an old wives' tale. Now, he was suddenly a believer.

He grabbed the girl under her arm and brought her to her feet.

"We need to go, now," he said, scanning the woods for whatever caused that noise. "Lexi, help me with her."

Lexi grabbed the girl by the other arm, and then they were stumbling through the forest in the direction Dylan best thought was away from the sound, even if it meant away from the trail. Right now, getting back on the trail was the least of their worries.

The girl whimpered—whether in pain or fear, it was impossible to tell—while Dylan and Lexi carried her. Her feet worked, but they mostly stumbled and tripped, causing all the weight to be on Lexi and Dylan. They were getting tired fast.

Every now and again, Dylan looked behind to see if whatever had screamed was following them. They were alone—for now. Or perhaps the thing was watching them, waiting until they were sufficiently tired to strike.

"We... can't... keep running," Lexi said with a bouncy voice between heavy breaths.

She was right. Dylan jutted his head toward a horizontal cleft on the side of the hill close by. "There. Let's stop there."

Lexi nodded. The woman looked at him in confusion then turned to Lexi, and then she let out a whimper when they trudged on. Dylan's concern was that the cleft wouldn't be wide enough for all of them. When they got closer, his concern was washed away because the gap was big enough, not just for all three of them to hide but also to stretch out.

Lexi was the first one to sidle into the crevice, followed by the girl, then Dylan. He gave the woods another once over before plopping to the ground next to the girl. He was still somewhat worried about her taking off again, so it was good that he and Lexi made a wall around her.

The ground was damp, but they didn't have the luxury of choosing at the moment. It took them a few seconds to settle down and their breathing to grow quiet. It was just in time because the scream came again, distant and faint.

Since Dylan was closest to the corner, he poked his head out to take another look. Nothing in sight. He felt too exposed sitting so close to the corner, but he knew that if they remained still, no one out there would be able to see them.

*Unless it uses something other than the eyes. Say, scent. Then it would be able to smell you—and the girl even more easily—miles away.*

Dylan breathed a sigh before turning to the girls. "It's best if we wait here for a little bit."

"What about Mickey? He could be in trouble, too," Lexi said.

Her eyes were bulging with fear. Dylan noticed her shoulders trembling ever so lightly.

"They'll have to fend for themselves for now. Going out there would be suicide," Dylan whispered.

Lexi seemed to consider this for a moment and then nodded. "You're probably right. Let me see if I can text him."

She pulled out her phone. Her trembling fingers flew across the screen before finishing the message, tapping a button, and continuing to stare. The dirty woman's gaze was fixed on the phone as well as if it was the first time she'd seen such technology.

"Nope." Lexi shook her head. "Shit."

"We'll look for them later. For now. We really should wait until the coast is clear."

"What if it doesn't go away?"

"It has to. Sooner or later, it has to."

He hoped that his words would reassure Lexi. She flashed him a small smile, indicating that they did. But he himself wasn't reassured.

The girl winced. Dylan looked at her. She was staring wide-eyed into the forest. Dylan followed her gaze. He couldn't see anything out there, but he heard it. A heavy patter of footsteps. Dylan turned to Lexi and the girl and motioned for them to get as low as possible.

The girls slinked into lying positions, pressed firmly against the ground. Dylan remained where he was, assuming the best position he could to block them out of view as he stared at the trees.

The footsteps drew closer and closer until they stopped. An eternity later, they proceeded but at a slow, cautious manner. *Tip-toeing,* Dylan realized. That itself wouldn't have frightened him that much were it not for the fact that the footsteps approached the hideout.

A wimpy hiccup came from the girl. Dylan pressed a hand on her thigh to indicate to her to be silent, his gaze still fixed on the trees. The footsteps were mere feet away now, each step crunching loudly, announcing its arrival, telling the trio that they'd been found and that it was coming for them.

Dylan pressed his back into the wall. What could he do? The only thing left to do was hope that the creature would walk past the hideout without noticing them.

The figure stepped into view, staring aside. Dylan's breath hitched in his throat. Even if he wanted to, he couldn't move.

Then, the creature turned its body toward the hideout.

***

"Down! Down here!" Bogdan dropped into the tall grass.

Mickey mimicked him then spat. "Fuck, there are a lot of bugs in here."

"Quiet. You want it to find us?" Bogdan hissed, angry at Mickey for talking too loudly at a time like this.

From here, they had a good view of the woods— particularly of the area where the scream had come from. Bogdan's heart raced fast. His eyes stung from the lack of blinking. He squeezed his eyes shut for a moment, then quickly opened them.

Something was close by, he could feel it. He couldn't see it, but a sort of presence lingered in the air. And then, he saw her.

Far off in the distance, a figure emerged from the trees, hunched over, its arms long and tense, its head jerking from side to side, looking for something. Bogdan heard a gasp escaping Mickey's mouth.

"Don't move a fucking muscle," Bogdan hissed through clenched teeth, spittle flying out of his mouth.

"Shit, shit, shit, shit," Mickey chanted like a mantra.

"Be quiet, you fool," Bogdan said, his tone louder.

The figure in the distance paced in random directions, its head constantly swiveling and searching, searching, searching. It was the old woman. It wasn't just the hunched back and the ape-like extremities that gave her away. It was the long, crooked nose that was impossible to miss whenever she looked to the side.

The image of Oscar being slaughtered right in front of him in a gruesome manner flashed before Bogdan's eyes. Bogdan's bladder threatened to go loose. He didn't want to die. He'd seen the fear on Oscar's face, but he hadn't truly comprehended what that emotion meant—to be afraid of dying.

Now that the woman was approaching, his mind came in close contact with that terrible fear, and he could almost smell it. It was the stench of piss and shit and tears and sweat and blood, all mixed together into a cocktail of death.

"Shit, you were right. You were right, you were right, you were right," Mickey never ceased to mumble. "You were right all along. It's *Baba*."

Bogdan's head turned slightly toward Mickey, but his eyes remained glued to the old woman.

"It's Baba Yaga," Mickey said with a calm inflection.

"Baba Yaga?" Bogdan had heard that name before, but he could not identify who or what it was.

The old woman was closer now. Bogdan didn't know what had happened when he'd kept a close eye on her the whole time. It was terrifying. Her features were more discernible now, like the anger in her eyes and the sack covering her torso.

Bogdan's heart skipped a beat when the woman looked directly at him. *Oh, no. She's found me,* he thought. But then her head continued pivoting. One thing was for sure. They couldn't stay here because she was headed straight for them. She would need to be completely blind to miss them, even in grass as tall as this.

"Mickey, listen. Listen. We have to move," Bogdan said.

"What?" Mickey jerked his head toward Bogdan, a look of disgust and horror on his face.

"If we don't move... if we don't move, she'll find us. We have to go when she's not looking."

"Okay. Okay." Mickey gave an energetic nod. "How do we do it?"

Bogdan looked at the old woman. She was close enough for him to see her long, pointy fingers wiggling. One swipe with those, and he would be on the ground just like Oscar, jawless, and with a gaping hole in his chest.

He looked toward Mickey's side. The tall grass continued there, and the ground fell into a ravine packed with trees. If they could at least break the line of sight with the woman, they'd be safe.

"Crawl over there when she's not looking. I'll follow when it's safe," Bogdan said, his voice barely above a whisper.

Mickey looked at the slope on his side, then back at Bogdan, and offered another enfeebled nod. Bogdan squinted at the old woman. Step after step, she drew closer and closer, stopping only for moments to turn to this side or that.

When she spun around to look at something, Bogdan tapped Mickey on the shoulder. Immediately, his friend began crawling across the grass. Arm after foot and vice versa. The rustle of the grass was minuscule, but Bogdan still worried they would be seen.

He kept his eyes trained on the woman, his pulse beating all the way to his neck at the tension that made him want to puke. Mickey stopped the moment the woman turned in their direction again and continued lumbering toward them.

When she looked to the side again, Mickey continued. He was making good progress, and the woman hadn't seen him. Good, good. One reason why Bogdan didn't want to go first was because he couldn't be sure if it would be safe. Between him and Mickey, he would rather have Mickey dead.

Mickey had managed to crawl to the start of the slope where the elevation provided cover. He was a good fifty feet away. He got up on his knees and peeked above the elevation at the woman before lowering his head down. His eyes locked with Bogdan's, and he motioned him to come over.

Bogdan nodded and looked at the old woman. His stomach lurched. The monster woman was too close now. Even if she stopped and looked elsewhere, he wouldn't be able to crawl away without being noticed. Damn him for playing himself like that. He should have been the one to crawl away first.

Panic swelled in his chest. What the hell was he supposed to do? He was going to die here, and he wasn't ready to die. He still had so many things he wanted to do in life, so many women to bang until he settled down with one and had a family, so many years to spend in the gym until his body was perfected, so many games of soccer he wanted to watch, so many joints he wanted to smoke...

No, he wasn't going to die here. He had to do something. Bogdan was a fighter, so he would fight!

The woman was close enough for him to hear her raspy, wheezy breathing.

Bogdan's eyes gravitated to the ground. His fingers closed around a pebble embedded in the dirt. He knew what he had to do. When he looked up, the woman was turned away, her fingers wiggling, as if itching to stab into something, her shoulders tensing and relaxing.

Bogdan looked at Mickey. Their eyes met, and it suddenly occurred to him that Mickey looked like a sheep. No, like a cow headed into the slaughterhouse that knew something was wrong but couldn't guess what because of its limited cattle intelligence.

*I'm sorry, man,* Bogdan thought. *But I'm not dying here.*

Mickey's eyes seemed to widen in realization just as Bogdan chucked the pebble in his direction. The tiny object landed directly on a rock at Mickey's feet, causing a tinny *clack* to explode in the area. Mickey's eyes fell on the pebble, a look of dismay on his face.

Then, the ear-splitting scream shook the earth.

Mickey was already running in the opposite direction, the woman's eyes trained on him as she dashed after her prey.

He barely managed to run ten meters before the woman pounced on him, knocking him headlong onto the ground.

For a moment, Mickey was dazed from the impact, but when the woman grabbed him by the ankle and dragged him back, he clawed at the ground, screaming a feeble "no" along the way. He got on his back and kicked with the remaining foot, but he was no more than a mosquito to this creature.

The woman gripped Mickey's foot with both hands, and then, with a simple but explosive twist, Mickey's ankle snapped loudly. He screamed a blood-curdling scream as his foot dangled uselessly, a sharp piece of bone protruding out of his ankle.

The creature let go of Mickey's foot. He held his shin, wailing in pain while the woman stared down at him. From here, Bogdan couldn't see her facial expression, but her semi-tense shoulders told him that she wore a hint of amusement on her features.

Mickey huddled into himself, crying and rocking back and forth, uttering words that Bogdan couldn't understand. The old woman took a fervent step toward him. An enormous hand squeezed around Mickey's throat. His pleas were replaced by gasping sounds.

Bogdan never once blinked as he watched Mickey's eyes bulging, his face growing red, thick veins worming down his forehead as he clawed at the woman's hand. Bogdan's fascination with violence outweighed his fears. He forgot all about his safety at that moment and stared at Mickey as the life drained out of him, right in front of his eyes.

The corner of Bogdan's lip danced with a smile. His crotch ached with excitement—like the first time he'd found out about porn and discovered that he liked what he was seeing there, no matter how repulsive some details were.

The woman squeezed Mickey's neck harder and harder until it looked like his eyes would pop out of his skull. His face took on a crimson color, and then—

A sickening *snap* exploded from his neck, and he went entirely limp. Bogdan realized how short-breathed he was, staring at Mickey's glassy eyes. His penis was so hard that it hurt.

The woman dropped Mickey on the ground, sat on top of him, and then she did exactly what she did to Oscar: She started digging through Mickey's chest. Sudden realization that he was almost out of time hit Bogdan. He had to escape before he was discovered. With the looming sense of danger slowly creeping back in, Bogdan's erection vanished, and he was left with one thought only.

*I have to get out of here.*

Luckily for him, the old woman was busy breaking through Mickey's ribs and burrowing her nails through his chest, trying to reach the grand prize. Bogdan crawled in the opposite direction, constantly looking over his shoulder. It would seem that the woman conveniently took her time with her meal this time.

When Bogdan was sufficiently distant, he stood up and continued tip-toeing across the ground, careful not to step on any twigs that would snap under his shoes. When he thought he'd put enough distance between himself and the woman, he slinked behind a tree and peeked back at the crime scene.

The woman stood and was walking back into the woods. Bogdan refused to look away from her this time. He had to make sure that he hadn't imagined the whole thing the last time. Sure enough, his eyes hadn't deceived him.

As the woman walked into the woods, she was no longer an old woman but young and beautiful as well as terrifying.

# CHAPTER 22

"Don't move!" an authoritative voice came from the figure standing in front of the cleft.

Dylan's hands instinctively shot up into the air. The image in front of him only just then crystallized, and he realized that an armed, uniformed person stood in front of him, the barrel of the gun pointed directly at Dylan's face. A mixture of fear and intense relief rose from Dylan's gut. Armed, uniformed people meant rescue!

The man's hand shot forward at incredible speed. Before Dylan realized what was going on, he was being yanked out of the hideout and forced face-down onto the ground.

"Hands on your head!" the man commanded.

Dylan complied without a second of hesitation. Multiple pairs of boots slinked out of his view. Then more authoritative voices shouted, and Lexi and the girl's frantic pleas sounded while they were being lined up next to Dylan on the ground.

"Shit. Survivor, these are civilians," one of the soldiers said.

"I'm aware of that," the one who pulled Dylan out responded.

They were speaking in English and in perfect American, Dylan realized.

"What the fuck do we do with them?" the third soldier asked.

"You guys are Americans," Dylan stated atonally. The point of the sentence was for them to know that he understood them and that he, too, was American.

The soldiers went mute for a moment. Then the one who pulled Dylan out, Survivor presumably, said, "You're not from around here."

"No, sir," Dylan stated. "Sparks, Nevada. My name's Dylan and I'm here on vacation."

"And these two?"

"Locals," Dylan said. "Lexi is my girlfriend. I don't know the other woman's name."

"What are you doing here?"

"We went on a hike, but then something..." He paused, knowing how absurd the rest of the story was going to sound. And yet, being pinned down by soldiers in the middle of a forest meant for hiking was already crazy enough. Something about the whole thing told Dylan they would believe him. "Something attacked us. Killed our friends. Then we ran into this woman. She's a hiker who's been missing for weeks. We were trying to hide."

"Who attacked you?"

Dylan hesitated for a moment. "We thought it was a bear or a cougar, but... There's a monster in these woods."

More silence. Dylan's heart raced while he waited to see what was going to happen next.

"What are you going to do to us?" Dylan asked.

"Berry, keep an eye on them," Survivor said.

"You got it," Berry said.

A pair of boots came into Dylan's view. He strained to look up at the soldier, but one shout at him to keep his head down was enough to pacify any attempt at movement. Footsteps receded in the distance.

***

Jackson looked at the lined-up civilians once he and Hoover put some distance between them. It was clear they were innocent people who had found themselves in the wrong place at the wrong time. They weren't supposed to see the Intervention Unit. The mission was going worse by the minute.

"This is Alpha Team. Respond," he said into the radio.

Seconds later, the tinny voice of the pilot came through. "I hear you, Alpha. Give me a sit-rep."

"Dixon and Trope have been killed. The target's still on the loose. We have three civilians in custody. They know about the existence of the target."

"Shit. I'll get in touch with HQ. Stand by."

Jackson shifted his weight from one foot to the other, scanning the horizon for the target. When he turned to Hoover, his voice was laced with worry. It was the face that most likely reflected what Jackson thought.

Not only was the situation FUBAR, but now they were faced with the dilemma of what to do with the civilians. Whatever HQ commanded, it wouldn't bode well for the unit. If they ordered them to evac, the civilians would slow them down. If they ordered termination... no one enjoyed doing that on the rare occasions that it happened, but it was necessary, and The Company made sure to stress it all the time.

During the first phase of training of new Intervention Unit cadets, the instructors always talked about the time one officer let a civilian leave the strike zone because it was a mother begging to go back to her two young children. The woman turned out to be a Code Red entity that proceeded to murder five people before being contained by the Fat Guys.

"Alpha, do you read me?" the pilot asked.

"Loud and clear. Status?"

"You are to evacuate the civilians. The guys at the borders will take care of the rest," the pilot said.

Hoover breathed an audible sigh of relief.

"Copy that," Jackson said. "And the target?"

"Your mission still stands."

"Goddammit," Hoover said.

Those orders were to be expected. HQ probably knew the risks when they sent a team to the mission, but it was too late to fall back. Dixon's tag gun was still strapped to Jackson's belt. Just one good shot and they could get out of the hot zone.

"Roger that. Heading to the LZ now," Jackson said.

He and Hoover exchanged a look with each other before heading back to Berry and the captive civilians.

***

Dylan watched the two soldiers talking to each other in the distance. He heard the distinct crackle of a radio and a voice talking to Survivor, but he couldn't discern the words. A few exchanges later, the soldiers returned.

"All right. Stand up," Survivor said.

No one moved. Dylan wanted to make sure the soldiers were talking to them, and not amongst each other.

"Hey. You can get up from the ground," the commanding soldiers said.

Dylan looked up to see Survivor staring down at him. That's how he knew it was okay to move again. He stood up, helped Lexi stand, and dusted himself off. Lexi, in turn, assisted the woman. Dylan breathed a sigh of relief.

"For a moment there, I thought you were going to execute us." Dylan scoffed.

Survivor stared at him cold-faced. Then his lips curved into a vague, lopsided smile. "Right. We're getting you out of here. Stick close. Do everything we tell you to, and you'll make it out of these woods alive. And if you see anything that we don't, shout. Cougars can be tricky motherfuckers."

"Cougars?" Lexi asked.

The soldier looked at her and then simply said, "Yes. Cougars. Move."

"Wait. She can't walk on her own." Lexi gestured to the girl. She was seated on the ground, her head slumping. She looked like she was going to lose consciousness.

"What's wrong with her?" Survivor asked.

"She's been lost in the woods for weeks. She's too weak to move."

"Berry." Survivor looked at one of the soldiers and jutted his head toward the woman.

The youngest-looking of them all approached the woman and effortlessly hoisted her over his shoulder.

"All right, move ou—" Survivor's sentence stopped when his eyes fixed on Dylan, growing narrow with focus.

No, not on Dylan.

On something behind him.

# CHAPTER 23

Jackson had noticed it right away. The bulbous shape that stuck out from the tree. It was so well blended into the environment that any person not specifically trained to look for such irregularities would have missed it easily.

The moment his eyes fixed on the shape peeking from behind the tree, Jackson's weapon was raised.

"Contact!" he shouted as he squeezed the trigger.

The young man—Dylan—crouched with a yelp that was drowned out by the ensuing gunshots. A banshee-like scream came from the trees. Jackson's hand was on the tag gun, ready to be fired at the target.

"Move, move!" Berry ushered the civilians out of the danger zone, the woman still over his shoulder, his sidearm drawn.

"Survivor, go! I'll distract it!" Hoover shouted as he fired off a few rounds into the trees.

He knew as well as Jackson that they stood no chance against the creature here, not among the trees that it loved so much. Maybe Jackson could get a clear shot and manage to tag the monster, but it would be wild luck. And it was risky. Not to mention he had civilians on him now, too.

"Don't fall behind, Hoover!" Jackson shouted.

Then, everyone except Hoover was running. Since Jackson was faster than Berry without the dead weight on his shoulders, he ran ahead and then stopped to cover the others. Far off in the distance, Hoover's gunshots boomed in the air while the target flew in and out of view.

"Hoover!" Jackson shouted.

Hoover reloaded, fired off a few more rounds, then turned to run toward the team. That was the moment the creature had been waiting for.

The moment Hoover turned his back, it sprang from the trees and leaped forward. Somehow, Hoover had sensed this. He turned around and pointed his rifle at the creature, firing a single shot before it knocked him down.

Jackson's finger was on the trigger, but there was no point in firing. It was already too late. One long finger had entered Hoover's eye and exited the back of his skull, and now, the monster was too preoccupied with its prey. It mauled Hoover even after he was dead, droplets of blood spraying in various directions like a brush paint from a soaked brush. And then the target assumed a relaxed, sitting stance on top of its dead prey.

"Shit!" Berry took a step forward, but Jackson placed a firm hand on his chest.

"It's too late. He's gone. Keep moving." He looked at the other two civilians, who were too shocked at the sight of the target and the dead soldier to move. "What the fuck are you waiting for?! I said, keep moving!"

He shoved Dylan and then Lexi in the opposite direction. That seemed to be enough to get them to start moving.

***

*Oh fuck, oh fuck, oh fuck!*

Those were the only thoughts that bounced in Lexi's head as they ran away from the monster.

*It's a monster! A fucking monster! And I just watched it kill another human being!*

It looked so human, and yet, there was no way that it could be. The appearance of the young woman with bedraggled black hair was marred by the vicious features of the face, the muscular, yet slim limbs, the fingers…

*The fingers…*

What the fuck was going on in these woods? This place was supposed to be peaceful. The legends talked about fairies and gnomes and…

*And Baba.*

The missing woman's words stirred in Lexi's mind and repeated like a kid hitting the same piano key over and over and over.

*Baba. Baba. Baba.*

"Faster!" the soldier with the woman on his back shouted.

Even with another person on top of him and with full military equipment, he was faster than Dylan and Lexi.

"Where?! Which way?!" Lexi whimpered but refused to stop.

"Move!" the soldier responded.

***

The closest exit of the strike zone was still far, far away. Jackson knew they would never be able to get the civilians there in time before the creature recuperated and went back after them. They had to stop, prepare properly, set up a perimeter, and ambush the fucker.

The civilians stopped all of a sudden. Jackson realized a second later why that was the case. They were standing in front of a hill leading down. It wasn't steep, but it appeared out of nowhere.

Jackson looked back. The creature was nowhere in sight, but that didn't mean they were safe.

"Go. Get the fuck down," Jackson ordered. "Berry, lead them. I'll cover you."

He got down on one knee and pointed the MP5 in front of himself. Berry and the others descended into the ravine, step by step. Jackson never for a second let his guard down. Minutes later, Berry shouted from the bottom of the ravine, "Survivor! Come on!"

Jackson stood up, dug his feet into the ground, and then slid down the slope. Even before reaching the bottom, he realized that the universe was listening to him and that it was giving him a little help.

At the bottom of the ravine was an old, wooden house.

# CHAPTER 24

The one they called Survivor kicked the door open and entered the cabin, his gun pointed in various directions.

"Clear!" he shouted.

Berry entered next, and then Dylan ushered Lexi in. He himself took a look at the top of the ravine before entering the house. The moment he was inside, Survivor slammed the door shut.

"All right. Everybody, keep it down. It could still be out there," Survivor said.

"The cougar, you mean?" Dylan jeered. "You fucking lied to us. That was no fucking cougar, man!"

Anger boiled in his skull. These soldiers knew what they were up against, and they deliberately kept Dylan and the others in the dark, compromising their safety.

"Keep it down! Unless you want to get everybody killed?" Survivor said, standing firm in front of Dylan.

Dylan wanted to punch the bastard in the face, but he knew that the moment his fist pulled back, he would be pinned to the ground and probably cuffed to prevent future retaliation. Right now, that would not help Dylan in protecting himself... or Lexi.

"Berry, tend to the civilian. I'll secure the house," Survivor said.

He walked past Dylan.

"I'm going with you," Dylan said.

Survivor turned around to look at him. *No, Dylan* expected Survivor to say. Instead, the soldier gave him a brusque nod of approval.

"Lexi, stay with them. We'll be right back." Dylan took Lexi's hand into his own, offering her a reassuring look. She nodded then knelt in front of the girl, who Berry had propped into a sitting position against the wall. Her head lolled to the side, her eyes half-closed like she was falling in and out of consciousness.

"She needs food and water," Lexi said.

Berry had already started digging through a pouch strapped to the back of his belt. Meanwhile, Dylan went after Survivor. The house itself seemed like anything but a regular cabin.

An old, wooden bed fitted with straws of hay and messy blankets that sat on top occupied the corner of the room. A small table and two chairs sat in the middle of the room. Plates rested atop the table, dirty with something old and meaty that crusted it, flies buzzing around the food. It wasn't until then that the putrid smell hit Dylan's nose. A barrel filled with some murky liquid that glistened from the light sat in the corner.

Survivor went through the doorframe leading to the next room. Dylan gave him enough space to clear the area and then went after him. A bevy of items cluttered this room. An old fireplace inside which sat the ashes of long-since burnt wood, a desk with old, tattered papers, a quill dipped in ink, and an oil lamp, a broom leaning in the corner of the room next to the small window.

The place looked old, and yet, not abandoned. The lack of dust and the haphazard order in which the items lay was proof of that. Someone not only tended to this place but also *lived* in it.

"What the hell is this place?" Dylan asked no one in particular.

Survivor's weapon never went down as he slowly scanned the room. When something clinked under his foot, he looked down to see an enormous hatch secured with a rusted padlock. Survivor got down on one knee and took the padlock into one hand. Turning the weapon around, he then smashed the lock with the butt of the rifle until the old lock came loose.

Survivor unhooked the padlock and tossed it aside. He stood up, pointed the gun at the hatch, and gestured with his head at Dylan. "Open it and step aside."

Dylan nodded. He grabbed the big ring that served as the handle. When he pulled with one hand, the hatch didn't budge. Survivor's impatient glare flitted to him for a moment. He grabbed the ring with both hands and tugged as hard as he could. Even using his full strength, he strained to crack it open.

Once the hatch door stood vertical, he let it fall over to the other side and backstepped.

***

Whatever Berry was injecting the girl with, it was helping. Probably fluids used for people who suffered from dehydration. The woman fell in and out of consciousness, her eyes mostly remaining closed, occasional moans escaping her mouth.

"Is she going to be okay?" Lexi asked.

Berry ignored her as he focused on pumping her with fluids in the syringes. He bit the cap of one of the injections and removed it from the needle before injecting the contents into the girl's thigh. She must have been asleep because she gave no reaction to the needle entering her body.

"Nothing like a little pick-me-up," Berry said. "She'll be okay for a while, but she'll need proper medical attention."

"I see."

Berry reached behind his back and brought forward a canteen that he promptly placed on the floor between himself and Lexi. "Here. Let her drink this when she wakes up. But make sure she's fully awake, got it?"

"Yeah." Lexi nodded. "Okay."

"If she asks for food, give her something light."

Lexi couldn't tell if she felt safer or not with the soldiers around. She was glad that they were here to help the girl and keep them all safe, but how much would they really be able to protect them? After what happened to their teammate back there... it was all questionable.

*Baba. Baba,* the words refused to leave Lexi's mind. They clung to her like mosquitos to a sweaty body. No matter how hard she tried not to think this way, the words bore a significance that she did not yet understand.

"Any idea who she is?" It took Lexi a moment to realize that Berry was talking to her.

"Um... yeah," she gave a belated answer. "Yes. She and her boyfriend had gone hiking a while ago, and then they went missing."

"Any sign of her boyfriend?"

"Not that we know. We were barely able to get a word out of her. She just kept saying "dangerous" and..." Lexi looked down, her sentence trailing off.

"And?" Berry asked.

"And *baba.*"

"Baba?"

"Yeah. It means grandma in our language. But I don't... I don't know." Lexi shook her head.

It was too difficult to think properly right now. Too many things floated in her mind. Among all the thoughts was a worry for Mickey. She wondered if he and Bogdan had managed to get out of the woods.

Berry shot up to his feet and approached the nearby window, cautiously peeking outside. Lexi cast another look at the girl then stood up as well. "Listen. My brother is still out there."

Berry gave her an indifferent look before focusing on the window without saying a word.

"He's in danger out there. We have to help him," Lexi insisted.

"Sorry. You saw what's out there. We can't go out. Not yet."

"Yes, I saw what's out there; all the more reason to go out there and help him."

"Not a chance, lady. It would be suicide."

Lexi gritted her teeth. Berry turned to her, his look of reticence turning into something akin to compassion. The moment he opened his mouth, she realized that it wasn't compassion but indignation. "Look. Five of us came here. Now there's only me and Survivor. I watched my teammates get killed in ways you can't possibly imagine." He stood so close to her that she could smell the gunpowder on him. "So, if you want to rescue your brother. Go on ahead. Knock yourself out. I'll even give you a gun."

With that, he turned back to the window.

***

The entrance to the basement was too dark. Jackson switched the light mounted to his gun on. The beam instantly illuminated the shabby wooden stairs. Before taking the first step down, Jackson looked up at Dylan and said, "If you wanna come with me, fine. But don't get in my way."

"Sure," Dylan said with a hint of defiance.

Jackson put his foot forward on the first step. As he descended, he had to stoop to avoid hitting his head on the edge of the hatch. A damp smell—damper than the one upstairs—entered his nostrils. The steps creaked under his heavy boots, but ten steps later, his feet were touching the basement floor.

It was then that the smell of dampness was replaced by a redolence he knew all too well. The stench carried with it a sense of fear, despair, and foreboding.

It was the smell of death.

***

Dylan suppressed a gag when his eyes fell on what Survivor's torch illuminated. The mess on the table was too difficult to identify at first, but it looked like something that would be found in a butcher's shop if all the meat was tossed carelessly on a pile.

"Oh, what the fuck?" he asked, his forearm pressed over his mouth and nose.

Survivor took a step forward, his torch mechanically rotating from one side to the other. Just before the light left the table, Dylan saw something that resembled a human foot. It was just his imagination. He hoped to God that it was— please, please—just his imagination because he didn't want to end up like that, just a dismembered corpse on the table of a basement in the middle of the woods.

The torch attached to Survivor's rifle illuminated more desks filled with vials and flasks and all sorts of strangely colored liquids that sat in them. Jars filled with viscous, dark matter and some kind of fleshy objects swimming in them sat on the tables. Thick, dusty tomes with tattered edges stood in piles like Jenga towers. More books covered the ancient bookshelf by the wall. At the center of it all stood a large, charred cauldron.

*What in the fuck did we stumble into?*

Survivor lowered his gun, and Dylan wanted to scream at him to keep it up and keep his finger on the trigger because, for the love of God, they were all in terrible, terrible danger.

"Let's get back up," Survivor said.

Dylan was glad to hear his voice because the silence was unnerving, and he felt like the tension was growing with each passing second. Survivor's voice broke that tension.

"Hey. You still with me?" He gave Dylan a pat on his chest.

"Yeah. Let's go back to the others," Dylan said, his tone ghastly.

Survivor nodded, and then they went back upstairs. Dylan couldn't close the hatch fast enough.

***

Lexi sat next to the woman, whose breathing had steadied. She looked like she was sleeping peacefully. Every now and again, she would stir or twitch, a word escaping her mouth before resuming her snoring. Berry continued staring out the window, tirelessly scanning the view outside.

It had been a few minutes since Survivor and Dylan left. There had been metallic smashing sounds in the other room, after which they spoke something she couldn't decipher. Then they went quiet.

Lexi wrapped her arms around her knees and leaned her chin on them. Now that the adrenaline had completely subsided, all she could think about was how coming here was a huge mistake. Of all the places she could have chosen—and there were many—why did she have to go with the one where some hikers had gone missing?

She was afraid of closing her eyes. Whenever she did, she saw that... thing mauling the soldier. She saw the features of the monster too clearly. It wasn't the long limbs or the claws that scared Lexi so much but the face that radiated pure, unfiltered hate.

Or maybe it wasn't hate. Maybe it was just a hunting instinct, just like all the predators living in the wilderness had. But it just looked so human, so... intelligent. Those eyes conveyed more than an instinct to eat and sleep.

There was more to it, and Lexi had seen it when the creature pinned down that soldier. It was an emotion that only humans were capable of expressing.

*Greed.*

The woman shot into a ramrod straight position with a start. Lexi recoiled at the abrupt movement. The girl's eyes were wide open as if she hadn't been asleep for the past few minutes. Her head frenetically jerked left and right, her eyes darting around the decrepit room. There was no surprise or unfamiliarity in those eyes, only shock.

When her eyes fell on Lexi, she began screaming.

"Hey, it's okay! It's all right!" Lexi grabbed the girl by the shoulders.

Berry was on his knee in front of her, too. The girl's scream turned into a whimper, and then she buried her face in her hands and sobbed.

"It's okay. You're fine. We're here to protect you." Lexi stroked the girl's back. It was tense like a rock.

The girl relaxed into Lexi's arms, which was a good sign. It meant she trusted Lexi enough. Lexi placed a hand on her hair. It was greasy and crusted with dried mud, tiny leaves, and twigs tangled inside her strands.

"Shh, it's okay. We're here. What's your name?" Lexi asked.

"Is-Isabella. But my friends call me Issie," she said.

It was the first coherent sentence that she had uttered that day. Lexi smiled at the progress they were making. Maybe being here today wasn't such a terrible thing after all. Maybe it was a sign from the one above.

"Issie, okay," Lexi repeated, mostly to make the girl feel safe at the sound of her own name. "You went missing in these woods some time ago."

Isabella looked down as if considering that for a moment, a frown creeping up on her face. A second later, she shook her head, her eyes meeting Lexi's again. "I'm sorry. I don't remember."

"What's she saying?" Berry asked.

"Wait," Lexi told him in English before turning back to Isabella. "Okay. You were with someone else. Do you remember that?"

"With... someone..." Isabella said as if uttering the words for the first time. She squeezed her eyes shut as if in pain. "I..."

"It's okay. Don't push yourself. The news said you were with your boyfriend. Do you remember?"

"The news... boyfriend..." She blinked sheepishly, and then pain washed over her face. "Jay. Jay. His name was Jayden. Oh God, he..."

She clamped a dirty hand over her mouth and sobbed into it for a moment.

"It's okay. You're safe with us," Lexi lied. She couldn't risk causing the girl to panic. "We'll keep you safe, okay?"

Isabella's hand dropped. She looked up at Lexi with a tear-stricken face. Her lips quivered. She sniveled a moment longer and then said, "It's not me I'm worried about."

"What do you mean?"

"Baba is coming. She's coming to get you," Isabella said, her breaths becoming shallower.

At that moment, Survivor and Dylan entered the room. Dylan looked surprised to see Isabella awake. Survivor was unfazed.

"Hey, look at me. We'll be fine. We're safe in here, okay?"

"No, you don't understand!" Isabella raised her voice, her hand firmly squeezing Lexi's forearm, jagged nails digging into her skin. "This is Baba's house! And she's coming back!"

# CHAPTER 25

"A claymore over there should do a number on it," Jackson said, pointing to the spot where Berry should place the landmine.

"Got it. Arming now," Berry hurried to the spot and got down to place the mine.

It was far enough from the house to give them time to prepare in case the claymore did nothing to the target but close enough for them to have their crosshairs on it once the explosion went off.

"I'll place a trip-wire here, here, and here," Jackson pointed to the spots then looked at the civilians. "If things go south, don't go running in those directions because you'll be blown to pieces."

Lexi bit her lip at that. Dylan's face was already drained of color, so the threat of a mine didn't seem to cause a reaction. The girl, Isabella, was still inside the house.

"You'll be fine," Jackson said. "Go back inside for now. We'll be there in a bit."

"Armed and ready to go." Berry stood.

"Berry, get over here." Jackson motioned him over.

The civilians were back inside the house by then.

"What's up?" Berry ran up to Jackson.

Jackson gave the top of the ravine a once over then put a hand on Berry's shoulder. "Listen, things may not go so well for us here."

"I'm aware of that, Survivor. Whatever you command, I'm seeing it through to the end."

"Cut the bullshit, Berry. You have a wife and a kid on the way. When the target arrives, and if things start to go bad for us, I want you to run back to the LZ. Tell HQ the mission was a failure and convince them to send the Fat Guys. This is way too big for one Intervention Unit. Got it?"

Berry's lips stiffened. "We're going to complete the mission."

"That's what every officer would like to believe. But we have to be realistic here. The odds are stacked against us. So if you see that we're in trouble, go. If you can save the civilians, do it, but if you have to choose, choose to save yourself."

Berry opened his mouth, and Jackson knew that he was about to disagree, so he quickly interrupted.

"Don't try to be a hero. Trust me. It never ends well. There's no shame in running. Retreat, recover, and live to fight another day."

Berry's lips turned into a smile. It was an unexpected gesture. "That's rich coming from Survivor. You always put the mission first. That's what the people say. And you always make it out alive. You're immortal."

Jackson grimaced. He could tell Berry that surviving was not always better; that surviving meant being left behind; that it meant going on mission after mission, an endless cycle, until Lady Luck finally gives up on you.

Instead, he simply said, "It's a curse, not a blessing. Remember that."

***

Dylan felt trapped, like finding himself at a party he didn't want to attend. Only this was a hundred times worse. Unlike the parties, he couldn't just make an excuse and leave. Unlike the parties, he wouldn't be met with judgmental glares, questions, and urges from people to stay this time. Here, he would be punished without warning.

The worry that invaded his mind made him feel like he was going crazy, and he desperately needed to distract himself. Either Lexi sensed this, or she wanted a distraction of her own because she sat next to him and put a hand on his knee.

"You okay?" Dylan asked.

"No." Lexi shook her head. "I don't think I am."

"We'll get out of here. Survivor and Berry are setting up defenses now."

"I guess."

"I'm sure Mickey and Bogdan are okay. They're probably far out of the woods already."

Lexi's hand pulled back, and she looked down at her lap. A little bit of silence ensued. The anxiety on Lexi's face was clear, but he didn't know what to say to make her feel better. It wasn't until her head rose that he realized that the worry was related to something else, and not the already known situation.

"I don't know what you think, but Bogdan and I were never a thing," she blurted.

Dylan blinked. He stared at her for a second, his lips slightly parted.

"What?" the single word came from his mouth.

"All he ever did was hit on me. Ever since I've known him. Even when Mickey told him to stop because I was uncomfortable, he said okay and then continued doing it. I never once responded to his remarks."

"You guys were never in a relationship?" Dylan asked.

His heart was beginning to beat faster because he sensed that he was still going to get a piece of information that he wouldn't like—something Lexi had kept from him.

"Never," Lexi said. "I don't think I've ever touched him before, even for a handshake. I'm repulsed by him."

"Not even a kiss on the mouth?"

"No."

"But Bogdan said…"

Dylan replayed Bogdan's words in his head. He tried to remember them exactly as they were.

*Oh, yes. Very close friends.*

*Forget past, American. It always full of pain.*

But he never really said it, did he? He hinted at it, but he never outright said it. Why? What the hell was his game plan?

"What did he say?" Lexi asked.

"I don't know. It's just… from his words, he sounded like you two used to be a thing. A huge one."

Lexi's gaze lingered on Dylan for a moment. Then her lips curved. She threw her head back and let out a guffaw. It was the first time today that he'd heard her laugh so heartily. It was as strange and unexpected as it was beautiful.

"Me and Bogdan?" Lexi asked. "Oh, God. I would sooner date an opossum."

She laughed a little more. Dylan smiled, too. It wasn't just the immense relief that flooded him. It was the sight of Lexi laughing. It was a beautiful sight, seeing the smile on his girlfriend's face. On top of all that, the candid laugh told him that he had nothing to worry about regarding Bogdan because Lexi was telling him the truth.

He squeezed her hand. "I love you."

And he knew, as the words left his mouth, he truly did. But he also didn't know if he would get another chance to tell her that, so even if he felt nothing, he would still say it. She smiled at him.

All at once, the door burst open, and Survivor and Berry waltzed inside.

"I doubt frags are gonna do anything to it. Flashbangs, though? Might at least distract it," Survivor said.

"Survivor. Survivor, listen." Dylan shot up to his feet. Survivor gave him an aloof glance. "You gotta give us some guns, man."

Berry snorted in laughter. Survivor coldly shook his head. "Out of the question."

"Come on. We can help you."

"No. Things are going to get crazy around here pretty soon, and giving guns to panicked kids wouldn't make me feel any safer."

He was about to walk past, but Dylan stepped in front of him. "Okay, listen. Just hear me out. That thing is too powerful for you to stop it on your own. You need help. Just let us pull our own weight. Don't leave us defenseless."

Survivor stared at Dylan with a bemused expression. His face said *Get the fuck out of my way before I knock some sense into you.* The soldier's hand reached up to his shoulder, and then he drew a knife from the hilt strapped there.

He pressed the butt of the knife into Dylan's chest, holding it there until Dylan took it. It was heavy, the blade long, but looking down at the MP5 in Survivor's hands, the knife felt insufficient.

"A knife? Really?" Dylan asked, sarcasm lacing his tone.

"Don't go trigger happy with it. It's sharp," Survivor said.

"This is bullshit."

"Cry me a river. If you don't like it, I'll be happy to take it off your hands."

Dylan pressed his lips together, no comeback coming to his mind. Berry offered his own knife to Lexi, but she already had one—the same one they'd used to cut the foliage blocking the church.

Before Dylan could say anything more regarding the choice of weapon he'd been given, Survivor walked past him and knelt in front of Isabella. Her eyes bore into his, wide and fearful.

"All right," Survivor said. "I need you to tell me everything you know about this *Baba.*"

# CHAPTER 26

Bogdan ran, jumped over roots and rocks, and sidled between trees. Every couple of seconds, he looked back to make sure the *thing* wasn't following him. He was alone in the woods, but it didn't feel that way. It felt as though eyes were everywhere, attached to him every step of the way.

He didn't even know where he was running. All he knew was he needed to get some distance from the thing that killed Mickey. That had been such a close call. It easily could have been Bogdan lying dead in the grass if it hadn't been for his wits.

It was better this way, anyway. Mickey was a nobody. He would never have amounted to anything anyway. Bogdan, on the other hand, had a future in front of him. He would make sure to live it to his fullest.

Starting right now.

As much as he wanted to put distance from the woman, he also didn't want to leave the woods because this was where he finally realized his identity. It was something Bogdan had known for a long time but refused to admit, something that showed through the cracks from time to time if he let it.

Whenever he saw a dead or dying animal on the street, whenever he saw another person's face contorting in pain at the words he inflicted, whenever he saw violence in movies, whenever he role-played rape with the women he dated...

But it was all superficial. Insufficient. A bad and watered-down mockery of the real thing. Like shooting zombies in a VR game. Like walking with a hard-on, but not doing anything about it.

Bogdan had felt his entire life like something was missing, like he was constantly searching for something to fulfill him, but no matter what he did, it wasn't enough. He had thought that lifting weights in the gym was *it*. He had thought that it would help him fill that void that he was so afraid of. But after today, he knew that he was only fooling himself.

He knew his true calling now. He knew it from the moment he saw Oscar's jaw getting ripped off his face. And he was tired of hiding from it any longer. Just because the fucking laws didn't allow for such things, what a bunch of bullshit.

But these woods were his safe haven. They were going to be the spot where he would be able to express himself—really express himself—without any repercussions and without anyone judging him. It was liberating. For the first time in his life, Bogdan felt enthusiastic about the future. He would even go as far as to say he was *happy*, which was something he didn't think he was capable of.

Being content, yes, but being happy? That was new for him.

He had to find Lexi, the American, and the girl. He would play along, and then when they trusted him enough, he would separate them and have fun with them one by one. The exhilaration that coursed through him was intoxicating. It made his crotch stir again, so he quickly suppressed those thoughts and trudged on.

He was running on fumes. It must have been hours since he'd last seen Lexi and the American. The blue sky that had taken on a tinge of orange was evidence of that, and so was the darkness that slowly crept into the forest.

A few times, Bogdan sat down to rest. It was supposed to be just a few minutes, but he ended up taking a break for what must have been well over half an hour. He had no sense of orientation. For all he knew, he could have been going deeper and deeper into the woods, putting more distance from the city with each step he took.

The forest was becoming darker with each passing minute. He was thirsty and hungry, and his steps turned into an unsteady stagger. The next time he looked up, the sky was dark, and the crickets had begun chittering.

Bogdan was about to collapse on the ground and try to sleep right there when his eyes fell on a house at the bottom of a ravine.

***

"Survivor, got eyes on someone out there," Berry said.

Jackson ran up to the window and peered outside. Sure enough, a figure lumbered toward the house.

"Gotta be the target. Get ready," he said.

Berry ran to the other side of the room, crouched next to the door, and wiggled the muzzle of his rifle into the hole they'd created in the wall for him to shoot through. Jackson himself took the safety on his MP5 off and pointed it at the figure, the crosshairs perfectly aligned. Earlier, he had taken the suppressor off his rifle. No need for it anymore.

"Claymore's going to go off when it gets closer. Once you hear the explosion, open fire," Jackson said.

The figure sauntered closer and closer, following the tiny trail of trampled grass. Jackson's finger was on the trigger. He didn't know what kind of damage the claymore would do, and he was ready for anything.

He heard stirring behind him. He could imagine the civilians poking their heads over Jackson's shoulder to see what was going on, but he didn't let that distract him. The silhouette was just a few feet away from the claymore now.

"Oh, shit," Lexi uttered. "That's not the monster. It's Bogdan!"

Jackson's finger eased on the trigger. The figure inched closer to the landmine. It was mere feet away from it now.

Sure enough, Jackson then saw it. The figure that walked down the path couldn't possibly be the creature because it was too... normal-looking, and too broad for the feminine features of the target.

"Stop right there!" Jackson shouted at the top of his lungs, the gun still trained on the figure.

The person stopped inches away from the claymore.

***

Bogdan froze at the voice. For a second, he thought that he was trespassing and that the person inside the cabin would threaten to call the cops. He looked up but couldn't see anyone in the dark window. He was about to continue forward while explaining his situation when the door burst open and two armed soldiers burst outside, their rifles pointed at him.

"Get back! Now! Step back!" one of them shouted.

"Don't shoot!" Bogdan's arms went up in the air as he backpedaled.

He realized in the back of his mind that the conversation was in English, but he couldn't understand what the soldiers were barking at him except that he should back away. Then his eyes fell on the cabin door behind them, and his arms eased down.

The American, Lexi, and the found girl stared at him.

***

Lexi's breath hitched. Bogdan was alone. *Alone.*

The flurry of questions that piled in her throat didn't leave her mouth because the air was filled with the shouting of the two soldiers. Everyone was confused, Bogdan most of all. The soldiers commanded Bogdan to step around into the grass and approach them. He did so, his hands raised at ear level again.

"Okay, okay!" Bogdan said as he approached.

Survivor pointed to the spot where Bogdan stood seconds ago. "Claymore. You almost blew your own leg off."

Only then did silence crash over the area again. Bogdan looked at the path, his eyes narrowed in confusion and rightly so. He couldn't see the claymore since it was so well hidden.

"Where's Mickey?" Lexi asked. The question just flew out of her mouth because she couldn't stand the tension. She had to know what happened to her brother and why the heck he wasn't with Bogdan.

Bogdan looked at her. It was the first time their eyes met since he arrived at the cabin. His chest inflated, and Lexi knew that bad news was going to come out of his mouth. Before he could say anything, Survivor interrupted.

"Back inside. Now," he commanded.

They had no choice but to listen. It was too dangerous to stay outside, anyway. Once the door was closed behind them, any vestiges of light that remained were snuffed out. As much as Lexi itched to turn on the torch of her phone to see Bogdan's face more clearly, she knew that Survivor and Berry would reprimand her the moment she did so.

"Bogdan. Where's Mickey?" Lexi stood in front of him in an akimbo position. Her entire body trembled violently.

Darkness obscured his face. He could have been harboring any facial expression.

"Sorry," was all he said.

The word cleaved Lexi's gut. Her arms drooped as she waited for a follow-up to that information, because what the hell did "sorry" mean? Why was Bogdan apologizing? Mickey was okay, right? He had to be. It was *Mickey*, her brother who dodged accidents dozens of times throughout her life. A family member doesn't just suddenly die like that.

"That woman... she killed him," Bogdan said, clearing all doubt.

"The hell she did," Lexi said. "What the fuck do you think you're saying? I'm going out there to find him."

The moment she took a step toward the door, voices in the cabin exploded, urging her to stop. The soldiers were already blocking her path.

"Move out of my way, dammit!" Lexi commanded, tears of anger blurring her vision.

Survivor refused to budge. She thought she could see the ghost of a compassionate look in his eyes.

"Lexi," Bogdan's stern voice grabbed her attention. She spun around to see what he wanted. He shook his head. "Don't."

The room's temperature seemed to drop by fifty degrees. Lexi felt dizzy. Buzzing filled her ears. She had to lean on her knees to stop herself from collapsing. Someone said something, but she couldn't hear it. Someone's hand touched her back, and she wanted to scream at the person to leave her the fuck alone and not touch her.

"I'm sorry," Bogdan said in their language. "I tried to help. She caught us off guard. I tried to save Mickey, but I couldn't do it. I did my best; I really did."

Lexi couldn't breathe. She only just then realized that she was crying. Her legs buckled, and she fell sideways on the floor, shrinking into a fetal position. Someone—Dylan, she assumed vaguely—knelt next to her and held her by the shoulder and back as she shuddered with uncontrollable sobs.

The world around her disappeared. The only thing that existed was the darkness around her and the pain that enveloped her. Then, there was nothing.

# CHAPTER 27

Lexi had passed out at some point. Dylan didn't want to wake her just yet, so he let her lie on the floor. He couldn't believe it. Mickey—gone. Dylan didn't know the guy too well, but he felt a fragment of Lexi's pain. He wished he could take all of it for her.

The cabin was deathly quiet. The only existing sound was the chittering of the insects and animals outside. It was the calm before the storm, Dylan realized. It wouldn't be long before the monster returned. That's what Isabella had said.

Baba, as Isabella called her, often wandered the woods during the daytime. Rarely, she went out at night in search for... something, but she didn't know what. The group couldn't get too many details out of Isabella before she broke into a panicked, sobbing fit. She kept telling them to get out of the cabin, to leave before it was too late, but Survivor and Berry wouldn't hear of it.

"She say you can't stop her," Bogdan translated Isabella's sentence.

"She's not indestructible," Survivor retorted. "We'll take care of her."

But there was uncertainty in his tone. It was vague, microscopic, barely noticeable. But Dylan noticed it because he'd been in Survivor's company for hours, and he'd heard him speak, so the change in his tone was easy to detect.

"She keeps calling her *Baba*. The hell does that mean?" Berry asked.

"Grandmother," Bogdan said. "But Mickey say something about Baba Yaga."

Isabella seemed to wince at that name, meaning that Bogdan was on to something.

"Baba Yaga?" Berry asked.

"Yes."

"I heard about that," Dylan said. "She's a witch of some sort from Slavic folklore."

Berry scoffed in ridicule. Dylan ignored that remark.

"So, what do we need to know about Baba Yaga?" Survivor asked.

"If I remember, she can be good or bad in stories. Sometimes, she helps people. But other times, she deceives them. That's all I know. Oh, and that she has a house that walks on giant chicken legs."

Survivor stared at Dylan incredulously for a moment. "What about combat details? How do the heroes of the story kill her?"

"I don't know, sorry. Lexi might know something."

Isabella rose to her feet. She began speaking frantically. Her words were all connected, not a second of pause between them. Everyone stared in confusion except Bogdan, who retained a focused look. When the girl was done speaking, Dylan jutted his head toward Bogdan.

"What did she say?" he asked.

"She say Baba must eat human hearts. It make her look young. She always want to look young."

"That explains the killings," Berry said.

"Doesn't change a thing," Survivor said. "We still don't know how to kill her."

"What must we do?" Bogdan asked.

"See if there are any weapons around. You might need something to defend yourselves with," Survivor said.

Bogdan nodded, seemingly agreeing with the soldier's idea. He stood up and sauntered into the other room. Dylan frowned. This might be the only chance he got to speak to Bogdan alone, and he wasn't going to pass it up.

He followed Bogdan into the room.

***

Bogdan's eyes flicked from object to object. The only thing that he could use as a weapon was the broom in the corner of the room, but that was ridiculous. The broom would not even annoy the old woman, let alone hurt her.

But Bogdan wasn't looking for a weapon that could hurt Baba Yaga. He was looking for a weapon that could hurt the others. The soldiers who were with them complicated things a little, but it didn't matter. Bogdan would find a way to get rid of them and then devote his time to the American and Lexi.

*Lexi.*

She would be his dessert. The thought of her in torn clothes, thrashing against him while he violently thrust into her over and over until climax caused his crotch to tingle... And then when he was done using her for his sexual pleasure, he would snuff out her life.

He imagined his hands wrapped around her neck, squeezing her throat and watching her eyes roll back, her resistance growing weaker, her screams mute. She would be forced to stare at Bogdan's face in those last few seconds of her life, and Bogdan would stare back, reveling in her inability to defend herself. He would finally show her that she wasn't better than him like she thought she was.

Bogdan shook his head to chase those fantasies away. Too early. Way too early. He would need to be patient and bide his time, and then he would get what he wanted.

A smile stretched his mouth when his eyes fell on the rusty axe under the desk. It was tucked away so close to the wall that he hadn't even noticed it at first. He took it into his hands, feeling the weight of it. It would be easy to swing. He gave it a small test swing, imagining the American's skull in the way. Even with the rusted blade, his head would crack open like a coconut.

"Hey," a voice startled him.

Bogdan craned his neck to see the American standing at the entrance.

"Hi," Bogdan said stupidly and lowered the axe, his gaze turned away from the American.

"Didn't think you'd made it out there," the American said.

"Yes. Me too. I thought you were dead."

The American paced around the room behind Bogdan. Bogdan didn't like being in his presence. He also didn't like the strong desire to split his head open with the axe.

"So, what happened out there? After we split, I mean," the American asked.

Bogdan turned around. The American was facing him, his eyes glued to him.

"I told you already. Baba Yaga killed Mickey."

"How did that happen?"

Bogdan didn't know if the questions were interrogational or if the American was simply curious. He assumed the former because Bogdan always kept his guard up and expected the worst from people.

"We were in woods, and then woman came out of nowhere," Bogdan said. "Mickey and I stay hidden, but woman saw him. She run after him and killed him, and I escaped."

The American ogled Bogdan for a moment then nodded. Content that the American's questions were answered, Bogdan turned around to continue looking for more weapons.

"I thought you said you tried saving Mickey," the American said.

*Darn it.*

Bogdan froze. He'd been caught in the lie. He had to think fast. He spun to face the American again. "Yes, I did."

"Well, did you?"

"Yes."

"But you just said you ran away."

"I tried to take woman off of Mickey, but she too strong. So, I ran."

Bogdan refused to look away. Looking away would mean he was weak, and Bogdan was anything but weak.

"I see. Are you sure there isn't something you're not telling me?"

Anger was starting to rise in the pit of Bogdan's stomach. "What that means? You say I'm liar?"

He pointed a finger at his own chest, his face contorted into a grimace. If the American was fazed by this display, then he did a pretty good job hiding it. A moment later, the American took a step closer to Bogdan. He was now inches from Bogdan's face.

"It wouldn't be the first time, would it?" the American asked.

Bogdan was taken aback by the American's display of courage, but he didn't let himself recoil in front of him. Still, even with the axe in his hand, Bogdan suddenly felt challenged, and he didn't like that. He didn't like that the

American was showing him that he would be difficult to tackle.

The feeling was familiar to Bogdan. The reason he had started going to the gym in the first place was to feel more powerful. And the packed muscles helped him with that until he once ran into a guy Mickey's size who didn't back down during an argument. Bogdan had seen in the little guy's eyes that he was ballsy enough to fight despite Bogdan's size.

The fight never came because the others at the party had intervened, but the little guy had more than enough time to throw colorful insults in Bogdan's direction while he stood silently and took it. The encounter had left Bogdan's ego bruised, and for many nights, he fantasized about running into the little shit on the street and knocking some sense into him.

He would not let the American give him the same feeling. Bogdan was the powerful one, and he would prove it. He couldn't wait to embed the axe in the American's neck.

"I think you're lying, Bogdan," the American said. "Just like you lied about Lexi."

Bogdan smiled. "Is that what you think?"

"Yeah. I don't know what your game plan is, but I'm keeping an eye on you."

Bogdan heaved the axe over one shoulder. The blade was facing the American. One tug of the axe down and he would be finished. And, in fact, he thought about doing it. Why not? He could say it was self-defense. He would have the perfect reason for killing him.

A crazed, panicked American thought his girlfriend was cheating with Bogdan and came after him, so Bogdan had to kill him. A simple story that could not be proven otherwise.

Not in this place. But how would the soldiers react? Would they shoot him on sight? Was the American the only one who suspected Bogdan? Or would Lexi fan the flames, too?

"You're focused on wrong man, American."

His hand squeezed the handle of the axe, his arm muscles flexing. Then, footsteps cut through the darkness. Just then, the old woman walked into the room. Bogdan's heart stopped for a moment. His eyes widened at the silhouette with frayed hair standing in the doorway until he realized that it was just Isabella. And then it hit him. It hit him so hard that he forgot the American was in the room with him. No, it wasn't just Isabella.

"Tell me what really happened," the American said.

Bogdan looked back at him, then his eyes flitted to Isabella. That was when an idea struck him. Yes, he could kill the American, but why do that when he could act like a player who moved the chess pieces? He had to be patient. He had to yield, pretend like the American had the upper hand. And when his guard was down, he would strike.

"Why blame me? I spent all day out in woods. I almost die out there." He raised his voice slightly. "Instead of blame me, you should to focus on monster. Or we will all die."

Isabella gave Bogdan a weird look before walking over to the other side of the room. Bogdan inched closer to the American. "Listen, American. We are all in danger. Greater danger than you can understand. It is in the room with us."

Dylan blinked, but his facial expression remained unchanged.

"She does not understand English, so act natural. The woman... she is the monster."

The American frowned, his mouth contorting into a jeering rictus. It was a look that said, "You did not just say something so stupid."

Before the American could interrupt him, Bogdan said, "I know you think I lie. But listen. It is her. She is Ba—"

He turned to the corner of the room where Isabella was inspecting the desk. She didn't seem to be paying attention to them.

"She said herself. She said the monster must eat hearts to become young. And I saw it!"

"Saw what?" the American asked.

Bogdan couldn't stomach his smug face. But at least he had his attention, which was good. The question he asked meant that he was at least willing to listen to Bogdan's story.

"I saw the monster. She is old lady. And when she eat Oscar's heart, I saw her. She become young woman."

"So what?" the American shrugged. "What does that have to do with her?"

"Are you blind?" Bogdan resisted the urge to gesture to Isabella. "She went missing long ago. She is supposed to be died! But she is alive! How?! I ask you, how?!"

Isabella briefly turned to face Bogdan and the American. He expected her eyes to turn white, fangs to grow out of her mouth. Instead, she turned back to the desk and fiddled with the tools on top of it.

She was Baba Yaga. He was sure of it. And if he was wrong? It didn't matter. She was unimportant anyway.

"Think about what I say," Bogdan continued. "We never see her..." His eyes shifted to Isabella, "...or the old woman at same place! And I see her turn into young woman who looks exactly like her!"

"That's ridiculous," the American said. Of course he would not believe Bogdan. "She has been with us the entire time. And we heard screams elsewhere. It's not her."

"Maybe there is more of them." Bogdan spread his arms. "I don't know. But I know she is involved."

His arms drooped, and he placed a hand on the American's shoulder. This next part was important. He had to be really convincing in showing emotions.

"I have seen her, Dylan. When she killed Mickey. When she killed Lexi's brother—my friend. One second, it was old woman. And then..." He ran a palm in front of his face. "Then it was her."

He couldn't, of course, be one hundred percent sure that it was Isabella, but it sure as hell looked like her: ragged, with disheveled hair, bruised and cut in places. The similarity was too uncanny.

The American's face slackened, just for a second. He looked at Isabella. He was starting to consider Bogdan's point. Good. It was so easy changing people's minds in distressing situations. Everyone was willing to jump so quickly at the suggestion of a scapegoat.

"We must kill her," Bogdan said, his eyes fixed on the American.

"You're out of your fucking mind," the American said.

"Are you willing to stay inside room with her? Because I would not. Not for one minute. She is the monster, no question. You will see. She will soon turn into old woman. And then, it will be late. We. Must. Kill her."

The American's eyes were fixed on Isabella. He was actually considering the possibility that Isabella was Baba Yaga. Good. Very good.

"We can't kill her until we're sure," the American said.

"We can wait. But then she will kill us all. We have to kill her while she distracted. Together." He gave the American a nod of approval.

The American sighed deeply. His eyes intermittently flitted from Isabella to Bogdan. "No. If you're wrong, we're going to kill an innocent person."

"And if I not?"

"We'll tie her up. See then what happens."

"Okay."

The American took a step past Bogdan and stared at Isabella—at Baba Yaga. Bogdan would wait until the American grabbed Isabella. If she turned into Baba Yaga, then he would run. And if she didn't… then he would bring the axe down on the American's head.

Bogdan could already imagine the scenario: the American dead on the floor, the soldiers and Lexi rushing in to see the dead body, Bogdan faking fear and distress, saying that he had no idea why the American had attacked Isabella, pointing at her to confirm what had happened, and saying that he had to kill him before he attacked the others. He might even have to cry a little for the others to believe him.

Then, he would just need to get rid of the soldiers and Isabella, and Lexi would be all his.

The American took another step closer to Isabella. She was humming something while leafing through a page, oblivious to the armed man approaching her. The American's shoulders tensed up. Bogdan's axe rose, aimed for the American's spine.

The American was a mere foot away from Isabella. She still seemed unaware. He was bracing himself to jump on her.

*Do it! Attack her!*

Bogdan's hands itched to bring the axe down on the American. The thought of the blade sinking into his vertebrae and flesh was so orgasmic. But at the same time, he kept an eye on Isabella, because he firmly believed that the missing woman was Baba Yaga.

Then, an explosion resounded in the air, way too close, way too loud.

And it was followed by a banshee scream.

# CHAPTER 28

"Open fire! Open fire!" Jackson shouted as he squeezed the trigger at the demonic creature that stood on all fours in front of the house.

Deafening gunshots and the scream—those were the only sounds that Jackson could hear. The claymore did barely any damage to it. Jackson could see the flesh on the side of the target's leg peeling off from the explosion, and the way the creature was thrown aside, but all limbs were still attached. And it stood right back up, effortlessly.

"Reloading!" Jackson shouted.

The target hissed and screamed, and then it was running toward the cabin. Even in the dark, Jackson could see it: the anger displayed on its face. The humans were inside its home, and no matter how feral or wild the creature was, it knew certain concepts like humans. And it did not appreciate having the battle taken to it.

The bullets tore at it, skin and flesh exploding on each impact, but still, it did not stop. It would have to stop at one point or another. Most of the targets that Jackson had faced so far got slowed down when enough bullets pelleted them.

But not all of them. Some had skin as thick as iron. Some had extreme regenerative abilities. Some were too fast even for bullets. But not this one. Not the target the civilians called Baba Yaga. She was tough, but the way the bullets penetrated her flesh told Jackson that she was vulnerable.

They were going to stop it.

***

Dylan's head turned toward the source of the explosion. Isabella did the same, her face covered in fear. Lexi was at the door, staring at Dylan. Her head focused on something else in the room. Her eyes went wide, and her mouth opened in a mute scream. Or perhaps she did scream, but the incessant gunshots drowned it out.

When Dylan looked behind, Bogdan held the axe raised above, his face twisted in an effort as he swung down. Dylan tottered to the side just in time for the axe to fly inches past his nose. The axe hit the floor, splintering the wood.

The motherfucker was trying to kill Dylan!

Dylan didn't think when he drew and swiped with the knife in his hand. Bogdan backstepped in time to dodge the swipe. A smile stretched Bogdan's face as he composed himself, the axe held firmly in both hands. The look said, "It is on now, asshole."

"What the fuck are you doing?!" Dylan shouted, but he barely heard his own voice over the gunshots and Baba Yaga's screaming.

Bogdan dashed toward Dylan, the axe raised above his head again. Before he could bring it down, Dylan jackknifed and propelled himself forward. His shoulder rammed Bogdan's stomach. He could practically feel the air being pushed out of him.

Then, they were on the floor, Dylan on top of Bogdan, wrestling for the axe. But Bogdan was too strong. He tugged then brought the wooden handle forward, smashing Dylan's nose. Dylan lost balance and fell backward, pain surging through his face.

In the moment that he blinked, Bogdan had found himself above him, the axe once again raised above. He was about to bring it down when Lexi crashed into Bogdan from the side. The axe fell out of his grip and clattered on the floor. Infuriated, Bogdan backhanded Lexi so hard that she half-twisted and fell on the floor, her forehead hitting the wood hard.

*That piece of shit!*

Dylan had never been so angry. He was running on pure adrenaline. His eyes locked with Bogdan's. And then their gazes unanimously fell on the axe.

***

"Fuck! I can't see it!" Berry shouted.

The target was nowhere in sight. It was running at the house, and then, gone.

"Eyes open!" Jackson shouted.

A loud crack above their heads exploded, and then chunks of the roof rained down on Berry, a pair of long, pointy-fingered hands grabbing hold of him and lifting him off the floor. Berry dropped his rifle. He pulled out his sidearm and shot at the thing above.

Jackson blindly aimed at the roof where he assumed the target was. It screeched, and then the hands were gone, Berry on the floor. Jackson rushed forward, hooked his arm around Berry's, and pulled him back.

A small person jostled past them, yanked the door wide open, and ran outside.

"Stop!" Jackson shouted at Isabella, but it was too late. She was already running across the ravine. "Shit!"

The ceiling above Jackson crunched, and the clawed hand appeared in the air, swiping, missing Jackson's head by inches. Jackson unloaded into it, and it retreated once more.

"On your feet, Berry!" Jackson shouted.

Berry skidded to his rifle on the ground and picked it up. "See it?!"

"No!" Survivor shouted back.

*Come on, you piece of shit! Show yourself so I can tag you and be done with this crap!*

Another scream came, and Jackson knew that the creature was getting ready to attack again.

"Heads up!" he shouted.

***

Dylan threw himself forward. He landed on his chest, his hands inches from the axe. His fingers brushed the edge of the wooden handle, and then he was sliding back, pulled by the ankle.

He bucked. The first kick missed. The second one connected with something hard, and Bogdan yelped. When Dylan looked to see if he'd done any damage, Bogdan was holding his knee, a painful expression on his face.

Dylan was about to use that opportunity to go after the axe, but before he could do that, Bogdan pulled him farther away from it, the look of pain replaced by fury. He shouted something that had the word "kill" in it, but Dylan couldn't make out the rest of the words from the explosive sounds around them.

Bogdan stepped closer, pulled back his fist, and then swung it at Dylan's face. The knuckles connected with his jaw, enough to disorient him for a moment. Dylan raised his arms in front of himself just when the next punch landed on his forearm.

Dylan kicked randomly again. His heel connected with something soft this time, and Bogdan backed up immediately, his hands over his crotch. Dylan's eyes briefly fell on Lexi. She was still on the ground, motionless. A pang of worry shot through him at the thought that she might be dead.

The axe was the solution.

He got on all fours and pushed himself toward it. Just as his hands were about to close around it for the second time, something crashed into him hard. Dylan's back slammed against the floor, and then he was face to face with *her*.

Her face was that of a young woman but contorted with monstrous features. Messy strands of bedraggled, black hair jutted out of her skull and fell down the sides of her face. The vertical, black slits of her pupils that resembled reptilian eyes were fixated on Dylan with a visible lust. Her cheekbones stuck out too much, the cheeks sunken, the jaw too long. Sharp rows of teeth peered out of her mouth.

She looked human, and yet she wasn't.

Baba Yaga opened her mouth, the teeth ready to sink into Dylan's face. One of Dylan's hands was pressed against the woman's forehead, the other on her neck as she effortlessly inched closer to him. Her skin felt surprisingly human to the touch. A metallic and putrid smell emanated with every hot breath she exhaled on his face, hot drool dribbling onto Dylan.

"Get off!" he groaned, his arms straining to push Baba Yaga as hard as he could, but it was to no avail.

With his peripheral vision, he noticed Bogdan curiously staring down at him. A smile stretched his lips.

"Well, as much as I should love to stick around and see her eating your face, I must to go," Bogdan said.

He bent down out of view, and when he stood up, Lexi was over his shoulder, the axe in one hand.

*No!*

"Thank you for letting me borrow Lexi," Bogdan said.

"Don't!" Dylan shouted.

Baba Yaga's face was inches from his. A long tongue that tapered protruded between her teeth. She was ready to tuck in. Bogdan was out of view with Lexi on his shoulder. A shatter of glass exploded, and then Dylan used his final efforts to scream at the top of his lungs.

"Survivor!"

***

The shattering of glass resounded in the other room. Berry and Jackson ran inside to see Dylan on the floor, struggling with the target. It was a miracle that he was still alive. Meanwhile, Bogdan was stepping out through the window with Lexi on his shoulder. No time to worry about them.

Berry and Jackson shot at the target. The moment the bullets hit her, she screamed and fell sideways off Dylan. Dylan assumed a fetal position, not that it would help in any way.

But the target was way too fast. She rolled backward and then lunged forward—right at Jackson. The next thing Jackson knew, he was pinned to the wall, his rifle pointed elsewhere because the target was holding it firmly. Trying to pry it away from her grip would be like trying to lift a truck.

The creature raised one clawed hand. The fingers wiggled, and then...

The creature threw its head back and wailed, dropping Jackson to the floor. It careened in this direction and that, Berry constantly at her back, holding firmly onto the knife that he had stabbed into her back. Then, they crashed backward, and the creature's limbs kicked as Berry held it in a chokehold.

"Tag it!" he shouted.

He didn't need to say it twice. Jackson drew Dixon's tag gun, pointed it at the creature's chest, and fired. A tiny dart shot forward, disappearing in the middle of the creature's chest covered by the rag. That was it. The mission was a success. Now, no matter what happened, The Company's job would be to do the rest.

The target screamed louder and bucked wildly. It stood up, Berry still stuck to its neck. It swung left and right, shrugging Berry off. He hit the wall and fell onto the floor. By the time Jackson switched to his main weapon, it was too late.

The creature was already in front of Berry, its long nails sinking inside his stomach. Berry let out a scream just as Jackson fired off an entire clip into the monster. Its back was riddled with bloody holes. It let out another caterwaul and turned to face Jackson.

Without warning, as he watched, her features started changing right before Jackson's eyes. The face of the young woman seemed to age within seconds, crags and age spots appearing on her cheeks, her skin growing flabby, her eyes milky, her hair pale.

But before the transformation could be complete, she turned around and hopped out of the window.

She was gone.

# CHAPTER 29

Jackson looked out the window in time to see the silhouette of the target disappearing. Good. A moan came next to him.

*Shit. Berry.*

Jackson fell in front of his teammate. One look was enough to determine that it was not looking good for Berry. An abundance of blood covered his stomach and thighs, an ever-expanding pool on the floor beneath him.

"Fuck," Jackson muttered.

Berry's hand closed around Jackson's wrist. Their eyes met, and time seemed to freeze in that instant. Although Jackson couldn't read his mind, Berry's face was clear with information that he wanted to communicate.

*Tell my wife I'm sorry. Tell her that I love her and our unborn child.*

The moment seemed to last forever. Then, Berry went still. His eyes remained open, but they were glossed over. *Dead.*

"I'm sorry, Berry. Rest in peace," Jackson said.

He closed his teammate's eyes and stood up. Cold and cruel? Perhaps. But there was nothing else he could do. He couldn't take back death. And when you worked for The Company, lingering on what could have been would only cause further deaths.

"Survivor! Bogdan's kidnapped Lexi! We have to go after her!" Dylan shouted, pointing out the window.

"No," Jackson said.

Dylan looked like he'd been slapped. "What?"

"This is Alpha Team. Come in," Jackson said into the radio.

"Read you loud and clear, Alpha."

"This is Survivor. The target has been tagged. Heading back to the LZ. Got one civilian with me. We're all that's left."

After a short moment of silence, the radio crackled. "Roger that, Survivor. Will standby."

"Let's move." Jackson looked at Dylan then motioned for him to follow him.

"Wait! You can't be serious!" Dylan caught up to Jackson and put a hand on his arm. "Lexi is still out there! You're out of your fucking mind if you think I'm going to—"

His sentence went mute when Jackson pinned him on the wall with an elbow pressed against his neck. For the first time in a while, an emotion jostled to the front of his mind.

Anger.

He didn't think Berry's death would hit him, but it did.

*Guess I'm human after all.*

"Have you not been paying attention this entire fucking time?! Did you not see what we were up against?!" Jackson shouted. "My entire team is dead! Berry had a pregnant wife who will never see him again!"

Dylan went still. His body was stiff, but he offered no resistance. He stared at Jackson with a mix of fear and disgust.

"You're lucky you're still alive." Jackson backed away then started to the door. "There's a helicopter close by, ready to take off the moment we enter. If you want to live, you can come with me, and we'll drop you off out of the hot zone. If not, suit yourself. I don't give a shit either way."

He didn't wait for Dylan to give him an answer before he was already out of the door.

***

Dylan stared down at his feet. He hated Survivor for doing this to them. To the soldier, Dylan, Lexi, and the others were just numbers. Dead weight that happened to tag along. Now that the mission was complete, Survivor didn't care what happened next.

Dylan's eyes flitted to the broken window. Bogdan was out there somewhere with Lexi. But so was Baba Yaga. And she would not give up so easily, Dylan was sure of that. What chance did he stand against her?

He approached the window and stared at the vast, endless darkness that swallowed the forest. He could go out there. He might even be able to find Lexi and Bogdan. He might even be able to save Lexi. But then they would be back at square one again.

Baba Yaga would still get them.

Even if he didn't manage to find them, she and Bogdan would still be dead by morning. The woods belonged to the witch. She knew them better than anyone, and she wasn't going to let any visitor escape. Not while they still had beating hearts in their chests.

Dylan bit his lip hard. He bent down to pick up the knife on the floor.

He hated himself so much in that moment. He hated himself even more when he turned around and went after Survivor.

***

Bogdan trekked through the woods, stumbling and tripping multiple times with the weight on his back, but he never once fell down. He knew exactly where he should go to have privacy with Lexi.

The village stood in front of him, engulfed in darkness. Bogdan could not wipe the smile off his face as he strode down the cobblestone path, looking for a good place to set Lexi down. Most of the houses were too dilapidated, too dirty, even for his standards.

Then his eyes fell on the derelict church. His smile stretched further. Lexi was somewhat religious, from what Bogdan could tell. What better place to desecrate her than in the house of God that she loved so much?

Yes, that was it. That was the place. Bogdan strode up the steps toward the church. Lexi stirred and moaned. Bogdan must have hit her hard to knock her out so cold. Once again, he couldn't help but be proud of himself and the way he'd managed to get everything working in his favor.

By now, Dylan was a heartless corpse inside the monster's cabin, and the soldiers were most likely dead, too. That would mean that Bogdan and Lexi were next, but Bogdan didn't care about that yet. Right now, he had only one plan in mind.

As he set Lexi down, he thought about the fun he was going to have with her. She was in for one hell of a wake-up call.

***

Dylan lumbered after Survivor, occasionally breaking into a jog to catch up with his fast pace. The looming sense of danger was gone for the moment. All that remained was shame. Dylan would need to live with what happened tonight for the rest of his life.

He would never return to this country. What he wanted to do was pretend nothing ever happened. For a second, he convinced himself that he could do that. Return to the United States, delete any evidence that Lexi ever existed, and start anew.

But he would never be able to erase the evidence from his head: all the memories they'd shared, all the laughs they'd had together, all the sensual kissing and touching, the way Lexi was so thoughtful toward him, the way she supported him every step of the way, no matter what problem he had.

Dylan stopped in his tracks. Survivor must have noticed that because he turned around to face Dylan.

"Come on, the LZ is close," Survivor said.

But Dylan didn't move. He couldn't move. An obvious realization crashed over him so hard that he wondered how he hadn't seen it before.

Lexi was in danger.

*Lexi.* His girlfriend. The love of his life. The person he wanted to spend the rest of his life with. All of a sudden, the emotions that he felt toward Lexi were ten times more powerful than they had ever been. They were potent enough to clear out the night and move every tree in the forest out of the way.

And with it came the impending sense of desperation. Lexi was in terrible, terrible trouble. Dylan couldn't leave her to die. No, he had to go back for her, right now.

"I can't leave." He shook his head.

Survivor's face contorted into shock. Dylan didn't even know he was capable of making such a face.

"Thank you for everything," Dylan said and then spun on the ball of his shoes and dashed in the opposite direction.

"What are you doing?! Get back here!" Survivor's voice echoed after him. "You're going to get yourself killed! Hey!"

But Dylan wasn't listening. With the knife firmly clenched in his hand, he was sprinting back; back to where the action was; back where Lexi was.

He was going to save his girlfriend.

***

"Stupid little fuck," Jackson muttered to himself, frustrated.

He had no intention of going after Dylan. That would be suicide. Plus, it wasn't part of the mission. The mission always came first. As Jackson stared at Dylan merging with the darkness, until his silhouette disappeared entirely, he couldn't help but admire Dylan's courage. He was a diamond in the rough, and with a little work, he would have been a great fit for the Intervention Unit.

"Survivor, you're late. Where the hell are you?" the tinny voice on the radio asked.

"Five minutes," Survivor said.

He gave the treeline a final once over. He shook his head, turned around, and continued toward the LZ.

# CHAPTER 30

Lexi opened her eyes. Her vision was blurry. She couldn't figure out where she was or what had happened. All she knew was that it was quiet. Too quiet.

A bright orange light stood in front of her. Lexi blinked. A groan came from somewhere, and then she realized it was her own. Then a voice cut through the blur, "Wakey wakey, sleepy head."

*Bogdan.*

The blur cleared out of Lexi's vision. The orange light was coming from a candlestand that Bogdan had lit. It took her some time to recognize the tall ceilings and the stained glass windows. They were in the church in the village. When and how did they get there? Where were the others?

It was all starting to come back to her. The screams, the gunshots, Bogdan attacking Dylan with an axe...

Bogdan was crouching in front of her. At first, she couldn't discern the features on his face properly, but then she noticed the puffed-up cheeks from the grin. His eyes came into focus next, and they glowed with an insanity that Lexi couldn't understand.

Lexi threw herself sideways to scoot away from Bogdan, but her jump quickly came to a halt. Something tugged at her wrists. She craned her neck but couldn't see what her hands were tied to.

"Don't resist it, Alexa. It's useless."

"Where's Dylan?" Lexi asked.

Breathing was becoming harder because of the panic that swelled in her chest. Bogdan's crooked smile didn't help alleviate that.

"He's dead, my dear," he said.

"No."

"Yes. Everyone is dead. Dylan, the soldiers, Mickey, Oscar, Hannah. Probably even Isabella. It's just you and me, all alone, in the middle of the woods. No one is coming to help you."

His hand brushed against Lexi's cheek. She recoiled. The crazed look in Bogdan's eyes was terrifying because he wasn't looking at Lexi like she was another human being. He was looking at her like she was a thing. A toy to be taken apart, put back together, taken apart again, and then thrown when done with.

Her heart hammered against her chest because she was starting to realize that what Bogdan was going to do to her was far worse than what the monster in the woods would.

She finally realized—but far too late—why she never liked Bogdan. It wasn't the fact that he was an obnoxious, brainless, shallow gym bro who always had to be the loudest in the group. It was because, deep down, she sensed that something was inherently wrong with him, that an unspeakable evil buried deep inside emanated from him.

And now, it was unchained, unrestricted by human laws.

Lexi wanted to scream and cry. She wanted to be out of here. She wanted to be home with her mother and Mickey. But she wouldn't show fear. Not in front of Bogdan. It's what he wanted, and she would not give him that pleasure, no matter what he did to her.

"I am really grateful to Mickey for introducing us," Bogdan said. "He was such a good friend. Oh, since we're talking about him, I might have lied a little."

*What are you talking about,* was what Lexi wanted to say, but her voice fell mute. Bogdan continued nonetheless.

"The old woman… she was going to kill me. But then I tossed a pebble in Mickey's direction, and she went after him instead. In a sense, Mickey saved my life."

"You son of a bitch!" Lexi jerked forward, her hands itching to claw at Bogdan's face but stopped by those damned restraints.

Bogdan seemed rather amused by this because he didn't even flinch. The anger that swaddled Lexi was quickly replaced by growing desperation.

"Let me go!" she said, her voice timid.

Bogdan looked at her curiously then smiled again. "You are so beautiful. You know that, right? You're too good for the American. I don't understand what you saw in him. But I guess it doesn't matter now that he's out of the way. Now, you're going to be all mine, all night long."

He leaned closer. Lexi moved her head away and closed her eyes, Bogdan's warm breath on her neck. His dry lips brushed against her neck. It felt like insects crawling over her skin. He then sniffed her as a hand traveled down her thigh.

"We are going to have so much fun. First, I am going to fuck you. And then I am going to fuck you some more. And then the real fun will begin."

Lexi's eyes drifted downward. She hadn't noticed the axe in Bogdan's hand until then. He gently ran a finger down the rusty blade then caressed Lexi's thigh with it, slowly gliding between her legs.

Bogdan spoke slowly, pausing between each word as if trying to achieve a dramatic effect. It was working. "You will beg me to stop and to let you go. And by the time I'm done, you will beg me to kill you. But I won't. I will savor every last moment until you can no longer scream. And only then, only when I have used every ounce of you for my own pleasure, and when I no longer find you amusing, will I kill you."

The blade of the axe retreated as Bogdan threw it aside. It clattered loudly in the spaciousness of the church. Lexi's eyes fell on the axe, and for a brief, futile moment, she thought about the advantage she would have if she could just get her hands on the axe.

Wishful thinking.

Bogdan reeled back, the intoxicated look on his face replaced by a frenzied one, like a piranha whose eyes locked with a piece of meat thrown into the aquarium. It was starting, she realized, the beginning of what would be the worst and last night in her life.

Bogdan's fingers wedged around the collar of Lexi's t-shirt. Lexi further stiffened, her hands uselessly tied behind her back, desperately twitching to get in front of her for defense.

"Feel free to scream. No one will hear you anyway," Bogdan said.

With a swift tug, the shirt tore with a sickening *rrriiip*.

Despite not wanting to give Bogdan that pleasure, she couldn't help it.

She screamed.

# CHAPTER 31

Dylan ignored the fatigue that held its clutches on him. He refused to stop running. But where was he supposed to go? At first, he ran in the direction of the cabin then continued down the undergrowth where he'd seen Bogdan taking off with Lexi on his shoulder.

He couldn't have gotten far. Not in the darkness, not with Lexi on his back.

Dylan plodded forward, desperation replacing the adrenaline. For all he knew, he could be going in the opposite direction of where Bogdan had gone. At one point, he stopped, not just to rest but to think as well. He couldn't think with the burning in his lungs and legs.

*Where would Bogdan go? Where would he stop? Come on, think, goddammit.*

Dylan climbed the hill, hoping to get a better view, even in such permeating darkness. He found a trail. Since it went in only one direction, the starting point being where he stood, he followed it. Bogdan might have used it, right?

"Lexi!" Dylan shouted, not caring that Baba Yaga would hear him. "Lexi! Where are you?!"

Surely he would have heard something by now if they were close by, right? No way would Lexi be quiet, and Dylan was sure that Bogdan didn't kidnap her just so he could kill her quickly. He could have done that back at the cabin, but he didn't. He wanted to have fun.

He was a psychopath.

*Mickey, you stupid fuck,* Dylan cursed and then stopped.

He was on the cobblestone path. Houses stretched on both sides, and that got his hopes surging. Of course, Bogdan would take Lexi to the village! What better place to have privacy, away from the monster, than inside one of the buildings?

But which one? Which one?

One look up was more than enough to give him his answer. The stained glass windows of the church glowed like a lighthouse in a stormy night.

And with it came the unmistakable scream that belonged to none other than Lexi.

***

Lexi's caterwaul was music to Bogdan's ears. The more she screamed and cried, the more it excited him. He had dreamed about using Lexi for so many nights. He had masturbated to the thought of her squirming against him countless times. Now, he would get to see the real thing.

Bogdan tore Lexi's shirt, revealing the bra that cradled her pert tits. He was going to enjoy cutting her skin, slice by slice. He could hardly contain himself. He had to have her *right now.*

Lexi kicked against him, but she was too weak. Even if her hands were free, she would not stand a chance against him. Bogdan undid Lexi's belt, and then—

A loud, ancient groan exploded in the church, freezing Bogdan instantly. He looked at the source of the sound. The entrance was opening.

*No. Not now. Come on, lady, I haven't even started!*

The American stepped into view.

***

"Lexi!" Dylan shouted when his eyes fell on Bogdan kneeling in front of her. Her face was contorted in fear unlike any she'd ever expressed before. Her shirt had been ripped at the collar, giving it a deep V-neck look. Bogdan's hands were on the belt of her jeans.

That's when anger once again overtook Dylan. He stepped forward, the knife pointed in front of him. "Get off of her, motherfucker!"

Bogdan's face was veiled with confusion. For a second, he remained frozen, and then... he smiled. He hung his head down and shook it then picked up the axe and stood up, turning to face Dylan.

"American. You don't know when to quit, no? You very tough to be still alive."

"Get the fuck away from Lexi," Dylan said.

"I will. But only so I can kill you myself."

Dylan's gaze briefly fell on Lexi. Their eyes locked for that moment, and he saw hope in those eyes—hope and fear. He couldn't let her down. If he lost to Bogdan, then he would still be able to have his way with her.

"I thought Baba Yaga kill you, American, but this... is even better. I will gut you in front of your bitch and then make you watch while I rape her."

"You're not yourself, Bogdan. Stop before it's too late," Dylan said.

He knew that talking to Bogdan was futile, but he had to try. If there was a way to avoid this fight, then Dylan had to find it. Bogdan scoffed, a gesture meant to ridicule Dylan for trying to persuade him.

He and Bogdan paced in a circle around each other. The duel was about to start, and one of them would not be leaving alive.

"I do not like interruptions, American. It is rude. Do they not teach manners in your country?"

"You're going to pay for what you've done, you piece of shit," Dylan responded.

He was looking for an opportunity to attack. Bogdan held the axe too firmly. He would be ready for Dylan's attack, and with such a big weapon, Dylan was at a disadvantage. He had to wait for Bogdan to attack first, then dodge the attack and go for a counter.

"Leave before it is late, American. You cannot win this fight," Bogdan said.

"You're afraid. That's your problem. You're chickening out."

Bogdan's features momentarily went rigid, the shadows cast over his face making him look like a zombie. Dylan wouldn't have noticed the subtle change in the expression had there not been the candlelight.

That's when he got the idea: He had to make Bogdan angry, make him lose control. Then he would attack Dylan without thinking, and Dylan would have an easier time beating him.

"Beneath those muscles, you're just a child," Dylan spat. "That's why you're doing these things. Because you're just a coward."

Bogdan's mouth scrunched. It was working. Good. Of course, the insult that would hurt someone who had big muscles was something denoting their femininity. They were all the same, Dylan realized.

There was a reason why someone who didn't do bodybuilding as a professional sport dedicated so much time and effort to building their body. It was a diversion from their insecurities. Deep down, Bogdan was a man-child with a frail ego, and no matter how many pounds of raw muscle he packed, those insecurities that hid under the chiseled abs and massive shoulders would remain.

"You're just a fucking pussy!" Dylan shouted.

That was what finally triggered Bogdan. He raised the axe above his head and charged at Dylan with a fierce cry. Dylan stepped backward, dodging the rusty blade by a lot of space. Bogdan didn't stop. He swung again, then again, swiping at the air, causing Dylan to retreat farther and farther.

Dylan's rear hit one of the pews. Bogdan brought the axe down just as Dylan propelled himself forward, out of danger's way. The sound of wood crunching under the axe's bite exploded inches behind him.

With a thrust, Dylan's knife sank into Bogdan's side. Blood drenched his shirt around the stab wound immediately as he wailed in pain. The axe cleaved the air once more, just as Dylan instinctively ducked. The blade missed his head by a thread.

He backed away to put some distance from his enemy, the bloodied knife in his hand. Bogdan's balance wobbled for a moment. He touched his side where he'd been stabbed and looked at the fingers. They glistened with his blood, and that only seemed to drive him even more insane.

He looked at Dylan, and his eyes were full of fiery hate. Dylan could see in Bogdan's eyes how much he wanted to destroy Dylan. It was past the point of murder now. It would be violent, gory revenge.

"Die!" Bogdan shouted as he rallied for another onslaught.

But he didn't try swinging the axe this time. Instead, he held out the handle in front of him and bull-rushed Dylan. Before Dylan knew it, the wooden handle slammed into his neck, and a sense of vertigo overcame him. The air in his lungs was forced out of him when his back hit the floor. The back of his head whacked the floor hard, causing the image in front of his eyes to spin.

It took him a moment to regain his bearings, but it was too late by then.

The handle of the axe was being pressed down onto his neck, squeezing his larynx, making breathing impossible. Bogdan's crazed face stared down at him, straining with effort, a vein bulging on his forehead and arms as he gave it all to choke Dylan.

Dylan closed his fist, but the knife in his hand was gone. His hands shot up to the handle, and he pushed hard to get it off his throat.

Somewhere in the distance, Dylan heard Lexi pleading with Bogdan to stop then Bogdan's laugh.

He couldn't budge the axe. The pressure on his neck was enormous, as if an elephant had stepped on it. He expected his neck to snap any moment, and then, it would all be over. To make things worse, Bogdan shoved harder and harder downward, grunting with each push.

The corner of Dylan's vision grew dark. He couldn't get the axe off his neck, no way. Bogdan was too strong. With nothing else left to do, his hand clawed at the floor, trying to grab hold of something—anything—that he could use for defense. His fingers touched only the marble floor.

"Die, already, you American scum!" Bogdan huffed.

Then, Dylan's hand touched something. A small object that his fingers could close around. The edge of the knife's blade cut his finger. His jittery hand closed around the handle, and then he thrust the knife at Bogdan's abdomen.

Bogdan's face went from furious to wide-eyed in confusion. But the pressure on Dylan's neck remained just as firm. If anything, it was even stronger. The darkness that occupied the corners of his vision spread toward the center. He could hardly see Bogdan's face.

He drew his hand back, then thrust again, then again, then again, many times over. Something warm slid down his hand. His stabbing grew slower and weaker. Then at one point, everything went dark.

***

Bogdan did not stop. He would not stop choking the American until he was dead. The American's face was red, veins decorating his forehead and the corners of his eyes like rivers on a map. Bogdan could see the life draining out of his eyes.

"Stop! You're killing him!" Lexi screamed.

A smile crept up on Bogdan's face.

Then, sharp pain seared through his stomach. He glanced down to see the knife sticking out of his abdomen. After the initial shock was over, anger took over. He pressed harder against the American's neck with an intention to crush his bones into fine dust.

But then another jolt of sharp pain flashed through his stomach, and another, and another. Bogdan clenched his jaw, refusing to let go. He was going to murder the American before he allowed him to breathe again.

For a very long moment, he was sure that the American's stabs did nothing to him. But then he noticed his head slumping forward, drool uncontrollably dripping out of his mouth, his arms going numb. When he looked down, his stomach was drenched with blood, the shirt riddled with dozens of holes.

*I am dying,* he realized as he toppled sideways. He coughed blood, and that's when his abdomen exploded with unimaginable pain.

***

Dylan couldn't tell how long it had been. It couldn't have been more than a few seconds between his vision growing dark and clearing up.

The axe was no longer on his neck, and he realized that he was able to breathe in, albeit with a painful throat. A coughing fit took over, and Dylan clawed at his throat, inhaling between each cough, savoring the tiny whiffs of fresh air that his lungs accepted into them.

Lexi was screaming something, but he couldn't focus on her words. Bogdan was on the floor next to him, on his back, his blood-drenched hands on his stomach. He was coughing and shaking, his face vacillating from one painful expression to another. Relish enveloped Dylan as he stood up. That feeling grew even stronger when his eyes locked with Bogdan's. They were pleading eyes, eyes that begged for mercy: mercy that he himself wouldn't have offered.

"Dylan!" Lexi cried out, and only then did Dylan's oxygen-deprived mind register her.

His eyes searched the floor—so much blood was smeared on it!—until he located the knife. He bent down and picked it up, his legs wobbly. He ignored how sticky it was from Bogdan's blood. He staggered to Lexi and dropped onto his knees. He dangerously tottered to the side before planting a palm on the floor to balance himself. Floaters still swam in his vision from the choking.

Dylan rebalanced himself and sawed through the binds that held Lexi.

As soon as her hands were free, she leaped into his arms and sobbed. He hugged her back, harder than ever before. For a while, all they did was hold each other because they couldn't do anything else. Dylan savored the ecstatic relief, enjoyed the warmth of Lexi's body, and reveled in her crying—because if she cried, it meant she was alive.

"You came back for me," Lexi said at one point, her head buried in Dylan's chest.

"Of course I did." Dylan forced a smile. "You're the love of my life. Did you think I'd just leave you behind?"

Lexi hugged him harder, and they spent some more time in each other's arms. Then, Dylan grabbed Lexi by the shoulders and said, "We have to go, Lexi. We have to get out of here."

She gave him a flurry of nods, and then they were on their feet, dragging themselves toward the exit. Dylan's entire body still felt weak.

Bogdan's cough caught their attention. Dylan looked at him. Bogdan stared directly at him, his head bobbing up and down like a bird's, his mouth working in words that never came because of the blood in his throat.

"What do we do with him?" Lexi asked.

"Help me. Plea—please," Bogdan uttered.

Dylan wanted to laugh at him. He shuffled to the axe on the floor, bent down, and picked it up, the blade dragged across the floor until it was up in his hands. The action took a lot of energy from him. Dylan stepped above Bogdan and stared down at his pathetic face.

"Do—" the word left his mouth, interrupted by a gurgle in his throat. "Pl—"

No mercy for this piece of shit. Dylan gripped the axe in both hands, raised it high above his head, then held it there.

No, he didn't hesitate. He enjoyed the look of fear in Bogdan's eyes.

Then, he brought the axe down.

The blade sank into Bogdan's chest with ease, despite the rust. His body jerked upright momentarily, a miserable "gah!" escaping his mouth before the back of his head hit the floor again. His eyes squeezed shut, his lips pulled back into a snarl. He looked like he was crying.

Dylan tried to pull the axe out, but it was stuck firmly in Bogdan's chest. He didn't know that could happen when the axe was used on humans, and he regretted ever having to learn that.

He wiggled the axe back and forth to loosen the grip. Blood gushed out of the wound. Dylan unstuck the axe. Bogdan's body spasmed as new blood dribbled out of the corners of his mouth. His eyes locked with Dylan's, and then he went still.

He was dead.

# CHAPTER 32

The cool night air felt good on Lexi's tear-stricken face. The moment she and Dylan exited the church, it hit her: She would be leaving the forest without Mickey. She would have thrown up had she not been so tired. Instead, she collapsed into a sitting position, buried her face in her hands, and dry-sobbed.

Dylan stroked her back and uttered words of comfort. Surprisingly, they helped a little. He was still by her side. They had survived a dance with the Grim Reaper together, and for that reason, Lexi somehow felt closer to Dylan. She knew that if their relationship was strong enough to survive a killing spree in the woods, it would be strong enough to survive anything.

"I love you," she said between hiccups.

"I love you too, baby. I'm sorry." Dylan wiped the remaining tears off Lexi's face.

"What are you sorry for?"

Dylan hung his head down. "I didn't appreciate you enough. I haven't told you, but... I wasn't sure about the future. About..."

"About us," Lexi finished the sentence for him.

"Yeah." He nodded.

Lexi swallowed, another wave of panic seizing her. "You don't love me anymore?"

His eyes flittered to her as if to ask, "How did you know that?" He then smiled and said, "I wasn't sure at times. Before tonight, I could never tell."

"And now?"

"Now I'm sure of one thing."

"And what's that?"

Dylan looked down again, a pensive gaze on his face. He then looked up, inhaled, and said, "I don't care where we live. I don't care if you never get your visa. I don't ever want to be away from you."

Lexi couldn't help it; a chuckle escaped her mouth. She leaned forward and hugged him. Whether this was Dylan's clumsy way of proposing to her or if he was just putting the idea out there for future consideration, Lexi didn't need to think about her answer.

Mickey popped into her mind. She could picture his reaction to Dylan's proposal. He would throw his hands up, shout at the top of his lungs, "My sister is getting married!" and then put on loud music and get the heavy drinks out.

New tears welled up in her eyes at the thought of her brother, and she could not stop them this time. She would never get to hear her brother's laugh again. She would never get to scold him over the stupid things he did or said without thinking.

She tried to remember what the last thing she said to him was. It was back when she and Dylan chased after Isabella. He had stared sheepishly at them, scared out of his wits. She might have yelled something like, "We'll be right back," or, "Wait for us," she couldn't remember.

If she'd known that it was the last time she'd ever see him, she'd have taken a few seconds to run up to him and hug him, and tell him to take care of himself, because he was her brother and she loved him. She hadn't done that in years because Lexi and Mickey just had that sort of tough love relationship: the one where they were like two brothers rather than a brother and sister.

And now, he was gone, just like that.

Lexi sobbed hard while Dylan held her. She was perfectly aware that sitting out in front of the church was not safe, but she couldn't will herself to move. She cried for Mickey. She cried for Hannah and Oscar. She cried for the soldiers who got caught up in the mess. She cried for Isabella and her boyfriend, wherever they were. She cried for everyone who had ever had the bad luck of running into Baba in these woods.

An eternity later, her eyes were dry, and the tears stopped coming—but the pain didn't. Still, she felt sufficiently strong enough to move again. She gave Dylan a nod to indicate that she was okay, and, with his help, she stood up on wobbly legs.

"Maybe we should find a place to stay in the village until morning. It's a long way back," Dylan suggested.

Lexi vigorously shook her head. "No. Please, let's just leave. I can't stay a second longer in these woods, please."

"Okay, Lexi. Yeah. Let's go, then," Dylan agreed without hesitation, and for that, she was immensely grateful.

Their walking pace was noticeably slower. Lexi could hardly raise her foot. As much as she wanted to collapse on the cobble street and close her eyes, the thought of plopping into a warm bed was a lot more appealing.

First, a warm shower to clean off all the muck, blood, and dirt. Then she would collapse in her bed. Her head would sink into the fluffy pillow. The soft blankets would rest over her like a gentle cloud. The cars outside her window would be white noise to help her fall asleep. She would drift into a fifteen-hour-long coma. And when she woke up—

An approaching patter of quick footsteps snatched Lexi's attention.

She turned around just in time to see an old, toothless woman dashing at her at incredible speed.

# CHAPTER 33

Dylan's head was killing him. Orange light that banged against his closed eyelids was what woke him up. He tried opening his eyes, but the light was too bright, so he spent a moment blinking, waiting for the stinging to go away.

"Ohh," he groaned, the back of his head throbbing insanely.

Shuffling came nearby, then a whimper, one that he recognized.

"Dylan!" Lexi's voice called out to him from the blur. "Dylan!"

Dylan tried to move, but he couldn't. He blinked hard a few times, and finally, his eyes cooperated and stayed open just a little longer.

The orange light was coming from an oil lamp. Everything else around was brown: the walls, the ceiling, the floor... The smell of must and copper wiggled into his nostrils.

Dylan was suddenly wide awake. His heart hammered inside his chest as he jerked his head up to see himself splayed on his back on a table of some sort, thick, iron shackles strapped to his ankles and wrists.

*We're back at the cabin!*

Dylan fought against the restraints, his arms and legs flailing and kicking, but it was no use.

"Dylan!" he heard on his left.

When he turned his head, Lexi was strapped next to him on a similar table. Long-since dried blood stained the wooden surface under and around Lexi. Dylan's breath hitched in his throat, and an overwhelming sense of desperation took him over when he realized what table that was.

It was the one inside the basement where he'd seen the human organs with Survivor.

*Oh God. Oh God! Please, no! Not this! No, no, no!*

Lexi was crying. Dylan wanted to cry, too, because he knew what was coming. He knew that there would be no happy ending for him and Lexi. As he stared at Lexi, he hated her for a moment because he had come back for her. But then he knew that he couldn't blame her. It wasn't her fault. It was his, and only his.

*You're going to get yourself killed,* Survivor had told him, but he didn't listen.

Survivor... where the hell was he now? Dylan raised his head, his eyes fixed on the stairs leading up—up, and to freedom. Any moment, Survivor was going to come down those stairs, a gun in his hand, and he was going to get Lexi and Dylan out of these shackles.

No. No, he wasn't. Dylan knew that. It was just his brain desperately clinging to hope.

"Shit," he threw his head back, hitting the table hard with it in frustration since he couldn't use his fists to punch stuff.

He squeezed his eyes firmly shut for a moment, not believing that any of this was real. This couldn't possibly be reality. Another infantile thought surged through his head, in which he convinced himself that this was all just a bad dream.

The pain in his head proved that it wasn't. The shackles on his wrists and ankles, too. And the smell of death that heavily hung in the air.

"Dylan..." Lexi sobbed. "What's going to happen to us?"

Dylan turned his head to face Lexi. In that moment, he needed her more than anyone or anything. He desperately wanted to hug her or even just touch her, but their tables were separated by at least a few feet. All he could do was watch.

"Lexi. Lexi, listen to me," Dylan said, tears streaming down his face. "We're going to be okay. All right? We're going to be okay."

A blatant lie, but he didn't know what else to say.

Lexi's lower lip quivered, and then she burst into another crying fit. A door opened somewhere. Both Lexi and Dylan went quiet. The stairs creaked as something descended. Dylan raised his head and watched as an elongated shadow danced on the wall.

*It's Survivor! It has to be him!*

The brain had an amazing ability to hang onto thin strands of hope. But even those hopes had to die when the evidence showing otherwise was in plain sight. For Dylan, the hope for Survivor to come to their rescue died when he saw the bare, dirty foot stepping down.

Lexi whimpered.

The steps creaked louder like a giant approaching, and then, Baba Yaga was at the base of the stairs, staring at her two captured humans. She was an old woman this time, and for the first time that night, Dylan saw her clearly, and not through blurry, erratic movement and rabid, murderous attempts.

Her grizzled hair covered half of her mottled scalp. The lines and crags made her face look like a raisin, like she was three hundred years old. Her lipless mouth was sucked inside. Her eyebrows were thick and white. Hair stuck out of her large nostrils. A long and crooked nose fell downward. A thick mole covered her elongated chin. Her milky eyes expressed indifference.

She slouched, the hump on her back standing taller than her head. Her arms were flabby, dotted with age spots, forearms riddled with a bevy of veins. Her oversized hands looked big enough to crush a skull. And yet, as she stood there, wheezy breaths coming out of her mouth, she looked so frail and vulnerable.

Briefly, her eyes locked with Dylan's. He couldn't bear to stare at her for longer than a second, so he averted his gaze to Lexi, who was staring back at him, probably for the same reason.

The old woman waddled between the two tables. An ancient smell wafted along with her. She walked out of view, and Dylan craned his neck to keep her in his sight. She stopped in front of something, and then rummaging noises came from where she paused.

Dylan's heart rate increased. When Baba Yaga turned around, an enormous tool akin to pliers, but with serrated blades, was held in her hand. Dylan felt sick. He felt like he was going to pass out.

Baba Yaga stared at the tool then looked at Dylan.

*Please, don't do this. Please, please, please,* he chanted in his mind, which he should have been doing aloud, but for some reason, he couldn't utter a word.

His prayers were answered when Baba Yaga looked at Lexi. Then, she made her way over to the side of her table. Lexi recoiled as much as her shackles allowed her to. She turned her head away from the woman. Baba Yaga opened and closed the plier-tool three times.

Those weren't pliers, Dylan realized. They worked in the opposite way. The tool was used for *opening* something.

"Hey, stop! Stop!" Dylan shouted. "Don't touch her! Please! Please, don't do this!"

His voice cracked at the end because he was crying, too, and because the old woman didn't even look at him, let alone listen to him.

Baba Yaga put a hand on Lexi's forehead and then moved her t-shirt down where it was already torn. Lexi screamed, her caterwaul mixed with sobbing. They both knew what was coming. Dylan opened his mouth, ready to direct more words at Baba Yaga, but he knew it wouldn't work.

There was only one thing he could do before the inevitable—talk to Lexi.

"Lexi! Lexi, look at me!" Dylan shouted. "Lexi!"

Hesitantly, Lexi turned to face Dylan. Their eyes locked, and for a moment, she calmed down.

"I love you, Lexi. I'll always love you," he said.

She smiled through tears. She actually smiled.

"I love you, too," she said.

Baba Yaga raised the tool then brought it down on Lexi's chest. The blade went deep inside Lexi's chest with a gruesome, squelching sound. Lexi's smile morphed into an "O" shape on her lips. Her back arched, and she twitched as Baba Yaga worked with the tool, embedding it deeper, but her eyes never left Dylan's.

"I'm here, Lexi! I'm here!" Dylan hysterically cried, his eyes fixed on Lexi's, but he could see everything else clearly in his peripheral vision.

She twitched harder when crunching and grinding sounds came from her chest. A trickle of blood appeared at the corner of her mouth, the spasming more and more violent. A sickening *snap* came distinctly from her ribs as

Baba Yaga spread open the tool, opening an enormous cavity in Lexi's chest.

And still, Lexi was alive, and her eyes refused to leave Dylan's, even as her twitching wound down, even as Baba Yaga reached a hand inside the hole that she had dug in Lexi, even as she pulled out her beating heart.

Then, and only then, did Lexi go entirely still. Her eyes remained glued to Dylan's, the final face she would see before her departure. It was a small and insignificant crumb of comfort against the waves of tragedies.

"Oh God... Lexi..." Dylan squeezed his eyes shut and turned his head away from Lexi's lifeless face, away from the old woman holding the still-beating heart in her hand.

In that instant, he wanted to be dead. He wanted Baba Yaga to finish him off right then.

The sound of wet chewing filled the air. Dylan looked at Baba Yaga, hate brimming from every pore in his body. Lexi's heart was raised up to the old woman's mouth, a distinct bite mark where a chunk of it was missing. Blood smeared Baba Yaga's mouth as her jaw worked until she swallowed loudly and took the next bite.

"You're a monster! A fucking monster!" Dylan rose as high up as he could then dropped back down.

Baba Yaga swallowed. And then she did something Dylan never would have expected in a hundred years.

She spoke.

"You are in my forest," she said in a gruff, raspy voice that sounded like it hadn't been used in years.

Her accent was strong. Dylan hated how it reminded him of Bogdan. All he could do was stare at Baba Yaga as she uttered that sentence, her eyes never trailing from the heart in her hand. For a moment, he wondered if he had really heard it or if it was another trick of Dylan's brain trying to do something to protect him from the immense trauma.

Then, Baba Yaga looked at Dylan as if to confirm it. *Yes, you heard that right. I did speak just now.*

"You can speak?"

"I have learned many things in my lifetime. I can speak any language humans share."

Dylan blinked, his brain trying to understand what was happening. Baba Yaga looked more human than he ever could have expected.

"What are you?" Dylan asked, his voice trembling.

Baba Yaga took another bite of the heart and chewed. For a moment, the wash of intelligence was gone from her eyes. Half the heart was already gone. And Baba Yaga was... was that Dylan's imagination?

When she swallowed and looked at Dylan, the intelligence was back.

"Your kind has called me many things throughout the centuries," she said. "Ever since I arrived, when your kind was still an embryo, they have given me names. I could tell you half of them, and we would still stand here when the month is over. But you know me by one."

*Baba Yaga.*

"Arrived? Arrived from where?" Dylan asked.

Baba Yaga stuffed the rest of the heart into her mouth, her cheeks bulging. She chewed, looked at Dylan, then pointed one long finger at the sky. Dylan blinked, expecting further explanation.

None came. Baba Yaga looked away and swallowed the last remnants of Lexi's heart.

Dylan blinked again. It wasn't his imagination. Baba Yaga's grizzled hair had gone black, the strands more lush.

The lines that adorned her face were gone, replaced by smooth skin belonging to a young person. It was the same monster that had attacked Dylan earlier when Bogdan took off with Lexi.

The transformation was so gradual that Dylan had hardly noticed it.

The young woman walked over to Dylan's table. He remained firmly in place as she stared down at him. The vestiges of the old woman who had the feeble appearance were gone. The woman standing in front of him could snap his neck with ease if she so much as wished it. Even without the shackles, Dylan would stand no chance against her.

Baba Yaga's fingers grew into long, pointy claws. Dylan thrashed and bucked against his restraints. Baba Yaga put one hand on the back of his head and raised it. Then, she ran the claw of one finger across his neck. Momentary pain shot through Dylan's neck, something warm trickling down it, but it was gone as quickly as it appeared.

His body went still. Baba Yaga gently placed his head back on the table. Dylan couldn't move a single muscle in his body. Why couldn't he move?

And then he realized the terrible truth. Baba Yaga had skillfully severed something in his spine, effectively making him a quadriplegic, just like that.

The panic that rose in Dylan's chest was abruptly halted. He was going to die, so he figured there was no need to plead with her. Instead, he wanted answers. He had to know why she was doing this. He desperately needed this all to make sense, so that all the deaths could be justified somehow.

At the same time, he was afraid of hearing her motives because, if they were useless motives, then all the deaths tonight had been in vain. Still, he had to know.

"Why?" he asked.

Baba Yaga canted her head.

"Why are you doing this?" Dylan asked.

Baba Yaga snarled. No, it was a smile, Dylan realized. She brought her spindly fingers to her face as if gesturing to it.

"To look beautiful," she said.

Dylan stared at her, expecting a follow-up, an extra explanation, anything really that would give him more conclusion as to why such a bloodbath was necessary.

But such an answer never came. Instead, the smile this time really did turn into a snarl.

And then she drove her fingers into Dylan's chest.

***

"About time, goddammit." The helicopter pilot tossed the cigarette on the ground and stubbed it with his boot. He turned around and hopped into the helicopter. "Where are the civvies?"

Jackson didn't answer. The pilot understood Jackson's look because he nodded. Jackson sat at the edge of the helicopter door and strapped the monkey harness to himself. He stared at the forest as the helicopter began whirring to life. It took a little until the rotor blades gained momentum, and then the aircraft left the ground.

"We'll be at the base in T minus sixty minutes," the pilot said.

Jackson didn't respond. He watched as the trees descended, until he was staring at the tops of the canopies that stretched as far as the eye could see. As the chopper lurched forward, Jackson got inside and grabbed the handle of the door. He gave the trees one final look.

Somewhere down there, Jackson was sure, nestled among the trees were the bodies of civilians who were unlucky enough to find themselves in the wrong place at the wrong time—and who would never be leaving the forest again.

He tried not to consider Dylan's admirable bravery as he closed the door and turned around. Brave or not, bravery meant nothing in the face of a Code Orange entity. But at least he died on his own terms.

Jackson took off his helmet and plopped into a seat. His eyes fell on the other empty seats inside the chopper.

Berry was supposed to be here with him. And so were Dixon, Trope, and Hoover. Any traces of sentimentality that Jackson was supposed to feel toward his former teammates were not there. He had stopped being sentimental long ago.

It was just like he said to Berry. He was cursed. But he'd long-since accepted that curse and used it to his advantage. It was his greatest strength and weakness at the same time.

Jackson closed his eyes.

He was Survivor. And the only thing that mattered during the mission was the mission.

# EPILOGUE

Isabella walked through the woods. It was late morning, and the sun that peered through the branches blinded her. She enjoyed the morning routine of walking through the woods. It gave her respite and the alone time she so desperately craved.

Lately, she didn't get too much privacy throughout the day, so she often dragged her feet when going out to check the snares in the morning. All of the snares she'd seen until that point were empty. That worried her immensely.

No animals trapped in the snares meant no hearts.

When Isabella looked under the last snare, a small rabbit came into view. Excitement surged through Isabella as she snatched the rabbit by the feet. She was clumsy doing so with one hand. The other hand was a stump that still radiated pain from time to time.

The rabbit wiggled and squealed, but it could do nothing to escape Isabella's grip. She'd gotten used to their cries of fear and pain by now. During the first few weeks, she cried whenever she had to bring a rabbit back to the cabin. Now, it was just a part of her routine; nothing emotional about it.

Isabella spun and sauntered back in the direction of the cabin. The snares had been placed some distance away since animals refused to come close to the vicinity of the cabin, but fewer and fewer showed up even there as of late. If it continued that way, the snares would need to be moved even farther away.

Isabella descended the hill and then climbed another elevation—her stamina was so much better lately—until she reached the abandoned village. She never got tired of its ancient beauty. Sometimes, she would sit in the middle of the cobblestone street and listen to the chirping of the birds. Those were fleeting moments that gave her repose from the daily chores.

She didn't think about running away. Not anymore. Not after that fateful night when Baba punished her for being disobedient. Isabella looked down at the stump of her hand. She could still feel her fingers there sometimes.

Phantom pain. That's what they called it.

Escape from Baba was impossible. This was her life now, and the moment she accepted it, living with that knowledge became a lot easier. Although, Isabella assumed that Baba's potions had something to do with that, too.

The village used to brim with life—that was what Baba had told her. It had been a happy bunch of people minding their business, just like Baba. They happened to build their village close to her hut, and being alone for so many years, Baba had gone to introduce herself. She was still young back then— young by Baba's standards, but way past the age of living for any mortal.

Baba wanted to introduce herself to the villagers. She ate the heart of an animal to assume her temporary young appearance and went to the village. She introduced herself to the villagers with gifts, but they were too distracted because the leatherworker's daughter had fallen ill with an unknown disease. Baba Yaga told the villagers not to worry. She used her knowledge to heal the little girl, and the villagers praised her as Yaga the Healer.

For many days, Yaga came back to the village and spent time with the little girl. They had become like grandmother and granddaughter, or more like mother and daughter, because the girl's mom had died years earlier. Baba Yaga had never loved anyone as much as she loved the girl.

But then, the little girl began behaving strangely. The villagers had found her one day in the woods, crouched over a dead rabbit. The heart of the animal had been ripped out, and the girl had eaten it. The villagers suspected black magic, and they gathered with torches and sickles and pitchforks, and they went to Baba's house.

Seeing the old woman, and not the young lady who had healed the little girl, the villagers' suspicions that she was a witch were seemingly confirmed.

Baba Yaga tried to explain herself, but the villagers wouldn't listen. They tied up Baba Yaga and then burned the little girl alive. Even her father watched as she burned at the stake. No one intervened. When all was done, they warned Baba Yaga never to come close to the village, or the same would happen to her.

The death of the little girl broke Baba Yaga. She tore free from her binds, and then she returned to the village, and then she slaughtered every man, woman, and child that lived there by tearing their hearts out and eating them. The population of the entire village had been wiped out in a single night.

Eating the hearts of humans had corrupted her. It showed her how beautiful she could be even if just for a fleeting moment. She had become addicted to it, and with each human that stepped into her domain, she would consume a heart, temporarily becoming young in appearance. At the same time, it was her revenge against humans.

But the more hearts she ate, the weaker the effect had become—the appearances not only lasted a shorter time, but they also disfigured her, made her into a terrible monster.

And still, she could not stop for years, decades, centuries. She still couldn't stop.

But she did change.

When she found Isabella, she saw that little girl in her, and that awoke a dormant protective instinct that she had long ago forgotten about. Isabella's resemblance to the girl was what made Baba Yaga spare her life in the first place. Now, she protected her even if it didn't feel like that at times. Baba Yaga loved Isabella because she was like the girl, and she hated her because she was a human.

Isabella descended the ravine and stopped in front of the door. The rabbit in her hand had gone limp. Isabella looked down at it to see if it was still alive. The quick rising and falling of its chest confirmed that it had simply given up resisting.

Isabella pushed the door open and stepped inside. Baba was in the working room, mixing something up at the desk.

"Baba?" Isabella timidly called out.

Baba jerked toward her, a wheezy gasp escaping her mouth. When she saw who stood at the doorstep, she turned back to the desk.

"Baba, there was one rabbit in the snares." Isabella raised the rabbit.

"Put him on the table, daughter," Baba said.

Isabella did as instructed but refused to let go of the rabbit. A moment later, Baba was next to Isabella, a flask of purple liquid in her old fingers. She threw her head back and imbibed until the concoction was entirely gone. She then nodded at Isabella, her eyes fixed on the rabbit. "Now. Do it like I taught you."

By now, Isabella knew how to rip the heart out. She pressed the rabbit onto its back with the forearm with the missing hand, picked up the knife on the table, and raised the blade. The rabbit knew what was coming. It squirmed and screamed until the blade went through its tiny body. It twitched a little and then ceased moving.

"Now, quickly. While it's still alive," Baba said.

Isabella carefully carved a hole in the rabbit's chest. Then she dropped the knife and dug her fingers inside. She pushed through the slippery liquid until she felt the lump that was the heart. She gently closed her fingers around it. Baba had said that one had to handle the heart like a butterfly: not squeezing too hard to damage it, and not too gently to let it get away.

The tiny heart pulsated in Isabella's hand.

"Good. Good. Give it here, daughter. Quickly, while it still beats," Baba gingerly said, a titter escaping her mouth as she brought her hands forward, her palms upturned.

Isabella dropped the heart in Baba's hands. Baba tossed the entire heart into her mouth. She gave it a few meager chews before swallowing it whole. She then froze, her eyes frenetically darting around the room. A hand rose to her face. Then the other.

She touched her sunken cheeks, her nose, her forehead, her hair...

"Is it working? Is there any difference?" Baba asked, her eyes wide like saucers as they trained on Isabella.

"Yes," Isabella lied. The word left her mouth before she could think because she knew that if she didn't answer fast enough, Baba would punish her.

"Liar!" Baba bellowed.

She let out a screech, slammed her oversized palms on the table, then grabbed the dead rabbit by the feet and flung it across the room. The rabbit's body whacked against the wall with a *thud,* leaving a stain of blood on the place of impact. Isabella's shoulders instinctively shrugged in startlement, but she didn't dare move. If she did, it would only infuriate Baba even more.

"It's not good! This is your fault!" Baba screamed at Isabella.

"I'm sorry, Baba!" Tears ran down Isabella's face.

"Do not cry with me, you little peasant! Shush!"

And then Baba's face went slack. She looked up and remained frozen like that for a moment. A smile stretched her lips. Only a few teeth remained in that mouth. Although Baba Yaga looked like she was in the grave with one foot, Isabella knew that she would continue to live for hundreds of years more.

Baba Yaga looked down at Isabella, her face full of joy. "Humans. Humans!"

She grabbed Isabella's hand and let out a shrill laugh while twirling in a dance. She then became serious as she said, "Daughter, go out there. Do your thing. Distract them just like you did with the ones before. I will do the rest. Do you understand?"

"Yes, Baba." Isabella nodded.

"Good. Good. Now, go." Baba pushed Isabella out the door.

Isabella was already making her way toward the village where she would wait for the passersby to approach. Then, she would fake being injured and needing help, and they would come to assist her. By then, it would be too late to leave Baba's woods.

"Daughter!" Baba called out.

Isabella turned around. "Yes, Baba?"

Baba stood at the door, glowering at Isabella. "Do not play any tricks this time. Because if you do, it will be you on that table again. And you will lose more than just a hand this time."

With that, she slammed the door shut before Isabella could respond.

What choice did Isabella have?

She went to do Baba Yaga's bidding.

# THE END

# ABOUT THE AUTHOR

Boris Bacic (spelled Bačić in his native tongue) was born in 1990 in Serbia, in a small Northern town called Subotica.

As a kid, he developed a passion for writing and drawing because it allowed him to dive into a world of his own. When he started going to high school, he stopped writing for a while and focused on fitness in hopes of becoming a police officer (or a soldier).

After serving in the army, he worked as a fitness coach for a few years before becoming interested in Creepypastas (short, scary stories found on the internet). He spent a long time reading horror stories and listening to Creepypasta narrations before deciding to post his own story on Reddit's Nosleep forum. He immediately got tons of recognition and praise from the frequent readers and had his stories narrated by prominent Youtubers – some of which include MrCreepypasta, MrCreeps, DarkSomnium, DrCreepen, etc. – translated into various languages, and his most popular Nosleep series, **Tales of a Security Guard**, is currently being made into a video game and short film.

Boris published his first book in 2019, titled **Scary Stories With B.B.**, and has since become an award-winning author with titles like **Apartment 401, Camp Firwood,** and **It Came With The Crash**. He has also reached #1 Bestseller in multiple categories on Amazon.

In his free time, he enjoys going to the gym, reading books, playing video games, exploring topics for his next book project, and occasionally, going to escape rooms.

Message from the author:

*Want to get in touch with me? Shoot me an email at:*
*boris@borisbacicbooks.com*
*I always love hearing from my readers.*
*BB*

# FINAL NOTES

Thank you for reading my book. If you enjoyed it, I would appreciate it if you left a review on the Amazon Product page. Your reviews help small-time authors like me grow and allow us to continue expanding our careers and bring you – the readers – more stories like these.

# MORE BOOKS IN THE SERIES

## Creature Encounters Book 1
## IT CAME WITH THE CRASH

*They thought the plane crash was the worst that could happen to them. They were dead wrong.*

# THEY CAME FROM THE OCEAN

## Creature Encounters Book 2

*Exploring the ocean is scary. It's worse when something's down there with you.*

# THEY CAME FROM THE MALL
## Creature Encounters Book 3

*Have you ever had the feeling of being watched by the mannequins at the mall?*

www.ingramcontent.com/pod-product-compliance
Lightning Source LLC
La Vergne TN
LVHW010313200726
843507LV00010B/1222